Pas de Deux

A DANGEROUS DANCE
BOOK ONE

LINA HARPER

Copyright © 2026 by Lina Harper

All rights reserved. No part of this publication may be reproduced, stored or transmitted in any form or by any means, electronic, mechanical, photocopying, recording, scanning, or otherwise without written permission from the publisher. It is illegal to copy this book, post it to a website, or distribute it by any other means without permission.

This novel is entirely a work of fiction. The names, characters and incidents portrayed in it are the work of the author's imagination. Any resemblance to actual persons, living or dead, events or localities is entirely coincidental.

First edition

authorlinaharper.com

Aleksandr Drakov was never meant to be my Prince Charming.

He's dark, ruthless, and powerful—and when he decides he wants something, he takes it. Including me.

I've survived my mental illness through rituals and rules, but he breaks every one. He buys my ballet theatre like it's nothing to remind me that every part of me belongs to him. I should be scared. Instead, I crave him. And that terrifies me more.

Because men like Aleksandr don't fall in love. They consume.

Evangeline Vale is forbidden in every way that matters.

She's too soft for my world. Too innocent. A ballerina on the edge of stardom, and the sister of the man I hate most.

I know I should leave her untouched. But I can't. I want her breathless. Ruined. *Mine.* And I'll destroy anything that stands between us.

Even her world.

Playlist

Pas de Deux (From "The Nutcracker") - Pyotr Ilyich Tchaikovsky
So Damn Into You - Vlad Holiday
Miracle - BAMBARA
Hayloft II - Mother Mother
Crazy In Love (From "Fifty Shades of Grey") - Beyonce
Call Me Devil - Friends In Tokyo
I Wanna Be Yours - Arctic Monkeys
Sweet - Cigarettes After Sex
Red Right Hand - Nick Cave & The Bad Seeds
Sea of Love (From "Maxton Hall) - Eli Riccardi
Bow - Slowed - Reyn Hartley
Prisoner - The Weeknd, Lana Del Rey
Bodies - Bryce Fox
Op. 64, Act 1: Balcony Scene (From "Romeo and Juliet") - Sergei Prokofiev

The complete playlist and more can be found on Spotify.

Author's Note

TRIGGER WARNINGS

This book falls under the dark romance genre and delves into intense themes, including violence, death, and off page death of a child.

OBSESSIVE COMPULSIVE DISORDER

One of the characters in this book struggles with obsessive-compulsive disorder. Please note that this disorder looks different from person to person, and Eva's struggles are based on my own. If you are struggling with OCD, please consider speaking with a therapist or psychologist.

SEXUAL CONTENT

This book contains strong sexual content, including praise kink, dom/sub, choking, biting/marking, and obsessive behavior. If you are related to me, please don't read chapters:

AUTHOR'S NOTE

- 10
- 12
- 16
- 17
- 18
- 28
- 30
- 35
- Bonus Epilogue (Paperback only)

But if you are not, have fun ;)

With love and death,
    Lina

For my husband. My forever pas de deux partner.

And to the girls who violently yearn for their ballet days to return.

EVANGELINE
CHAPTER ONE

There was something magical about fresh snowfall in the air, something beautifully magnificent and ethereal about seeing those tiny flakes fall from the sky, settling on my lashes and coating my skin in winter's magic. The city park practically glittered in the cold, December air, and for a moment, I could almost pretend that I was the main character in a romance book about to kiss my one true love.

But, alas, my real life was far from romantic.

In fact, the only reason I was even at the park wasn't that *I* was on a date, but that my *best friend* was on a date, and for some reason, I'd agreed to tag along with her. I was really regretting my decision now as the three of us walked down the slick sidewalk, the two of them huddled in close conversation while I hovered on the outskirts.

Should I go home? I don't think she needs me here, I thought as the two of them started to kiss.

Or, at least, it was probably supposed to be a kiss—though it looked more like he was trying to consume her soul or something. I wasn't exactly the most experienced with kissing, but I didn't think it was supposed to look like *that*.

"What do you know?" a nasty voice inside of me snapped. *"You've never kissed anyone in your life."*

Which, unfortunately, was true.

When I was a little girl, I used to dream of my wedding day, of the prince I would one day marry. He would be tall and handsome, charming and considerate, kind and brave. Someone safe. We'd fall in love at first sight before riding happily into the sunset on our wedding day, probably on a horse and carriage.

Now, as an adult, I wanted the same things—though I was a little less set on the horse and carriage, mostly because I got way too motion sick to do something like that. But a Prince Charming, true love, and a sunset-colored happy ending sounded wonderful.

To my brother, though... that was his worst nightmare.

And in my family, what Jules said went, and he had declared I wasn't allowed to date without his express permission. I was beginning to accept that I would need to purchase a cat or ten at some point in time.

Yes, that was a little dramatic. Yes, I was only twenty-one, and I still had plenty of my life left to find my Prince Charming. But anyone who tried to remind me of those things—namely Mia, my best friend—usually shut up when they met Jules for the first time. According to him, he didn't ever plan on changing his mind.

Hence the plan to get a cat.

What would I name a cat? I wondered. *Maybe Odette... Clara? Sylvie?*

I distracted myself with thoughts of the cute baby animals —*Oh, maybe I could get one of those super fluffy cats!*—while we continued through the park. It was certainly better than trying to think of my nonexistent Prince Charming, who was probably never going to come for me.

Thick flakes of snow settled in my soft curls, and my boots

crunched with each step. Skeletal tree branches swayed in the wind, their boughs strung with warm white lights. Iron fences were adorned with garlands made of holly and fir, and each gate held a sprig of mistletoe, perfect for the kissing I would never have.

Sugar Plum, I decided. That would be my cat's name, based on one of my many favorite ballets, because how could I have possibly picked just one? Every show I danced in became my favorite, which meant that right now, *The Nutcracker* was at the top of my list. Sure, I wasn't a big part, but the fact that I was dancing in the most prestigious ballet company in the country made being in the background completely worth it.

Plus, it was how I met Mia.

"Isn't this so fun, Evie?" she asked, reaching over to squeeze my hand.

No. Despite my fascination with the year's first snowfall, I wasn't having fun. It sucked to be constantly reminded of something I longed for but didn't have, not to mention I was freezing *and* exhausted from a gruesome morning rehearsal followed by a chaotic afternoon shift. I wasn't planning on coming at all—who wants to third-wheel a first date?—but Mia gave me one look with her wide, gray eyes and suddenly, I couldn't say no.

Not that I would have anyway. I had an issue with telling people how I felt, which is why I said yes when Mia was too nervous to go out with Whatever-His-Name-Was, and why I kept trying to gather the nerve to tell her I *hated* the nickname Evie, yet failing every time.

I was always like this. Constantly sacrificing myself to make others happy—whether that was my brother, Mia, the other City Ballet Company dancers, or my coworkers at the cafe I worked at—was easier than dealing with what happened when I didn't.

Because what if they needed me to say yes? What if their

happiness rode on a *teensy* bit of mine? How could I put myself above them like that?

I couldn't.

Which was why I plastered a big smile on my face and said, "Yup! So fun."

"Carmelo," she said, turning back to her date. "Tell me about your job again."

Oh, yeah. Carmelo, I thought, though I didn't feel too bad for not remembering. Mia was the type to fall in love on a Friday and fall out of it by Monday, which meant that Carmelo had two more days to go before he received a breakup text. *Poor guy.*

I hoped I was wrong. I hoped Mia could find the happiness she deserved—for both of our sakes. I was tired of tagging along on first dates, even though I knew she was probably inviting me because she hated thinking of me sitting all alone in my apartment.

Which, yes, would have been a *little* sad, but that was why I was going to get Sugar Plum, and everything was going to be absolutely amazing again.

Carmelo's voice was impossibly deep as he recounted his job at a warehouse outside of the city, tracking shipping logistics. That was about all I got from what he said because my mind began to wander shortly after he began, which it did often. My thoughts were a labyrinth, and I followed every golden string in hopes that I would one day be able to escape it.

The snow looks so beautiful. It's like I'm in a fairytale.

If I were a princess, I wonder which one I would be... Maybe the Swan Princess? No, I'm not brave enough... The Little Mermaid? Yuck, then I have to be around fish. Oh! Maybe I'm Snow White. I do like apples...

Gosh. My feet hurt so bad. I really need to stop agreeing to cover Sam's shifts after rehearsal, but they have a lot more friends than I do, so it wouldn't be fair to keep them from them when I see Mia all the time.

Oh my God. What if that bump I just stepped on was actually a baby rabbit? What if I killed it?

Am I going to get arrested for bunny murder? Do they arrest people for that?

I have to go back to save it. I have to help it. I—

"Evangeline," Mia said softly, wrapping her hand around my arm and squeezing gently with a tight smile that showed her worry in the corners of her eyes. "You all right?"

My head whipped around to the bump only to find nothing there at all. I blinked a few times to make sure I hadn't missed anything, but when no dead baby bunny appeared, I let out a gentle exhale. "Yeah... Yeah, I'm fine."

Mia's eyes were all-knowing before she turned back to her date, thankfully giving me space to exit the labyrinth on my own.

I tried to please everyone. Even my own head. But there, I always failed, no matter how hard I tried.

Most people, when I told them I had obsessive-compulsive disorder, or OCD, always chuckled to themselves before saying, "Yeah, I'm pretty organized, too." And while I could definitely see why they thought that OCD was just being clean or tidy—because I was both of those, as were many people in my online support group—that wasn't everything.

OCD felt like... Well, it felt like living with a constant swarm of bees surrounding my head, each of them a different thought or anxiety that would sting and sting me until I fell to the ground. Sometimes, I would try to swat a bee away, but that would only make it angrier. It would attack me harder and harder and harder until I screamed and begged for it to leave me alone. So it was easier to live with the buzzing and hope I didn't get stung.

It wasn't just noise. It was a *threat*.

My thoughts latched onto things. Little bumps in the road, something someone said to me earlier in the day, the feeling that I would never be good enough to make my dreams come true. It was all about fear. Fear that I wouldn't amount to anything, fear that I would hurt others, fear that I would hurt myself. I couldn't pick up a knife without being terrified I would slit my own throat. I couldn't drive a car without having a panic attack, because every pothole was a person. I couldn't do anything without being *afraid*. The fear had become so normal that it controlled every part of me.

Mia knew this about me and had trained herself to watch for the signs that I was on the verge of a spiral. I suspected that her younger sister, Charlotte, who was one year below me in the dance program at my former university, had asked Mia to keep an eye on me. Though she was a few years older and a few years deeper into her ballet career, we went together like silk and glitter.

So I didn't mind it when she tore me from my thoughts, even if sometimes ignoring them with her made them louder.

"Let's do something fun!" she said, clearly trying to distract me. "How about a snowball fight? It's perfect weather."

I glanced down at my outfit. It was adorable, but if I got hit with one snowball, I would be soaked to the bone. My fur-lined coat was the perfect shade of ballet pink, my favorite color, matching the cute bow I tied half of my hair up with. My white tights completed the outfit along with my pink boots. Jules had practically shoved a pair of gloves on my hands, so I did have those, but they were made of delicate, white lace—not good for a snowball fight.

But me being me, I just smiled and said, "Sure! Sounds like a great time."

When Carmelo nodded his agreement, we all split up. I

ducked behind a streetlight and began to imagine myself caught in the warm, yellow glow by a handsome man who would wrap me in his arms and kiss me until my whole body flushed. A man who'd take control from my wretched illness and leave my mind empty and my body breathless.

I tried to picture a face for my prince, but whenever I tried to think about it, the details went fuzzy. Like I hadn't yet seen the one who would be right.

I was so caught up in my daydreams that I failed to notice a snowball flying my way until it landed on the back of my head, covering me in white.

"AH!" I screamed when the cold dripped down the back of my coat and beneath my dress—again, I *really* didn't dress practically.

Mia, who was hiding behind a majestic elm tree, giggled before crying out, "Oops! Sorry, Eva! If it makes you feel better, your hair still totally looks amazing."

"I know, but— urgh! I'm all cold now!"

Mia opened her mouth to reply, but was interrupted by a snowball hitting her square in the chest. Carmelo laughed loudly, and I took that as my cue to run. If I got far enough, Mia wouldn't be able to hit me. Her tall, lithe body contained absolutely no muscles outside of the ones she used for dancing.

I turned around to check if they were running after me when—

BAM!

I ran into something hard, something very, very, *very* hard and immovable. I smacked into the ground, knocking my head against the hard thing I ran into, which I was beginning to realize, despite my slight concussion, was a person cursing under their breath.

Crap.

"Oh…" I moaned, rubbing at my forehead. "I'm so sorry. I wasn't—"

But then my eyes slowly fluttered open. And I saw him.

My Prince Charming.

December 10th

MOTHER

Aleksandr. When are you going to bring a nice girl home?

ALEKSANDR

I am too busy for women, Mother.

MOTHER

Too busy for women??? You know I am not getting any younger. You are twenty-nine years old, Aleksandr, and you have not brought one woman home to meet your family. Can you not find one nice date?

ALEKSANDR

I don't want to date. And stop texting me. I am working.

MOTHER

You work too much. No wonder you haven't found your future wife. You need to get out of that bloody warehouse and out into the world.

ALEKSANDR

No.

MOTHER

Has no one caught your eye in all this time? You know your cousins in Italy have started hunting for wives. Maybe you should follow their leads.

Aleksandr

No.

MOTHER

Do you prefer men, Aleksandr? Your father and I will support you in anything.

ALEKSANDR

Mother.

Stop.

ALEKSANDR
CHAPTER TWO

Death was silent. It came in shallow breaths, in little sounds like the slice of a knife across a trembling neck. Sometimes, it could be dramatic—a fire in a warehouse, a gunfight in the park—yet I rarely deigned to attend to those. I preferred the hush afterward, the fragile moments when my ears rang with the buzz of a fresh kill, and my demons became silent.

Tonight, I was not as lucky.

The man begged and pleaded, voice raw from hours of screaming for mercy. As if my family were known for such a weak thing. The Drakovs were dark dragons, and dragons did not shy from their nature.

Besides, any tenderness I may have once had died years ago, replaced by a cool persona that gave me my nickname.

The Reaper.

I held the pistol to the back of the man's head. And the man looked at me before whispering brokenly, "You are Death."

And then, like Death, I slaughtered him.

The sound of the bullet echoed from the warehouse, the

stone floors hungering for the warm blood now spilling from his temple.

Normally, I might have relished the kill, yet today, I only frowned. I wasn't sure why. This was not the first body I would put into the ground, nor would it be the last.

But the man's words rang in my head even after he was gone. *You are Death.*

I snapped at my men to remove the corpse while my second-in-command—my cousin, Nikolai—walked over with a bunch of papers in his hand. "That was the last of the Vallen scum who took our shipments, boss. But we'll keep an eye out for anyone else who might be interested in trying to take more. And we've replaced most of the commodities, though the weapons are taking longer than…"

My mind wandered away from my cousin, listening only to three words.

You are Death.

"Are you even listening to me?" Nikolai asked as I scrubbed my fingers of any blood splatters before drying them with a decorative towel that had my mother's tastes written all over it. I watched as the last bits of blood flowed down the drain, all evidence of what transpired now gone.

You are Death.

"Aleksandr! Pay attention!" Nikolai snapped his fingers several times while I glared at him.

How the two of us were related, I had no idea. Our blood was the only thing we shared. That, and our violent… *proclivities*. His dirty blond hair and bright sky-colored eyes were a contrast to my dark locks and midnight blue irises, and his pale skin was unlike the dark olive tone I'd inherited from my mother's side. His shirts were always falling off his body, and they were usually stained with dark liquor, unlike my pristine black suits.

Nikolai's constant, shit-eating grin looked odd compared

to my cold scowl. But maybe that was because he was the most passionate man I knew, while I couldn't remember the last time I cared about anything.

"Have you heard anything I've said?"

"Was any of it important?"

"Yes, I was talking about the ballet—"

I held up a hand, and he wisely stopped talking. A rarity, unfortunately. "So, no. I don't care about a fucking dance."

Nikolai waggled his eyebrows. "But the dance is full of women in short skirts and tights. And men with even tighter ones."

"I don't care."

My cousin scoffed. "You like a pretty woman, cousin. Admit it."

"No."

Because while Nikolai consumed sex like it was air, I regarded it like paperwork. It was a means to an end, another box to tick so I could move on with my life. A sense of control that helped hold the demons back until they raged at me again. My only experiences were with the women who worked in my clubs, the ones who knew I was leaving as soon as my dick was empty. I didn't need anyone thinking I would get attached.

You are Death.

My cousin scoffed. "You're extra grumpy tonight."

"I am. Because I could have been creating new plans to infiltrate the Vallens tonight, but instead, I had to clean up after someone else when they failed to account for some inventory."

"You mess up a few numbers, and suddenly it's all 'Niko doesn't know how to do his job!'" he exclaimed, throwing up his arms dramatically. "But let me tell you the numbers for the City Ballet. I think it's a wise investment if you—"

"Enough," I muttered, waving Nikolai off with a sharp gesture, dismissing whatever sexy ballerina nonsense my cousin was about to tell me. He grumbled something under his breath, probably about my lack of decency or manners, which was true. But the Vallens were my family's greatest enemy, and because of my idiot relative, any plans I created to get an advantage over them now had to be redone.

Soon, I told the darkness that had resided within me ever since I was twelve. *We will get our vengeance soon.*

The delay was fine. I wouldn't stop until that entire family was destroyed, no matter how long it took.

I dressed for the frigid temperatures, turning to Nikolai. "Do not follow me," I said to him before slamming the door behind me.

Despite my gruff—all right, *grumpy*—personality and my anger, I did actually like Nikolai. But tonight, I needed this walk to clear my mind in peace and quiet—and if he was there, it was sure to be anything but.

My feet led me to the city park, which was decorated for the holiday season. I fucking hated this time of year. It reminded me of when I lost Liza, my sister, on another cold December night like this one.

I fell into an easy stride, my guards flanking me a few steps behind. Close enough to act if anyone tried to attack me, but far enough to give me the illusion of privacy. It wasn't as if I truly needed them. I had two small guns concealed on me—one tucked into my waistband, the other in a holster on my ankle. And if neither of those somehow worked, I kept a switchblade in my pocket for emergencies.

Or for fun.

But tonight, the only other people in the park were several feet away, a trio that was screaming, laughing, and generally interrupting my brooding.

You are Death.

I must have been too stuck in my head because, without warning, something collided into me, soft but solid, knocking me off balance and onto the ground. The thick snow softened my fall, cold and wet as it soaked through my coat and gloves. I hissed through clenched teeth at the sudden impact, holding whatever was on top of me with a tight grip, ready to destroy it.

"What the—" But my words froze in my throat, buried underneath my surprise.

It was the most beautiful fucking woman I'd ever seen.

Her soft, flushed cheeks, sprinkled with freckles, combined with her heart-stopping smile, sucked all the air from my lungs. Then, my eyes went to her brown hair. Snow dotted it like tiny stars, clinging to her fluttering lashes. The street caught her in a halo of gold, making her look even more like something that didn't belong anywhere near a man like me.

"Ow..." she moaned, rubbing at her forehead, where a white scar traveled along her hairline. "I'm so sorry. I wasn't watching—"

Behind me, the crunch of boots in the snow told me the guards were approaching, ready to intervene and throw this random woman off of me. Normally, I would have let them come and sort out any threat. But then she opened her eyes for a fraction of a second, allowing me a glimpse of chocolate-brown eyes that were so warm and unguarded, it made me pause. My world had never been full of anything but darkness, yet these were bright. Happy, even. So stunning that my mouth parted, and my hand came up to hold back my guards.

"Are you hurt?"

"My pride? Yes. My head? It's nothing a little makeup won't fix."

Despite the soft giggles beneath her words, I touched it anyway, memorizing the place I'd made contact with her. There would be a bump there in the morning. The thought of her with even the smallest of injuries stoked something dark inside of me. For the first time, my hunger changed shape, twisting, wanting not just to kill, but to hurt. To own.

To make her *mine*.

I craved the way she looked at me, her eyes wide and trusting, lips parted as if she, too, was mesmerized by what she saw. I wanted to claim that look, for her to whimper my name under her breath in her nightingale voice, for her to belong to me and only me.

You are Death.

Yes, I thought, finally shoving the voice away from my mind. *I am Death. I have tasted Life. And I want more.*

No matter what it took.

"Let me help you stand." I looked away because I knew that if I saw her lips looking so damn kissable, I would slam her to the snow and find out what those brown eyes looked like when they rolled into the back of her head.

Sliding my arms around her and helping her up, I studied her a moment longer than was polite, committing every facet of her to memory. I had memorized building plans faster than this, cataloged men's faces in seconds before ending their lives. But her, I took my time with.

There was something about her that was familiar, some part of her that tugged at the edges of my memory. But I pushed the feeling aside, because hers was a face I would not forget.

"Are you cold?" I asked, frowning at her thin coat and reddened cheeks.

She shook her head, though the slight tremble in her body suggested otherwise. Without a second thought, I slipped off my cream-colored scarf and wrapped it around her neck. I wondered what her pale skin would look like covered in bite marks and bruises. Evidence that I owned her.

The woman's eyes widened. "I can't accept this."

"Of course you can. It matches your outfit perfectly."

She beamed, spinning for me. My cock hardened at the sight of it, her performing for me. "It does, doesn't it?" she giggled. "Though I promise I'll return it."

I liked that promise. It meant she wanted to see me again. Because, despite our already apparent differences, I could only bring myself to think of beginnings rather than endings. Reasons to stay instead of reasons to go.

"My name is Alek," I said, voice low as I stuck out my hand.

She didn't hesitate to accept it. "I'm Eva."

Eva.

Eva.

Eva, Eva, Eva, Eva, Eva, my mind replayed over and over while my fingers lingered around hers, unwilling to let her go yet.

"That's a beautiful name. It suits you."

Soft. Delicate. *Breakable.*

Her cheeks pinked further, and she laughed quietly, tugging the scarf closer. "You're very kind for someone I nearly knocked flat, Alek."

My name on her lips did something violent to my chest.

"You didn't," I said smoothly despite the frantic beating behind my ribcage, the one that insisted I take her innocence and taint it with my sin. "I wasn't watching where I was going either."

"Still, I'm sorry. And grateful for the scarf. It's really warm, and I can tell the fabric is expensive." Eva giggled. "I might accidentally forget to give it back to you. No one's ever given me something so nice."

The thought of Eva walking around the city with something of mine—something to claim any little part of her that I could—made my cock harden in my pants. I wanted to use that scarf to tie her to my bedposts so she could never leave. I wanted to do a lot of things to this woman.

Like make her mine.

My soul had been marred by shadows for over a decade, controlled by demons who wanted to hurt the world around me. But Eva? I wanted to find out what she looked like when her light was smothered by my darkness. I wanted her to be trembling and sobbing for mercy. I wanted her to be so addicted to me that she would do anything for another taste.

In the minutes I had known her, my soul had become obsessed. It didn't care who or what she was. I craved her. And when I craved something, I would do *anything* to have it.

I reached forward and cupped her cheek with my hand, stroking her soft, petal-pink lips with my thumb. The sudden touch shocked both of us, though I couldn't bring myself to stop, and apparently neither could Eva, whose breath hitched.

Yes, I thought. *I want you breathless for me.*

"They're fools," I mumbled.

"For?"

"Not giving you what you deserve."

But I could. I had an entire empire at my disposal—hotels, bars, clubs, property management, shipping and logistics, weaponry, and many more. If I had to call upon that empire to get her, to serve her properly, I would.

Eva swallowed. "And how do you know what I deserve, Alek?"

I leaned forward, preparing to find out if she tasted how she smelled—like vanilla with a hint of sugar, warmth in winter. Something soft I could bury myself in.

But a laugh behind us made her blink before pulling back, looking apologetic. I wanted to kill whoever interrupted us. I *would* kill them as soon as I pulled her to me and finished what we never got to start. Their blood would coat my hands while I took her to the underworld with me—the Persephone to my Hades.

"Sorry. I'd better get back to my friends. We were having a

snowball fight. They're probably starting to get worried." Eva turned to look at the only other couple in the park, yet instead of going over to them, she frowned.

"What is it?" I asked.

I took a closer look and noticed her "friends" were not worrying, but making out against a tree. Her nose wrinkled, disappointment thinly veiled with amusement.

"Wow. Traitors."

"They seem occupied. Is it like that a lot with them?"

She shook her head. "Well... no. Not really. Mia is my best friend, but this is our first time meeting Carmelo."

Eva gave me a fake smile, and I'd never hated the sight of something more. It stirred something restless in me, something sharp and yearning to kill someone to bring back the real one.

"It's fine," she said, even though it was clearly not. "I hope this one works out. I'd better leave them to it. They don't need a third wheel hanging around."

"Can I take you home?" *Say yes, Eva.* "My car isn't far."

It would be much easier to convince her to come back to my home once I got her in my backseat, where prying eyes and idiot couples couldn't interrupt what I had planned.

"Thanks, but no. I'm not far."

"Can I walk you, then?"

To my dismay, she shook her head again. "Sorry, but my brother is pretty protective. I don't think he'd approve of strangers knowing where I live."

I bit back a scowl because the news was both irritating and relieving. I was glad she had someone looking out for her, but he was in my way, and I wouldn't allow that.

"All right. But at least let me walk you to the gates."

Where I would follow her home, learn everything about her, and use it to make her mine.

Poor Eva. She had no idea she'd walked into the spider's

web. Into the cave of a vicious monster who decided he wanted to savor the taste of her.

Eva smiled gently—that damned smile had me on my knees—and nodded. "Fine. But only to the gates. And only because you are loaning me such a nice scarf."

I held out my arm and relished the feeling of her arm slipping through mine, her petite body brushing against me with every step. Eva giggled to herself as she attempted to catch snowflakes.

My lips almost curved upward watching her. I couldn't remember the last time I smiled, yet she made me want to.

I brushed back a lock of hair that had fallen out of her ribbon. Eva startled, her brown eyes coming back to me with curiosity. My gaze held hers, and I allowed some of the desire I'd been attempting to hide peek through the cracks, the demons that had begun to crave her. "You're very beautiful."

Something softened in her eyes at that, something fragile and real. She ducked her head, a smile curving her mouth. "Well, thank you. That's kind of you."

I had never been described as kind. A killer, a monster, death maybe. But I wasn't interested in saving her from my world. I wanted to drag her into it. I wanted to see if her tears tasted delicious. If her pain sounded as sweet as her voice. Eva would call the things I planned to do to her kindness.

By the time she realized the truth, it would be too late for her to escape me.

"I'm glad you weren't watching where you were going, Alek," she whispered as we neared the gates.

"So am I."

We stood there a moment longer than necessary, each drinking the other in. Finally, Eva looked above and smiled to herself. I followed her gaze and almost smirked when I found a bough of mistletoe dangling above us.

And maybe it was too hasty of me, but I shot forward and grabbed the back of her neck, hauling her lips to mine.

Eva gasped, her hands wrapping around my middle, gripping my blood-stained shirt with all her might. Her open mouth was an opportunity that I greedily took, thrusting my tongue inside and groaning at the taste of her.

Sweet, like candy.

She was soft and warm, everything I imagined her to be. My other hand, the one not gripping her neck, found the curve of her waist and pulled her impossibly closer. Stray locks of hair brushed against my nose, assaulting me with the smell of vanilla shampoo and pure temptation.

Mine... mine... mine... I wanted to growl when I lightly bit her lip, giving her a taste of pain with her pleasure. She was going to be all fucking *mine*.

I ended it when I decided I'd taken enough, when my control frayed just enough to make me consider trapping her under me. But I had to be smart about this. Games of chess were not won by irrational first moves. To own the board, I would play as the white knight. And then I would reveal myself as her dark king.

Eva took a step back, eyes dazed, fingers tightening around the scarf as if anchoring herself back to reality.

"I'll return this," she said, voice cracking. "I swear."

"I'll hold you to it, solnyshka."

And before I could say goodbye, before I could order one of my guards to silently follow her, Eva leaned forward one more time and placed a brief but searing kiss on my lips, pulling away with amusement dancing across her face.

I reached up to touch my mouth, smirking to myself when my fingers came away covered with faint traces of her pink lip gloss. The same color as her ribbons, her coat. It was becoming my favorite.

I turned to my guards, my face once again cold. They

studied me unnervingly. I couldn't blame them. After all, I'd spent my entire life completely uninterested in women, unlike my soft, sweet, gentle Eva. She wore her naivety like a diamond necklace, her innocence shining, calling to the parts of me that wanted to break her into submission and show her how good darkness tasted.

One guard, Ilya, cleared his throat. "Sir... that was—"

"Not another word," I said quietly, the threat more than apparent in my voice. "Follow her."

Their eyes widened with panic as they looked to the dark path Eva had vanished down. I followed their gazes and found nothing. No pink coat, no sign of the silhouette I just held in my arms. It was as if she'd never been there at all.

And then Ilya voiced the words I hadn't dared to think. The ones that had the potential to ruin everything.

"Sir. W-we can't. She's gone."

I turned back to them, jaw clenched to the point of breaking, eyes cold with fury. She didn't get to disappear. Not from me.

"Then fucking *find her*."

December 10th

ALEKSANDR
Want to redeem your utter failure at the shipyards?

NIKOLAI
Will it get you to stop glaring at me?

ALEKSANDR
No.

NIKOLAI
Fineeeeee.

But whatever favor you want is going to be your Christmas gift.

ALEKSANDR
Fine.

I need you to find a girl.

NIKOLAI
Oooh! A scavenger hunt. How exciting!

ALEKSANDR
This isn't one of your fucking games, Nikolai.

NIKOLAI
All right, all right. Don't get your panties in a twist. Who am I looking for?

ALEKSANDR
Name is Eva. About five two. Petite. Brown hair, most likely wearing pink.

NIKOLAI

That's it?

That's all you're giving me?

There are millions of people in this city, and you're giving me the most basic ass description?

ALEKSANDR

I would watch how you talk about her. She's not fucking basic.

NIKOLAI

Sheesh, Aleksandr. You're even grumpier than normal.

ALEKSANDR

Find her, Nikolai.

NIKOLAI

Don't worry, cuz. I will.

EVANGELINE
CHAPTER THREE

"And run, and run... Arabesque... Mia, stop giggling, you're a snowflake. Act like one... I want to see clean footwork, now... Beautiful, Evangeline. Chin up, my darling..." Madame Germaine accentuated her words with a tap of her cane as we soared across the studio, our bullet pointe skirts fluttering while we moved. "Excellent, Evangeline! Arms up high for this next eight-count..."

I smiled in the mirror while the teenager playing Clara leaped across the room, the Nutcracker following behind her. But instead of seeing the choreography I'd spent months perfecting, instead of seeing what Madame Germaine saw, I only noticed the flaws.

My skirt was slightly wrinkled. A single flyaway escaped my bun, smudged lipstick streaked the corner of my mouth, and my leotard dug into my skin just enough to feel wrong.

A voice in the back of my mind hissed, *"You are not enough. You are not perfect."* The voice kept repeating, sharper with each heartbeat, until my chest ached.

Another layer to the mental illness that had been buried inside of me for years.

We finished the dance, and Mia spun onto her toes as she

bounded over to the side. Her body looked otherworldly as she practiced one of her moves as the sultry Arabian dancer, bending and turning into impossible form.

"See. She is perfect," the voice said. *"You are not."*

Mia pinched my cheeks. "Well, you're a sad-looking snowflake, aren't you? Why are you frowning so much?"

"I'm not frowning. I'm concentrating."

"Sure." Mia laughed, giving my shoulder a playful shove. "Look at you, Eva. You've been staring at your reflection like it's personally offended you for at least fifteen minutes. You're obsessed with... what? Your hair? Your outfit?"

"Maybe both," I said with a shrug, retying my ribbon.

Glancing at my reflection one more time, I corrected a slight tilt in my shoulders and cursed at a small spot of sweat on my skirt.

"Not perfect... Not perfect... Not perfect..."

"You're ridiculous," Mia said, shaking her head. I couldn't help but notice how wonderfully in place all her golden hairs were. What did she do that I didn't? Was it a different hairspray?

"Hey, princess," she continued, snapping me out of a spiral before it began. "You've been acting weird for the past couple of days. I've given you space. Now I want you to spill."

"I'm fine, Mia. Really. Don't worry about me."

"Uh-huh," she said, not buying it for a second. She patted me on the shoulder like a doting older sister. "Tell me right now, Evangeline Vale, or so help me God: I will tell your brother that you have nasty blisters all over your feet. Or maybe a fungus...."

My eyes widened. My hands trembled as I clutched her arm, every thought spiraling into worst-case scenarios. "No, Mia, you really can't. If he thinks something is wrong with me, he won't let me dance in the show! He's already upset about the little bruise on my head."

That was an understatement. When Jules saw the teensy little bump on my forehead, he went ballistic, even though I told him I'd tripped and fallen. Last night was the first night he let me stay in my apartment again.

Though it was a little overboard, I enjoyed our time together—Jules caving and watching rom-coms with me every night. Despite his sometimes stubborn ways, he cared for me. We'd never fought, never argued. So I knew what he was doing was probably best for me, even if I didn't agree with it.

Mia rolled her eyes. "Relax, Evie. I know. But you're telling me when we leave. Okay?"

Instead of letting myself burn under her questioning gaze, I faced the rest of the studio, which was lined with mirrors, reflecting the dozens of dancers standing against the walls while the Prince and the Sugar Plum Fairy danced in perfect harmony.

So romantic, I thought with a sigh as I watched their pas de deux. I wanted someone to dance with me like that, to look into my eyes, pull me close, and—

There was a loud banging sound as the Fairy fell to the ground, rubbing at her ankle.

"Are you all right?" I mouthed to Elsie, one of my brother's oldest childhood friends and prima of the City Ballet Company. I itched to run to her, but a part of me remembered that Elsie wouldn't want me to make a big deal out of her injury as it healed. She kept her emotions locked in a box even more than I did.

Elsie was the reason I'd always dreamed of auditioning—which I did as soon as I was invited to, even though it meant leaving university a year early. The close-knit dancers, the glittering costumes, the graceful choreography sounded like a dream, and I'd loved the idea of getting to dance alongside her even though she'd talked of retiring for years.

But when she badly sprained her ankle right before the

season began, I thought she'd finally make the leap. Though she was young, ballet was incredibly hard on our bodies. Our feet were covered in blisters, the skin sometimes falling off when I took off my pointe shoes, and our muscles were almost always sore. Despite this, Madame Germaine somehow convinced Elsie to come back for one last season. It was nice to have a familiar face when I first joined, but I still didn't like knowing she was in pain every time she danced.

And my brother *really* wouldn't like it if he knew how hard it was on her.

He said they were just friends, but I had my doubts. Jules was Elsie's Prince Charming... if only he would acknowledge it.

"I'm fine. Go," Elsie mouthed before getting back into position while Madame Germaine dismissed the rest of us.

Mia slung her arm through mine and led me to the dressing room, which was steadily filling with loud voices laughing and talking about the upcoming show. The Nutcracker was every ballet's biggest show—generating enough revenue and interest to keep the theater going for the rest of the year—and the excitement for the upcoming shows reflected it clearly.

I arranged my shoes with exact spacing, adjusted the hems of my skirt three times, and smoothed the tiniest crease in my costume, my hands trembling until everything felt right. When I looked perfect once more, I slipped my coat on and reached for my scarf.

Well, not my scarf.

His.

It still smelled like him—like winter and leather and the faint hint of soap. The cream-colored fabric was much too warm for the studio, but I looped it around my neck anyway and savored the feel of it against my skin. Soft, unlike his body underneath mine.

The memory of him made my cheeks heat.

A lightly tanned hand slapped against my assigned vanity. "Rehearsal is over. Now *spill*."

I sighed. "I'm just nervous for *The Nutcracker*. I don't want to mess up."

But Mia clearly didn't buy it.

"Liar," she said. "You did great today. Madame Germaine called you excellent, which is practically a promise to be a principal next year. And though you like to pretend that you do, you don't have to earn your place here every second. You're incredible, Evangeline. We all know it."

Mia's reassurance loosened some of the knots in my chest, but only a little. Compliments always did that to me. They always felt like things people had to say to me, not ever anything they actually meant. Maybe that was me being insecure, my childhood catching up to me.

"What's wrong? Really?" Mia asked again, this time much softer.

The truth was that, while I was nervous about the ballet, my mind was a tempest. And at its center was *him*.

My Prince Charming.

His hard face, chiseled as if formed underneath a sculptor's hands. His body, warm and safe and *so muscular*, filling out his suit in the most delicious of ways. His eyes, which were the color of the sky in the middle of the night when my dreams of him were strongest. His dark, swirling tattoos peeking out from under his collar. His presence, which sucked all the air out of my lungs, leaving my soul to crave him instead. His velvet soft lips pressing into mine and devouring my every uncertainty.

I bit my lip. "Can I tell you another time? I'm really tired. I think I just want to chill. But I promise I will tell you *if* you can keep a secret."

"Um... do you even have to ask that? Bitch, I'm your *best*

friend. Of course, I can keep a secret—as long as you agree to tell me when you're ready. For now, though, want to come over and rot our brains with cheap wine and reality TV?" Mia asked, wincing as the bitter winter wind greeted us outside the studio.

"Sure. Let me call and tell Jules."

Her groan echoed all the way to the metro station. "No! He's a buzzkill who's gonna say no."

"You don't know that."

"I'd have to be an idiot not to! Your brother and fun go along together like peanut butter and drywall. Not at all, Eva. Not at all."

I shook my head as I fumbled in my bag for my phone to call Jules, who was supposed to be picking me up.

Was it a little embarrassing to be picked up by my big brother when I wasn't in school anymore? Yes, a little. But even without my anxieties around driving—I still flinched whenever Jules hit a small bump—I didn't have the money for a car of my own. I could barely afford my apartment that, sure, had the occasional rodent and roach and, yeah, sometimes had people that terrified me digging through the discarded needles in the nearby alley, and, yes, wasn't nice even remotely. But I was sure there were worse options out there.

Every princess had to live in squalor before finding her castle... at least I thought so. I usually liked to skip ahead to the happy endings with all the kissing and weddings and pretty dresses.

Mia waited impatiently as I turned my phone on, only to find several missed calls from my brother.

Crap.

"Hey, Jules," I greeted him after he picked up on the first ring, no doubt seething by the phone while he waited for me.

"What is the point of purchasing you a phone if you aren't going to call me with it?"

"To get cute cases and take lots of pictures of puppies and kittens. Oh! And play those cozy restaurant games."

"How are we related?" he grumbled. "You were supposed to call me an hour ago, so I could pick you up from rehearsal. Are you all right? Did something happen? Do I need to—"

"Nothing happened. We got let out late. Ask Elsie if you don't believe me." Because he wouldn't.

Jules always insisted I was too optimistic for this world, too easy for people to take advantage of. We chose to move through the world in different ways. While he barreled through it, doing whatever he needed to do to get what he wanted, I'd spent it wearing a hundred different faces, my smiles always enough to keep the peace. People pleasing was a language I spoke fluently, one I'd learned early and never quite forgotten. It was easier that way.

And maybe some of what he said was true. Mia kept trying to instruct me on how to grow a backbone, though it wasn't really working, and I often found myself believing every sob story on the internet. But I didn't consider myself naive. I knew there was darkness in the world. I just chose to ignore it in favor of all the light it had to offer instead.

"All right. Well, I'll come pick you up—"

"That's okay. I'm going to Mia's tonight."

"And how are you getting to her house?"

"We can take the metro."

"*WHAT?!*" he screeched so loud I had to rub my ears to get the ringing to stop. "No way, Evangeline. You are not riding that death trap train in those sketchy tunnels. Not at night— scratch that. Not at *all*."

I sighed. Our conversations always went like this—me trying to be a little more independent and Jules shooting me down while I bit back tears. I knew Jules still saw me as his baby sister, but if I was old enough to consume a questionable amount of liquor in Mia's living room while watching reruns of reality TV, then I was old enough to figure things out on my own. Things like taking the metro or working a dead-end job or...

Or finding my Prince Charming. A guy like Alek.

But I didn't say any of that to Jules. Because I would do anything to make sure the people I cared about had their happiness. Even if that came at the expense of my own.

Still, I thought it wouldn't hurt to try one more time. "I'm twenty-one years old. I'm old enough to ride a train to a friend's house. Mia lives in a nice neighborhood. It can't be that bad."

"No."

"Jules, please—"

"No. I'll come and pick you up right now."

"But—"

"No buts, Annie," he said, using the childhood nickname my whole family called me. The one he *knew* would soften me to the point of caving in. "Don't fight me on this. Love you."

And then he hung up.

Mia sighed. "See! Buzzkill."

December 14th

ALEKSANDR

Have you found her?

NIKOLAI

Hello, Nikolai, how are you?

I'm fabulous, thank you. I just made passionate love to a redhead with the largest tits I've ever seen. How are you, Aleksandr?

Oh, it's great to hear that you are doing well.

ALEKSANDR

What the fuck are you talking about?

NIKOLAI

Just teaching you how to have a proper conversation since it seems like you've forgotten.

Thank God you have your attractive, intelligent older cousin around.

ALEKSANDR

Don't make me ask again.

NIKOLAI

No, I have not. But I'm looking.

December 21st

ALEKSANDR

Have you found her?

NIKOLAI

Perfection takes time, Aleksandr. No.

ALEKSANDR

Look harder. Unless you changed your mind about wanting to live.

NIKOLAI

A please would have sufficed, dear cousin.

ALEKSANDR

Fuck you.

December 25th

NIKOLAI

Merry Christmas, cousin!

ALEKSANDR

Have you found her?

NIKOLAI

No "Happy Holidays" back?

ALEKSANDR

Have. You. Found. Her.

NIKOLAI

No. She's proving to be exceedingly difficult to find. Not spotted on any city cameras, and no digital footprint that we can find. It's like she doesn't exist. Did you make out with a ghost or something?

ALEKSANDR

No.

Find her, Nikolai.

NIKOLAI

sighs

I will.

...

ALEKSANDR

Merry Christmas, asshole.

EVANGELINE
CHAPTER FOUR

A FEW WEEKS LATER, I WAS BACK IN THE CAR ON THE way to Mia's apartment—the only place I went beyond the theater, the cafe, and *occasionally* Jules's house.

Lately, I'd been staying there more often than at my own apartment, mostly because with Mia, it was easier to fall asleep. Easier to pretend that my life wasn't a cage, that I wasn't the only bird in there, both lonely and alone.

Mia, the human equivalent of a hummingbird, might not have been in the cage with me, but she was hovering outside of it with all her might, trying to break me out with every glare aimed at the back of Jules's head while he drove us carefully down the streets, which were alight with holiday glow.

It was a magical time of year, one of my *favorite* times of year. And this year, it was even better because I got to perform in a show I'd always wanted to be a part of—even if I was just a snowflake and a flower. Perhaps next year, if our stern director's looks were anything to go by, I would be more.

I hoped I would. But hope was a fickle thing in a mind like mine. A ticking clock that would eventually run out of time.

"*Not perfect... Not perfect... Not perfect...*"

I tried to tear my mind away from the voice, instead turning to Mia, who was miming strangling my brother. I elbowed her to knock it off, and she rolled her eyes like a sullen teenager.

Which made sense considering I felt a *lot* like a teenager right now, sitting in the back seat of my brother's car on my way to a sleepover. But in my defense, I was only in the backseat because Elsie was in the front.

Elsie came over for dinner more often than she didn't, especially when I wasn't home. She'd cut off her family long ago, and my parents were off gallivanting around the world, uncaring of what Jules and I were up to. Jules's dinners with Elsie were special to him, and he was always a little more lenient with me going to Mia's when she was coming over.

Just friends, my butt, I thought. I watched through the rearview mirror as my brother's eyes continued to go to her like a sunflower following the sun.

"All right," he said, pulling up to Mia's familiar building. "You'll call me in the morning to take you back?"

"Yes, Jules," I huffed. "See you later."

"Bye, Buzzkill," Mia sneered under her breath before skipping to the door arm in arm with me. As soon as we stepped inside, I breathed a sigh of relief. I loved my brother, but his overprotectiveness sometimes made me feel like I was suffocating.

"I don't get where he gets the *nerve,*" Mia grumbled, waving to her doorman before clicking the elevator button, flipping off my brother's sports car as he pulled away.

Her glower followed us inside and up to her apartment door. "I mean... is it his ass? Does he shove the audacity clear up there for safekeeping?"

"Mia, be nice. He's my brother."

"This *is* me being nice. Because I'm this close—" She held up her fingers barely a millimeter apart. "—to beating his ass until he lets you behave like a grown ass woman. So, really, me holding myself back *is* being nice."

I looked at her while we walked down the hallway. Mia wasn't going to be fighting anyone, anytime. Especially not my stocky brother with a temper issue. She lost every battle with a Sephora makeup sale. One promise of a brand new eyeshadow palette from him, and she would be toast.

"I mean, if you're old enough to get a tramp stamp that you later regret, you're old enough to live without someone constantly surveilling you!"

My brows knitted together. "What's a tramp stamp?"

Mia froze in the midst of jingling her keys in her lock before sighing and turning. She squeezed my cheeks with a gentle smile. "Oh, you sweet summer child."

"What is it?"

"Never mind," she laughed. "Come on."

I followed her into her apartment, which was decorated with an eclectic assortment of prints, knick-knacks, and far too many throw pillows. Despite our almost laughable salary from the City Ballet Company, Mia always seemed to have enough budget for a little trinket wherever we went.

Not that Jules let us go many places. But sometimes he took us to the mall, so I took that as a win.

I smiled at the view out her floor-to-ceiling windows, the city lit up like a Christmas tree. The world was so wide I could hardly believe it sometimes. My little corner of it felt so small.

Mia flicked on her large television before stalking to her modern kitchen and setting a bag of popcorn in the microwave. Our dinner on nights like this, when we couldn't bring ourselves to cook after a performance, nor order takeout that we couldn't afford. Mia's parents might have subsidized her luxury apartment while she danced for the Company, but they weren't paying for her food delivery fees.

"So," she began later, flopping onto the couch, a bottle of

wine in one hand and a bowl of popcorn in the other. She patted the spot next to her. "I've given you a couple of weeks. When are you finally going to tell me why you've been acting so *weird* lately?'

I was in the middle of wrapping myself in a pink fuzzy blanket—one she kept here just for me, knowing they were my favorite—when I stilled, my eyes dragging over to Mia, whose hardened expression told me I wasn't getting out of it this time. I'd been putting off her many questions for months, and I knew I would soon be reaching the limits of her patience.

I just wished it had lasted a *little* longer.

With a sigh, I scooted closer to her, grabbing the bottle from her hands and taking a direct swig. The sickly sweet taste burned the back of my throat, and I coughed. Drinking was never really my thing. I was always too focused on dancing to go out with friends, and I hadn't been twenty-one for long anyway. Plus, it wasn't like Jules was offering me his liquor to try.

Needless to say, that was something Mia changed shortly after we met. Now, I still didn't *love* drinking—who likes dealing with headaches and regrets in the morning?—but I didn't abhor every second of the nights she dragged me out to the clubs either.

"Spill, Evangeline."

"Fine," I groaned. "But you can't tell anyone. *And* you can't judge me. Or react. Or ever bring this up again."

"The only one of those I'm actually agreeing to is to never tell anyone. But I will be judging, reacting, and most certainly bringing this up again because you never have secrets, ever, and I plan on taking full advantage of this."

I tried to glare at her, but she looked at me like I was a wet kitten—angry yet adorable. "Fine. I kissed someone."

True to her word, Mia *did* react.

A lot.

First, she threw the popcorn bowl up, kernels launching into the air and landing like snowflakes around us. Then, she screamed, clapped her hands, did a few laps around the room, sat back down on the couch, squealed and jumped up again, and did a few more laps before wrapping me in a hug and pulling me back down with her, giggling like a madwoman.

"Eva! You kissed someone! You *kissed* someone! Oh my God, oh my God, oh my God. That was your first kiss, right?"

My cheeks burned as I nodded. I didn't love to be reminded of how inexperienced I was, because it wasn't like I *wanted* to be a lame, unkissed virgin with no knowledge of what things like tramp stamps were. But with my sheltered upbringing, going to a small, women-only boarding school for high school, then dedicating my entire universe to ballet as soon as I was old enough to fully commit to it, there hadn't been time or space for love to blossom. Plus, there was no one I ever *wanted* to make my first kiss.

But I'd kissed Alek twice.

The first time, he caught me off guard. I was too busy staring at his long, black lashes, the dark sapphires they lined, and the way his skin looked like rich caramel under the glowing streetlights.

But the second time, I'd kissed him first because I *wanted* to kiss him again. I wanted to taste him, to feel his body pressed against mine, to inhale him until my head spun. Already, I felt the pull of something I couldn't name, some dark hunger that seemed to come from him alone. If I saw him again, I didn't know if I'd run—or if I'd let him own me entirely. Because a large part of me was ready to do a *lot* more than kiss him.

Only the reminder that Jules would kill Alek if he found out we'd even talked pulled me back from our second peck. I'd had to run away before I got tempted again, but if I saw Alek again?

I wasn't sure what I'd do.

I needed to distance myself from him. For both my sake and Alek's. Jules would never allow us to be together, especially since Alek was radiating danger from his expensive suit to the tattoos beneath it to the hardened glint in his eyes. There was too much in the way, too many rules that a relationship like ours broke.

"Okay, okay," Mia said. "Tell me everything."

So I did. I told her about the snowball fight, the collision, Alek's hands making sure I was okay, the way he looked at me like he'd never wanted anything more, him loaning me the scarf, and our kiss. And, finally, I told her about the way I ran away like a coward, unwilling to face the idea that Jules wouldn't let us be together.

"I'm gonna die alone, Mia," I groaned.

She clicked her tongue. "No, you're not. Men like that don't just vanish."

"You don't know that."

"From what you've told me, I know enough. You might be convinced he's your perfect Prince Charming, but it seems pretty clear to me that he's a starving man, and what he's craving is you. You know who that sounds like to me? *The villain.*"

I gaped. "But I don't want to end up with the villain!"

"Do you?" she raised a brow. "You want a Prince Charming, but would a prince be willing to go against your brother? Would a prince *win*?"

I frowned because she had a good point. Jules was stubborn like fire—unpredictable, raging, consuming everything in its path once it caught a spark. He wasn't the kind of man who cooled down with time or reason. He burned hotter when challenged, met darkness head-on with his temper blazing until there was nothing left but ash.

Maybe Mia was right. Maybe this wasn't something that

could be soothed with gentleness or patience. You didn't smother a wildfire with soft words. You either let it burn itself out...

Or you met it with something strong enough to withstand it.

And I didn't know Alek very well, but I knew this much: he wasn't fire. He was ice. Cold, relentless, and deadly in its own way. And for me, he would hold his ground until the flames had nothing left to feed on.

If I hadn't messed things up already.

"No," I finally replied to Mia, chewing my lip while I tried to think about anything I could do to fix the mess I'd created.

The problem was: I wasn't sure I *could* fix it—and even if I could, I needed to slow down and think about not only our last show tomorrow, but our auditions for the spring show, *Romeo and Juliet*, the day after. I figured I would be a background dancer, but a part of me hoped I had proven myself in *The Nutcracker* to get more of a lead role. I needed to focus on my career, on my dancing, for the next few days. Afterward, I would worry about Alek.

"Exactly. The villain is the one who will do anything for you, who will give you the world if you ask for it. He'll take everything from you and leave you desperate for more, which is scary and a little hot. But I guess it fits because the villain is going to be the one to fuck you into oblivion. *Not* your Prince Charming."

I was pretty sure that, at that moment, my face resembled a bright red Christmas ornament. "*Mia*! I-I... um... I mean... ugh! Don't say things like that!"

"Why?" she grinned knowingly. "Is it because you want him to? You want Alek to shove you against the wall and show you what a good time is?"

"No!" I lied, turning away before I turned into a tomato. *God*, this was so embarrassing. Why did I even tell her this?

"Uh-huh. Anyway, let me tell you *all* about protection. Are you on the pill?"

"I am *not* answering that!" I stood, stomping over to the kitchen while clutching my blanket and one of her pillows shaped like a disco ball. I desperately needed some water.

Was it hot in there? Did I need to turn on the air conditioning?

"Alek and Eva, sitting in a tree. F-U-C-K-I—"

Mia's song was cut off by the sound of a pillow hitting her in the side of the head. She lost herself in a fit of laughter, clutching at her stomach while she rolled in pure glee. Despite her teasing, I couldn't help but laugh alongside her, some of the heaviness I'd felt since Alek and I met finally alleviating. My lungs screamed for a reprieve, and my cheeks ached from smiling so hard.

After the laughter faded and the wine dulled to a pleasant warmth in my chest, we curled up together beneath the blankets, the city humming softly beyond the glass. Mia eventually fell asleep with her head on my shoulder, breathing slow and even, like nothing in the world could touch us.

I stared at the ceiling long after, tracing invisible lines between the shadows.

A villain. A man willing to burn the world for me.

The thought should have scared me. Instead, it settled deep in my bones, warm and dangerous yet magnetizing in a way, drawing me closer to something I both feared and craved.

If Alek really was a villain, if he wanted me like Mia said, nothing would stand in his way. I couldn't hide from him, and the longer I went without him, the more I wasn't sure I wanted to.

December 26th

ALEKSANDR
Have you found her?

NIKOLAI
Yes.

MISSED CALL FROM ALEKSANDR
MISSED CALL FROM ALEKSANDR
MISSED CALL FROM ALEKSANDR

ALEKSANDR
Answer, Nikolai.

NIKOLAI
Dude, I'm in the shower. Stop interrupting my music. My shampoo is in desperate need of a good concert.

MISSED CALL FROM ALEKSANDR
MISSED CALL FROM ALEKSANDR
MISSED CALL FROM ALEKSANDR

NIKOLAI
Stop, you asshole! I'm getting ready and coming over. Be patient for once in your life.

MISSED CALL FROM ALEKSANDR

ALEKSANDR
Tell me where she is, Nikolai.

NIKOLAI
I will in 15 minutes. See you soon, cousin!

MISSED CALL FROM ALEKSANDR

ALEKSANDR
Nikolai.

MISSED CALL FROM ALEKSANDR

Nikolai.

MISSED CALL FROM ALEKSANDR

Nikolai.

MISSED CALL FROM ALEKSANDR
MISSED CALL FROM ALEKSANDR
MISSED CALL FROM ALEKSANDR

NIKOLAI

:)

ALEKSANDR
CHAPTER FIVE

Nikolai wasn't inside my door before my hand was wrapped around his throat, shoving him against the wall. The little bitch had the nerve to look amused as I growled, "Give me one good reason why I shouldn't strangle you where you stand."

"Because the world would miss my dashing good looks and striking wit?"

I narrowed my eyes and tightened my grip. "Strike one."

How had someone not killed him before? I'd been around him for almost thirty years, and I was ready to bury him six feet under so he'd finally shut up.

"Because Aunt Maria would be very upset if you killed her darling nephew?"

"She can cry on my shoulder at the funeral."

Niko's eyes widened when he realized I was serious—something he should have considered earlier. It had been almost three weeks since I met Eva, and I had gone past being impatient and straight to feral.

Where the fuck was she? I knew I didn't have much information about her, but with every Drakov man scouring camera footage, returning to the park where we met, skulking about city records, it shouldn't have been possible for her to hide from me. And yet she remained out of reach.

It drove me off the cliff toward madness.

Every night, I replayed our kiss over and over in my mind, wondering why I was so obsessed with a girl I barely knew.

Her light pulled at my darkness, igniting a hunger I hadn't felt for years. I needed to consume her—not just her body, but her mind, her very essence—until the thought of leaving me became impossible. She would belong entirely to me.

Logic screamed that a weakness like her should be snuffed out. But desire—possessive, raw, unforgiving desire—roared louder. I would burn the city, crush anyone who stood in my way, and drag her into my world whether she wanted it or not.

The captive men currently tied up in my warehouse, their blood still crusted under my nails, were the only things keeping me from actually doing it. They did not fully satisfy the beast, but they pacified it. For now.

Was she a ghost? A figment of my tired imagination?

No. I wasn't sure what she was, or what kept her hidden from me. But it didn't matter. Eva was mine. Every thought, every breath she took, every secret she clung to. All of it belonged to me. Whether she realized it or not, she would not escape me again. I would see to that.

"Fine, fine, fine," Nikolai gasped, face beginning to turn a sickly gray-blue. "But I haven't told anyone where your girl is, so if you kill me, you'll never know."

My scowl must have been a terrifying sight to Nikolai, who stepped back as soon as I let go of him, putting several feet of distance between us in case I got the urge to kill him again.

"You have five minutes to convince me you know where she is," I growled, running my hands through my hair. The dark brown strands had been standing straight up since I woke up the morning after meeting Eva, expecting to get a call that they'd found her, only to hear radio silence for days.

Nikolai fixed his rumpled clothes with much exaggeration. "Hello to you, too, cousin. I see you've been working on your hospitality."

"Where is she?"

"God, you used to at least pretend to be normal. Now it's 'Niko, find her', 'Niko, where is she?', 'Niko, I'll kill you.' You know, you could at least take me to dinner before you threaten me."

I watched Niko's pulse jump as I turned to face him. And considering what he saw—what I saw every day in the mirror—I couldn't blame him. My eyes were bloodshot and red, the bags beneath them dark as bruises. My jaw was locked so tight it ached, and my usually put-together ensemble was covered in blood and probably a little urine from one of the captives.

"I am not in the mood, Niko," I seethed.

"That much is clear. Are you ever in the mood?"

"Where," I said, grinding my molars to dust, "is Eva?"

Nikolai gulped. He lifted both hands slowly, palms out in surrender. "Easy, dude. Don't start killing me yet. I have a feeling you're not going to like what I have to say."

"I don't like anything you say. Start talking."

"You're going to need a coat. And probably a shower."

"No."

"Aleksandr—"

My fingers flexed. "Tick tock, Nikolai. You're running your mouth a lot for someone who's running out of time."

Niko's mouth twitched, like he was fighting a smile. "See, but if I tell you where she is, you're either going to go all crazy and fuck things up for yourself, or you won't come with me. So rinse off, put on something presentable, and meet me back at the door."

"No."

"I haven't even said where!"

"I don't care."

Nikolai sighed, flopping backward onto the couch that I, unfortunately, liked too much to stain it with his blood. "Then I suppose you don't want to see her."

That made me still. "Are you saying you'll bring me to her if I come with you?"

A slow smile unfurled across his face. He had me, and he knew it. "I'm not saying anything until you put on your coat and rinse whatever is causing that horrible smell off you."

"That's not an answer."

"It's the only one you're getting."

I stared at him for a long moment, weighing my options. Killing him would feel good—but it would also end my chances of seeing Eva tonight. And that, I couldn't risk.

"Give me one hour," Nikolai added, softer now. "One hour where you trust me. And if I'm wrong, you can throw me off the balcony, or whatever it is you want to do."

I exhaled through my teeth and began stomping to the stairs. "Fine. But I won't enjoy it."

December 26th

JULES
Good luck tonight, Annie.

EVANGELINE
The correct phrase is "break a leg." :)

JULES
If someone breaks your leg, I will fucking destroy them.

EVANGELINE
Jeez, Jules...

ALEKSANDR
CHAPTER SIX

Fifteen minutes later, my scowl was deeper yet my mind was swimming in hope. Nikolai led me outside to a black car where his driver waited. The car rumbled against the cold, late-December winds.

"And where have I agreed to go for the next hour?" I grumbled.

Nikolai grinned. "To the City Ballet."

"Oh, fuck me."

It was a short drive to the theater, where a well-dressed crowd lined the sidewalk, waiting eagerly to get tickets. I was suddenly glad that Nikolai insisted I showered if she were one of the many people standing underneath the bright lights. I didn't want to see Eva looking like the Reaper, with blood splattered on my face and my hair in disarray.

"It's the last night of the show," Nikolai said, referring to the many people scrambling to get inside. "They've had a good turnout."

"And you know this because..."

"Because I've gone every night. You know that redhead I mentioned?" Nikolai mentioned many conquests, including many redheads. It was impossible to keep track of them all, but I nodded my head anyway in hopes he would get to the point sooner. "Well, she must have been pretty impressed with my performance. I mean, who wouldn't be? My cock is—"

"Niko."

"Right. Anyway, she wanted me to come see the show, and I told her I had expensive tastes because I wasn't going to sit with *regular people* with some child kicking my seat and another person smelling like cheap cologne and mildly stale popcorn. I can just see it now, liquor spilling all over my cashmere—"

"Nikolai. The point. Find it."

My cousin leaned in and gave me a sly smile. "What's the magic word?"

I narrowed my eyes. "*Now*."

"Well, she gave me box seats, and I came here one night. During intermission, I got to thinking about your darling Eva girl—"

"Don't fucking call her that," I growled, hands tightening on the seats until my knuckles were white and there were little crescent moons on the leather. If the driver hadn't opened the door right at that moment, I might have punched my cousin.

"—and anyway, I think the rest is better said inside. Just follow me."

The building was a monument to excess, all marble columns, warm golden light, and flickering lights that were in desperate need of an update. People clustered beneath the overhang, bundled in wool and fur, breath fogging the air while they eagerly grabbed their tickets and programs. They looked untouched. Soft. The kind of people who believed violence only existed on stages and screens, neatly choreographed and contained.

They were wrong. I knew the truth.

I followed my cousin inside, coat collar turned up against the cold as if it could hide my displeasure. I'd never been to the ballet before, and I'd never anticipated breaking that streak. Yet here I was, enduring an hour for Eva.

The sound was what hit me first. Music swelled from somewhere deep inside the building. There were strings tuning, clarinets trilling, and a timpani drum playing in a slow, booming rhythm. The sound grew louder while an usher led us to a small grouping of plush seats in a private balcony overlooking the stage, where two glasses of whiskey sat as if waiting for us. I grabbed one of them and downed it whole before gesturing to the attendant for another.

If I was going to spend my evening here, it would at least be with liquor.

The air in this stuffy theater was thick with perfume, polished wood, and anticipation. The dark red carpet looked so soaked with spilled liquor that it was practically a fire hazard. Crystal glasses chimed softly at the bar, and everywhere I looked, there were people. I felt more exposed than I had in years, staring at my little sister's broken body in the mangled car while people in uniforms swarmed like wasps.

"This is a waste of my time," I muttered, settling into the uncomfortable chair. Where the fuck was my drink?

Nikolai laughed deeply, clapping his hands together once as if we were about to attend a party instead of my personal hell. "Relax. It's culture."

"It's torture."

"Yes, yes," he said, waving me off. "Poor Aleksandr, forced to see one of the most moving art forms with some of the best seats in the house, surrounded by velvet and a server bringing you champagne. What a tragic life."

If you murder him, it will be difficult to clean the chairs, I reminded myself while the beast inside me raged in a storm of fury. "Are you going to tell me why I'm here now? Where is Eva?"

"Patience, Aleksandr. You agreed to one hour. At least wait until closer to the end before bombarding me with questions."

I scowled. "Fine."

The orchestra began to rise, their instruments now playing a sweeping song, growing and growing while the chandeliers slowly dimmed. The curtain was still drawn, but I could now make out faint rustling behind it, the little shadows of shoes coming to the edge as if trying to peek out. People were filling the seats, eagerly leaning forward, their programs rustling. Somewhere below, a woman shushed her children.

Finally, the curtains were pulled back, and dancers filled the stage, beginning the opening number. Their actions were controlled like pieces on a board. Nothing was out of place.

They moved throughout the music, their bodies portraying a story with grace and precision. Party guests, children, soldiers—characters I was unfamiliar with, but who Nikolai was trying to teach me about through his constantly whispered commentary. And though I could admit that they were impressive, I was utterly bored with it all.

Every second stretched my patience to a razor's edge. My jaw ached, and my blood thundered. My mind refused to focus on the stage, drifting instead to her—her pink coat, her snow-dusted curls, the way her body had fit beneath mine, soft and unresisting. The knowledge that she was out of reach, untouched and unmarked, made me want to tear the world apart.

Eva.

Where was she? Why the fuck was I here?

Beside me, Nikolai was explaining how the main character was about to go on a journey through this wonderful world. He was clearly enjoying himself far too much, and for a moment, I imagined pushing him over the balcony ledge. It could look like an accident, the crack in his neck timed with the timpani drum, the applause drowning out the ringing in my ears.

A pleasant thought. I almost smiled, savoring it.

Too bad I actually liked him.

The scene shifted once again, music softening, the stage darkening. They were no longer at a party, but in a world of white. Flakes fell around a dancer in a sparkling tutu, glittering lights spreading across to reveal a corps de ballet fluttering around her. Their costumes caught the lights like frost, and I realized they were meant to be snowflakes—or snow fairies or whatever the hell Nikolai was telling me.

"This is the Land of Snow. The Snow Queen lives there with her fairies," he murmured. "There's the redhead!"

I barely heard him, my gaze sweeping over the quick dance without interest.

Until my heart stopped in my chest, my body chilling.

The back row. The closest side of the stage.

Her brown hair was pulled tightly into a bun, a miniature white crown pinned atop it, transforming her into the princess she was destined to be. She was smaller than the others, her movements softer and more precise. Her arms curved with grace, lips teetering on the edge of a smile.

My breath hitched. The stage lights caught her face as she turned, and for half a second, I saw her eyes.

Chocolate brown and utterly unmistakable.

Eva.

A smile curved the edges of my lips as I leaned forward and whispered, *"Finally."*

December 26th

MIA

How you feeling, bestie?

EVANGELINE

Mia!!!

We're not supposed to have our phones backstage.

MIA

It's intermission, Evie. And anyway, you're clearly on your phone too.

EVANGELINE

Because I saw it light up!!

MIA

Well...

How are you feeling?

EVANGELINE

Weird.

I feel like someone is watching me.

MIA

Babe...

There's an entire audience watching you.

EVANGELINE

No. This feels different...

Am I being paranoid?

I feel like someone is here. Someone important.

MIA

Me, duh.

Anyway, that's odd. I dunno. Better get to the stage soon!

EVANGELINE

Yeah... odd...

ALEKSANDR
CHAPTER SEVEN

She was beautiful. She was so fucking beautiful it made my eyes hurt, and my heart pound, and my icy heart feel like it was on fire. I leaned forward without thinking of it, my body like a puppet whose strings were controlled by Eva. Every demon inside of me silenced itself so it could listen to the music as she moved.

"Wow," I whispered. "She's amazing."

My fixed attention on the dancing wasn't respect for technique or appreciation for choreography, or whatever other words Nikolai kept using to compliment them. No, it was sharper. Hungrier. Because I had found my snowflake in a storm, and part of me was worried that if I looked away, she would disappear.

And I would never let that happen again.

Unlike Nikolai, who considered himself a patron of the arts, I couldn't care less about paintings and dancing and shit. There was probably a wing with my cousin's name on it at every museum in the city. Our family was certainly wealthy enough to do it, though most of my charitable donations were made to the city police in return for their... *disinterest* in my family's activities. Never something as silly as a ballet.

Yet watching Eva dancing, a white and silver skirt flowing around her rapidly moving legs, leaping and turning like it was second nature, I found myself unable to look away. She was a natural, her feet moving at angles that were surely painful. There was discipline in her body—years of it, etched into muscle and bone. Suffering, sacrifice, and obedience. And I realized, then, that maybe the arts could be beautiful. I only needed a muse.

"Does it hurt her?" I asked Nikolai as she elevated to her toes once more.

"Certainly," he said, his expression unbearably smug, knowing that he pleased me. "That sort of thing can't feel pleasant. Their feet certainly reflect the toll. The redhead I fucked—she's the one on the far left—had disgusting feet, but it was kind of a turn on. Sort of a reminder that she's trained her body to be able to handle it."

I didn't like that. I didn't like the idea of Eva hurting herself for a show, of making herself bleed and bruise in the name of beauty. Yet I couldn't judge her for such a thing, because I could tell now, watching her on the stage, that this was her home.

But I wanted to be her home. I wanted every ache, every turn, every breath she drew to belong to me. If anyone dared to step between us, I would end them without mercy.

"And anyway, Eva can definitely stand these movements. I mean, look at her legs. They're fantastic. I bet—"

But he was cut off by my hand wrapping around his throat and squeezing until his lips turned a pale shade of blue.

Nikolai's eyes widened as I aimed a dark glare at him. "Don't you *ever* talk about my future wife's legs—or any other part of her fucking body—that way again. Or you'll find out firsthand why they call me the Reaper."

He nodded quickly. "Got it, got it. What body? I'm so blind I can't see it."

"Smartass," I grumbled, shoving him away, but not before I saw the stupid, arrogant grin he flashed my way.

"Future wife, huh?"

"Do you have a problem with that, Nikolai?"

"No, no." He chuckled under his breath. "But does this bride of yours know she's engaged?"

"She'll figure it out."

Whether that was sooner, as I preferred it, or later, after some convincing, was a mere detail. When I wanted something, I got it.

And I wanted her. She was fucking *mine*.

I didn't care if I had to be a monster to keep her.

"I think the scarier question is: does *Maria* know she'll be getting a daughter-in-law. You can't tell her, Aleksandr. She'll suffocate the poor girl under a mountain of tiramisu and embarrassing stories of your family members!" Though Nikolai wasn't related to my mother by blood, I had to give it to him: he knew the woman well. She was overbearing, nosy, and sometimes completely unbearable. Yet besides Eva and my sister, she was the only woman I'd ever truly cared for. A detestable feeling, though I knew my father could protect her enough to let the attachment slide.

"Details, Niko. Details."

I rested my chin on my hand as I continued to watch Eva, enraptured by her grace and skill. There was something almost sacred in the way she moved. I found myself cataloging her movements with the same attention I gave to weapons and strategy, ready to build an altar and worship her as my goddess divine. Because I would. I would worship Eva on my knees and sing my praises with my tongue.

"Speaking of details," he said, leaning forward as the snowflakes exited the stage. "Want to know how your brilliant cousin pulled this off?"

"No."

"Well, your curiosity need not worry, because I'll tell you. So I was at the show two days ago—the fifth time I've seen it, and I must admit: they only get better—when I finally thought to myself, 'You know, I've never read the program before.' I figured I should probably learn the redhead's name after all, but I wasn't sure I wanted to see her again at this point anyway. Got a little boring for my tastes, but she was fun while it lasted. So I opened up the little paper thing, which is full of way too many ads, and I read the bios for all the dancers, moving down the line alphabetically—"

"Are you capable of telling a story without an excessive amount of information?"

"No, and anyway, I get down to the V's, and I see..."

He slapped a program into my hands and opened the page he's referencing. There, the final dancer is listed:

Evangeline Vale.

My Eva.

Her headshot is next to a short biography, and I study the words over and over and over. It says little about her—that she went to a small private school upstate for university, where she held honors for three years, and that *The Nutcracker* was her first full production for the Company. It also said, to my amusement, that her greatest weakness was her sweet tooth. I tucked the knowledge away for later and looked back at Nikolai, wishing I could smack the smirk off his face. Yet I held myself back because I, unfortunately, owed him.

"I thought to myself," he continued, "that maybe Eva is short for something. After all, we've been looking for an Eva with absolutely no success for weeks. And I hate to typecast someone, but you said she loves pink and was wearing ribbons, and that sounds like a ballerina to me. I figured this might be our girl."

"*My* girl."

"Details. So after the show, I followed her for a little bit yesterday. She went to this dingy cafe, and when she came out in her uniform, *BAM*! She was wearing a name-tag that said Eva. I spent some time there—your girl is *terrible* at making coffee, by the way. I think they only hired her because she's much more attractive than anyone else there, and the other customers certainly think so by the way they tip her and try to get her attention."

"That will stop," I hissed under my breath, my fists already tightening with the need to kill someone.

The thought of men looking at her—smiling at her, lingering too long, daring to believe she might want them—lit something vicious in my chest. The world had a way of tearing through things like Eva—gentle things, bright things—and I had spent my life being the thing that tore back.

Anyone who touched her would pay. Blood. Bone. Pain. And I would savor it.

I would rip them to fucking shreds.

"Oh, definitely," Nikolai said. "I tried to scare off as many as I could. Can't have my future cousin-in-law treated like that. But if it makes you feel better, I don't think she notices. Just continues making her shitty coffee and sneaking stale pastries from the case."

That didn't make me feel better.

"Is ballet not her job?"

He shrugged. "Honestly, I doubt the corps members get paid much. Maybe she works there to get a little extra money."

I nodded. That was fixable. One little raise and she would never need to work at the cafe again. Besides, she was probably exhausted from doing two jobs. I would have to find a way to increase her salary, even if it meant sneaking money into her bank myself.

The curtains pulled shut as Act One ended, sending the theater into a short intermission. I motioned for our private server to come forward. It was a teenage boy, a nervous one who clearly tried his hardest to comb back his hair and look presentable. "I want flowers sent to that dancer," I said, pointing at Eva's picture in the program.

"But, sir, that's not my job—"

I shoved a wad of bills into his chest, more than he was probably making that night. "Now, it is. I want them delivered to the dressing room by the end of the show."

He looked as if he were going to argue once more before clutching the cash to his chest and nodding. "Any requests for the flowers, sir?"

"Pink."

"Oh! You should get her those flowers that look like roses mixed with clouds!" Nikolai interjected. "They'd look like her costume in Act Two."

"What the fuck are you talking about?"

"Erm, peonies, sir?" the boy asked.

I waved my hand. "Yes, yes. Something big with lots of pink. Nothing is too much."

He scampered off, and a few minutes later, he came back, red-faced, saying that they'd be on her dresser by the show's end. I tore off a piece of the program, hastily scrawled a note to include with them, and handed it back to the boy with another thing of cash.

The strings rising again while the flutes began to trill were a hint that the intermission was ending. That and Nikolai squealing like an infant pig, leaning forward and exclaiming, "This is the best act! The Sugar Plum Fairy's pas de deux is stunning."

"Pas de deux?"

"Technically, it's just French for 'a dance of two,'" he

explained. "But, really, it's the most intimate part of the entire ballet. The whole stage narrows to two dancers who trust completely and complement each other well. The man might be strong with his legs, while the woman is graceful with arms, or something like that. One leads, one follows, but both are a part of the dance. One dancer is all lightness. She's ethereal, she's weightless, she's unbound by gravity. And then there's the anchor. He's the force of nature that keeps her from flying away or falling apart. It requires a whole lot of trust because if that anchor falters, the whole thing collapses. It's a thing of instinct, of *passion*. It's all very romantic."

"Yes," I murmured as the curtains opened, revealing Eva and the other dancers once more, this time dressed as members of some fairytale world that the main character and Nutcracker passed through. She held her position so still, I briefly worried she wasn't breathing. But then her eyes flicked to the audience, and I relaxed back into my seat.

A pas de deux.

Yes, I thought, smiling to myself as I watched my Eva. *A dance of two, indeed.*

I realized suddenly that watching wasn't enough. The distance between us—rows of velvet seats, gold railings, a grand stage—felt like an insult to our connection. I didn't like barriers between us, didn't like that I couldn't go to her whenever I wanted to taste her vanilla lip gloss again. And I especially didn't like the idea of her walking off that stage, potentially disappearing into a world I couldn't be present in.

The final notes of a song rang out, and one piece of candy —God, this ballet made no sense to me—was replaced by another. I leaned back, folding my arms across my chest, and said, "I'm buying the ballet."

The thought settled into me with frightening ease. Right now, when she stepped off that stage, she belonged to the world. Sharing dressing rooms with a dozen other dancers, meandering her way through crowds, visiting with strangers who somehow thought they had a right to her attention. The idea of anyone being able to access her—anyone but me—curdled into something sharp and territorial.

If Eva was going to be surrounded, it would be by walls I built. Doors I could close. People who would bleed and die for her. She would not belong to the world, but to the one I created. Every move, every action, would revolve around mine.

Like a pas de deux.

Nikolai blinked once. Then twice. "You're joking."

"Have I ever joked?"

He studied me for a long moment, something like awe creeping into his expression. "You know," he said slowly, leaning back into his seat, arms crossing his chest, "most men would start with a first date. Flowers and a nice dinner."

"I've already sent her flowers. And we will have several dinners together. This moves much quicker."

He laughed loudly, drawing the ire of many other patrons near us. "My, my. You are a *sucker* for this girl. You know, in an asshole-y way, it's kind of sweet—"

I ignored him, too busy pulling my phone from my pocket, dialing a number I had memorized. He answered on the second ring, his thickly accented voice gruff. "Reaper."

"How quickly can you purchase a majority stakeholder position in the City Ballet?"

He considered my demand for a moment, probably scratching his beard and leaving his wife at the dinner table. Tzotzi was an... interesting man. He'd worked for my father and my grandfather, and while none of us knew much about him, we knew he did a damn good job. He was discreet in everything he did and more efficient than a hundred men. Which is why I trusted him to make me the theater's new owner by the end of the night.

"I'd say... about thirty minutes. Perhaps less."

"I'll be awaiting your text."

Tzotzi hung up, and I sat back in my chair while Nikolai stared at me, mouth agape. "You're really fucking buying the damn ballet."

"I'm not buying just the ballet," I said, my voice sharp. "I'm buying *her*."

December 26th

NIKOLAI

Aunt Maria, help me!

It's your son!

He's gone CRAZY!!!!

ALEKSANDR

Wrong number, asshole.

EVANGELINE
CHAPTER EIGHT

My chest was still heaving as the curtain fell, the cast members remaining perfectly posed while the audience's applause echoed around us. It was an intoxicating feeling—their praise, their excitement. Producing something beautiful, something that moved people, was a big part of why I loved performing.

I'd always loved to dance. The studio was the place I could express myself using my body rather than with words that never got listened to at home. And my parents encouraged it because it meant getting me away from the house and away from them. When I expressed interest in a school several hours away—where one of the most robust dance programs in the world was—they were more than eager to sign their names on the checks.

Anything to make me disappear.

Ballet was everything to me. I'd sacrificed so much to be there. My school, my friends, even my true name. All so I could be here, on the stage, feeling the applause rattle my bones.

Mia wrapped her arms around my shoulders and squeezed tightly. "You did it, Evie! Your first show is done!"

"Here's to many more, Vale." Another dancer squeezed my wrist, though with the blinding lights and raucous noise, I couldn't tell who it was. It was such a close-knit community of people supporting each other that it could have been anyone.

Mia and I hugged each other behind the curtain for a few more moments before we made our way into the crowded dressing room, where every dancer swarmed a small area, gasping and pointing.

"What are they looking at?" Mia mused, her hands already tugging at her perfect blonde bun and the many pins keeping it in place.

"I don't know... wait, is that *my* mirror?" I asked. The crowd must have heard me because they parted as soon as I got close.

The largest bouquet I'd ever seen sat atop my station, swallowing the mirror and all of my belongings whole. It was an explosion of pink, soft blushes, and deeper rouge layered together in perfect harmony. Like something torn straight out of a painting of the Garden of Eden. Part of me wondered if the city had any flowers left after someone created this. There had to be hundreds, if not thousands, of dollars' worth of flowers here.

The stems were wrapped in heavy cream paper, crisp and expensive, tied off with a ballet pink silk ribbon. Hydrangeas the size of my head pressed against pale ranunculus, spray roses spilling outward in careful excess, and woven through it all were thick clouds of peonies, full and lush. My breath caught at the sight of the cloud-like flowers. They were my favorite, reminding me of a spring-filled world covered in coquette ecstasy.

"Oh my God," someone whispered behind me. Probably Mia, judging from the crassness of their next question. "Eva, who the fuck did you sleep with?"

"I didn't," I said automatically, though my voice came out

thin. My fingers hovered before finally brushing the petals of a peony, soft and cool beneath my touch.

Who would do such a thing? My brother was out of the question. Jules had come to my opening night with a lovely bouquet of pink roses for me and an equally large one of sunflowers for Elsie. He wouldn't have gone from something nice and simple to *this*.

Mia stepped forward and pulled a ripped piece of something that looked a lot like our program. I took it from her with shaking fingers.

> To my solnyshka.
> Mine.

No name. No flourish. Just neat, confident lettering, like whoever wrote it never doubted I'd know it was meant for me. A strange warmth unfurled low in my stomach, equal parts thrill and unease.

"Solnyshka?" I murmured, that word tugging at the edges of my memory.

"It means 'Little sun' in Russian," another dancer piped up from the back. I glanced around the room again, suddenly aware of everyone watching me. This moment felt intimate, though I couldn't explain why.

"All right, everyone," Mia said, sensing my discomfort and unwillingness to voice it. "Move on. Leave Eva to her secret admirers in peace. I'm sure you nosy bitches will hear about this soon."

As soon as they'd gone back to their own mirrors, Mia grabbed my arm and pulled me close, hissing underneath her breath, "Who did this?"

"I don't know," I said softly, looking back to the flowers. I hadn't been on a date in... ever. The closest thing I'd ever come to one was tagging along with Mia on some of hers.

Her eyes narrowed to sharp slits. "Okay, well. Someone with money did this. Like, *real* money." She touched one of the tulips nestled between some peonies. "And taste. Very good taste. This is the most beautiful bouquet I've ever seen."

"That doesn't mean I know who it is. Everyone I know has money!"

Which was true. My family was well off, which meant that all the families I was allowed to know were too. And the friends I made in adulthood, friends like Mia, came from wealthy backgrounds too. Unfortunately, ballet wasn't very accessible. Shoes, costumes, recital fees, dance lessons—all of it was extremely expensive. Growing up, my academy had scholarships available to those in financial need, but without access to learn dance in the first place, how would they ever gain the passion to try? It was something I knew the dance world needed to do better. Maybe one day, when I could finally stop paying my bills slightly late, I could help with that.

Mia tilted her head. "On the contrary, you know he's not a creep. Probably. Or if he is, at least he's a creep with cash, which is my favorite kind... You didn't notice anyone in the audience?"

I shook my head, though an image flashed unbidden—dark eyes, the weight of being watched. I'd assumed it was pre-show nerves, but what if it wasn't?

I shoved the thought away quickly. "I wasn't looking. It's hard to see with all the lights."

She hummed, unconvinced. "Well, whoever he is, he's clearly obsessed. *Wait.* Could it be Alek?"

"I don't think so. I mean... I remember him having an accent, but how would he find me here? And why would he even want to deal with me, Mia? I totally ghosted him."

"I told you, Evie: *villain*. Villains don't care about ghosting."

My gaze drifted back to the bouquet. "This seems like something a prince would do, not a villain. So does that mean it's not Alek? Should I try to figure out who it is? I feel like I should write a thank-you note or *something* showing my gratitude."

"Um, you can express it by having the best sex of your life with the hot guy who sent you these!"

A few of the other dancers side-eyed us, chuckling under their breath, used to Mia's antics.

I gaped at my friend, my cheeks burning. "You have no idea these came from Alek! They could be from my *mom*!"

She rolled her eyes. "The same mom who's been ignoring you since you were four? Yeah, these are totally from her. Face it, Evangeline. These are definitely from Alek!"

I wished she were right, I really did. But the voice inside of me kept saying I messed everything up, that I wasn't perfect enough for him. And unfortunately, that voice was much louder than my friend's.

"Maybe," I said, not wanting to discuss it anymore. "I'll see you at auditions tomorrow?"

Mia sighed, though she thankfully let it go. "Yeah, babes. See you bright and early!"

Other people may not have understood why we were having auditions the day after a major show, but those people hadn't met Madame Germaine, the fiercest woman I'd ever met and the director of the City Ballet Company. She didn't believe in things like rest, not in the middle of our season. We had a show to put together by mid-March, which meant that every day was a day dedicated to the ballet. We could rest in the off-season.

I changed quickly into a simple pair of sweatpants and a

hoodie. My hands lingered over my costume and my hair accessories while I tucked them into the costume closet.

I was going to miss this show. Though we'd be doing it again next Christmas, a secret part of me hoped that I would be in a larger role, which meant that this could have been my last performance as a snowflake and flower. Madame Germaine said I was showing promise, and my hopeful heart ran with that.

I slung my duffel bag over my shoulder and grabbed the bouquet, careful not to crush the flowers against my chest. They were heavier than they looked, substantial in a way that made my arms ache as I carried them down the hall.

I felt eyes on me as I carried the bouquet. Not theirs, not the dancers. Someone else was watching, waiting. I shivered under the weight of the nameless gaze and hurried my steps.

Outside, the cold slapped me back into reality. To my left, I could hear the sounds of the crowd cheering, of cameras snapping photos with some of the other dancers for the meet and greet. I could have gone, but no one would be there. Jules had been to several shows, but after the fourth, I told him he didn't need to anymore, and my parents had never come to a single show, not even when I was a kid. I guessed I could go see Charlotte, who was in town to visit Mia, but honestly, I just wanted to go home so I could get the night over with.

Was that all my life was? Forcing a smile and getting things over with?

No, I told myself, plastering another big one across my cheeks. *Of course not. You're just tired from such an amazing day! Tomorrow will be even better!*

Still, a part of me hurt as I left all the lights behind for the darkness of the metro.

The word *solnyshka* replayed in my head over and over. I kept imagining my secret admirer whispering it in my ear over and over and over, his voice sounding a lot like Alek's.

To my solnyshka. Mine.

So what if I was stressed? So what if my feet bled almost every day, and my head was pounding with an ever-increasing migraine? So what if my apartment smelled a little like mold and the cafe kept shrinking the hemline of the skirts I was forced to wear in front of dusty men? How could I complain about all of those things when I was living my *dream*—dancing in the City Ballet with a life that could only get better from here?

It was my negativity talking, the post-holiday blues pulling me down. I just needed to remind myself of all the wonderful things in my world, things like flowers and best friends and new auditions.

My life wasn't perfect, but maybe one day, I would finally learn how to write my own rules for it.

December 27th

JULES

Good luck with auditions today, Annie.

Love you.

EVANGELINE

Aw, Jules!

Are you feeling gushy today?

I wanna be gushy, too!!!

I love you, big brother. :)))

#BestBigBrotherEver

#SibsForLife

cat gif

JULES

EVANGELINE
CHAPTER NINE

My nerves were suffocating the air the next morning as I blew my big brother at least ten kisses. Through his sports car's tinted windows, I could make out his eye roll followed by an embarrassed flush of his cheeks, the red overtaking his freckles. But I didn't apologize because it was his fault for starting it.

He knew what he was doing when he woke me up with affectionate texts.

At one point, my family used to be somewhat normal. I didn't have a whole lot of memories of this time in my life, but Jules would sometimes tell me about it—how my mom would brush my hair every night, how my dad let me sit on his lap during business meetings, the family trips we went on together.

But when I was four, all of that changed.

My parents became harder. They started stealing Jules—who was only eleven—away from me, instructing him in the ways of the family business. And me?

They shipped me away.

To ballet lessons. Boarding school. University. Anywhere that wasn't with them.

I didn't know what caused my life to crack, but I saw the shards of whatever it was every day. I spent most of my life without affection, and whenever I got it, I was determined to keep it forever.

One day, my Prince Charming would fix the holes inside of me, the ones that begged to be loved.

Maybe that would be Alek.

Or maybe I should have been looking harder for my cat.

My therapist said my OCD—and my people-pleasing tendencies—were because I was desperate to earn love and approval. And sometimes, when I offered to cover too many shifts or give away what little money I had to someone on the street who needed it more, I thought she might be right. Maybe I was someone craving reassurance and a gentle touch.

But other times, I wondered if I was more of a masochist. Because I wasn't sure anyone who wanted love and approval would join the ballet.

"EEK!" Mia screamed, running over to me and wrapping me tightly in her arms as soon as I entered the main theater. "You're here!"

I hugged her back, though my brows furrowed against where I was pressed to her shoulder. Even with my shoes on, Mia practically towered over me. "Um... Mia? You saw me yesterday."

"Ugh, and it's been too long! Come on. Let's go warm up."

My chest loosened a fraction as I set my bag backstage and followed Mia to a makeshift set of barres where we began to stretch together. My hips groaned in protest as I held my leg almost as high as my head, yet it was a good pain, the kind that meant I was back where I belonged.

While I stretched, I moved on autopilot. I switched out of my flimsy sneakers and tied my pointe shoes. I smoothed my pink leotard and tights before slipping on a matching short skirt. Our clothes had to be tight and somewhat revealing so Madame Germaine could watch our movements closely, pointing out all of our mistakes with her scary-looking black cane.

I fidgeted with the straps of my tank top before pulling my hair back into a ponytail and wrapping a ribbon around the tie, fixing it into a cute bow that sat neatly on top of my head. I smiled at my reflection, urging myself to actually like what I saw, while Mia giggled.

My smile instantly dropped. "What?"

"You are so cute. I can't believe you think Alek is actually staying away from you."

I opened my mouth to question her, but before I could, Madame Germaine's voice rang out. Our accompanist began to play trilling notes on the piano in the corner. The director clapped her hands, gesturing for us to surround her in a semicircle.

The room quieted instantly. I felt the silence down to my marrow.

"Today is important," she said. "Auditions for our leads, Romeo and Juliet, will begin shortly. I expect professionalism, focus, and courage. Even if you are not selected as principal, today will determine your role in the show."

My pulse quickened. *You got this,* I tried to tell myself. *It's just an audition. You've had tons of those.*

"*You are not good enough to be here,*" a voice inside of me trilled.

"And," Madame Germaine added, "we will have a guest observing."

A ripple went through the room as we all wondered who the guest would be. Company auditions and rehearsals were always kept far from the public eye. We wanted people to see us at our best—not the weeks it took to get there. Even I, as a newbie, knew that.

"The Company has recently acquired a new investor," our director explained, her lips almost twitching down in the corners. "He will be watching today's audition and, if he so chooses, giving feedback on the roles selected."

The room shifted to the darkened rows of seats beyond the stage, where we all knew our new investor would be sitting. I tried to peek beyond the curtain, but the lights were too bright and the chairs too dark. All I could make out was a silhouette of shadows.

My skin prickled with awareness. Like there was a monster out there, inhaling all the atmosphere until the only thing I could breathe was the sensation that they were watching me like they hungered for me. My chest tightened, breath coming shallow as my thoughts scattered like birds.

"*Not perfect.*"

"*Not perfect.*"

"*Not perfect.*"

"*Not perfect.*"

I pressed my thumb into the inside of my wrist, grounding myself in the sharp sensation. Once. Twice. Three times.

Breathe, Eva.

Without meaning to, my mind drifted to several weeks ago. To Alek's hands steadying me against the cold, making me feel desired for the first time in years. Desire and a flicker of something sharper—unease, maybe—wrapped around me like armor. Somewhere beyond the music and mirrors, I felt a trace of him, a shadow at the edge of the room, and though I didn't want to admit it, it made me braver.

I straightened my spine and prepared myself to dance. Whatever today held—whether that was a role or a rejection—I could do this.

We started the auditions with warmups, all of the dancers splitting into two lines where we would perform classic leaps and turns to jaunty music, one after another after another, like an assembly line of ballet.

My nerves began to flare up once more while I watched the older, more experienced dancers move with grace and poise. While these were just warmups, everyone knew that Madame Germaine was already beginning to form her finalists. We were lucky to be given the chance to audition with each show, the principals ever changing. Not every theater was like that.

I pressed my palms briefly to the wall before falling into the back of the line, grounding myself in the familiar coolness of the wood. The buzzing inside my chest hadn't gone away—not exactly—but it dulled, like static turned down a notch.

The dancers continued moving through calypsos until it was only Mia and me left to go. We gave each other soft smiles before taking our place.

And then my body started to move before my mind could interfere anymore. My arms lifted, my spine lengthened, and my feet found their marks. Instinct had taken over, almost two decades of dance experience winning out over my fear of not being good enough. The nerves tried to claw their way back in, whispering *too stiff, too slow, too much*, but I drowned them out with breath and rhythm.

On and on through warmups. *Turn. Leap. Land. Pose.* I felt centered, strong, and powerful. Everything a dancer always dreamed of being.

By the time we moved on to choreography, my lungs burned, and sweat dampened the back of my neck, yet I had never felt better. I no longer had the voice nagging me to prove that I was perfect, to knock against the floors or pick at the skin of my hands.

We began to move through the audition dances, twisting

and turning over and over again while Madame Germaine watched. I heard the sound of her heels clicking against the floor before I felt her presence behind me. I stiffened, bracing myself for her corrections.

But to my surprise, she stepped in front of me and tilted her head.

"Evangeline," she said, her voice shockingly warm despite her cold face. "You're dancing well today."

My chest fluttered. "Thank you," I murmured, my face dropping automatically to the floor.

She lifted my chin with two fingers, raising my eyes to meet hers. She studied me for a few moments before clicking her tongue and shuffling forward.

My heart was going haywire—butterflies practically slaughtering each other—when she ordered us to repeat the combination, this time keeping her gaze solely on me. I raised into an arabesque, then dropped into a dégagé, arabesque, then dégagé, Juliet's variation settling inside my bones. And when the music slowed and the combination ended, I looked to Madame Germaine, only to find her watching me with a subtle smile. She nodded before telling us to get a drink and ordering the men out for their piece.

While we sipped our water, Mia pulled me to the side and squealed under her breath. "Evie!! Oh my God, she *smiled!* Do you know what this means?"

"That her facial muscles work correctly?"

"No! Madame Germaine only smiles when she sees something she really, really, really likes. I think you have a chance at a lead role!"

Something tight loosened inside of me like the ribbons of a corseted dress had been undone. *A lead.* That was more than I ever could have dreamed of. *Me.* A lead?

What if I were Lady Capulet? Or Lady Montague? Perhaps Rosaline? Or—

I swallowed.

What if I were Juliet?

I shook my head before the dream could intoxicate me too much. "No. It's my first year, Mia. There are more deserving people out there. People like you!"

She rolled her eyes. "Madame Germaine will never make me a lead. And anyway, I don't want to be one. I like being in the corps de ballet, shining without the spotlight. But you? I think you'd be *perfect* center stage."

Mia moved on to a different topic—namely, one of the male dancers' *extremely* tight tights—but her reassurance stayed, settling deep in my bones. For the first time in years, my chest ached with want. Not with the feeling of not being good enough, but with the feeling that I could belong here.

After a quick water break for everyone, Madame Germaine thumped her cane on the stage floor three times, gathering our attention quickly. She called forth four male dancers to be considered for Romeo, and I politely clapped after each one. We weren't supposed to show favoritism to anyone during auditions, which I guessed was good considering I kept wanting to scream in delight after each one.

A restless energy settled beneath my skin as Madame Germaine announced Raphael as Romeo, the same principal who played the Prince in *The Nutcracker*.

"Congrats, Rapha." I smiled at him as he joined the rest of us, waiting for the director to speak once more.

Madame Germaine rose from her chair. "And for Juliet, I'd like to watch Elsie, Jeanine, Alexandra, and... Evangeline."

My world froze.

My name.

Did she say *my name*?

I bit my lip to contain the biggest smile I'd ever had before turning to Mia, who gave me a thumbs up.

"*Told you,*" she mouthed as she was swallowed by the

crowd of people who came to congratulate me, apparently uncaring of the etiquette rules Madame Germaine had set.

"Congrats, Evangeline."

"Way to go, Rookie!"

"Good luck!"

Madame Germaine tapped her cane three times as a call for the celebration to finish and for the finals to begin. She nodded toward the accompanist. And in a voice I felt down to my core, she said, "Let's begin."

December 27th

NIKOLAI

Yo, cuz.

Wanna come over and play video games?

ALEKSANDR

No.

MISSED CALL FROM NIKOLAI
NIKOLAI

Answer me, damn it.

I'm lonely.

ALEKSANDR

No.

MISSED CALL FROM NIKOLAI
NIKOLAI

Rude.

MISSED CALL FROM NIKOLAI

Alekkkkkkkk.

MISSED CALL FROM NIKOLAI

Pay attention to meeeee.

ALEKSANDR

No.

NIKOLAI

Are you with Eva?

…

YOU DIDN'T SAY NO.

Are you going to finally get her?

…

YOU DIDN'T SAY NO AGAIN.

YOU'RE WITH HER.

ALEKSANDR

I'm about to be.

Now shut the fuck up.

EVANGELINE
CHAPTER TEN

My lungs were burning as the music wound down to a few gentle notes before disappearing altogether, leaving me with the rush of blood in my ears and the feeling that my life was about to completely change.

I knew—I just *knew*—that I had done it. That I had danced the best I ever had, that I had captured Juliet's youthfulness, her technique, her love for life, all with my body. Though I was sure I could later pick out many flaws, right now I couldn't.

The voice was completely quiet as if to say, "*Well done. Perfect.*"

I held my final pose for a heartbeat longer than necessary, chest heaving, sweat cooling along my spine as the silence stretched. Then, Madame Germaine's cane tapped once against the floor, the sound sharp and final. I released my body, gracefully landing off my burning toes onto my feet.

The crowd clapped, though I couldn't bring myself to look at any of their faces. Would they look proud? Disappointed? Unimpressed? I didn't want to know.

But for some reason, my gaze drifted to the darkened theater, drawn to the slow, deliberate clap of a shadowy figure.

My entire body went cold, but not in a bad way. No, this was with the knowledge that I was being watched—and the freezing realization that I liked it. The silhouette was all shadow, all hunger, and yet a twisted part of me couldn't look away.

I swallowed. Only Alek had ever left me unsettled like this, a tangle of desire and something sharper—danger, maybe—curling through me.

Maybe I was missing him too much.

I stepped back into line amongst the others, my legs still trembling, and my heart racing so fast I worried it would fall out of my chest. I'd given everything, and for the first time since I'd joined the Company, I thought I might have a chance.

Madame Germaine rose, surveying us with her hawk-like gaze. The room stilled immediately.

"Thank you, my darlings," she said. "You've all danced beautifully. Now, who will play our Juliet?"

My stomach flipped violently. *Please be me. Please be me.*

Madame Germaine's lips parted, and for a moment, I swore I saw the beginning of an E shape, like she was about to say either my name or Elsie's—and though I loved my friend, a selfish part of me hoped it was me. A trickle of noise escaped Madame Germaine.

Then a voice cut through the theater.

It was low. Smooth. Dark as sin, deep as the Mariana Trench, richer than any chocolate. Part of me recognized it, but another part of me could barely hear it through the dramatic pounding of my pulse.

"Evangeline. The role of Juliet will be played by Evangeline," the man said.

My head snapped toward the audience, my breath caught somewhere between my ribs and my throat. Was that the investor? Were they asking *me* to play the lead role?

Why?

We all turned to Madame Germaine, not used to anyone making decisions for her. I expected her to frown and refute them, telling us who was *actually* Juliet. But to my surprise, she nodded once before saying, "Yes. Evangeline Vale will dance as Juliet."

For half a second, my world stopped.

Then it crashed back in all at once.

Mia screamed, running at me from the side of the stage before wrapping me in the tightest hug I'd ever had. Someone else came up and hugged me from behind—Elsie, if I had to guess. Another dancer grabbed my hands, babbling congratulations, and the rest piled on. In an industry like ours, it was easy to feel jealousy. But the fact that everyone was nothing but happy for me made me unbelievably warm. My vision blurred as my chest filled with something bright and overwhelming and unreal.

Juliet.

I was Juliet.

I laughed, my hands flying to my mouth as tears stung my eyes. I felt like I was vibrating out of my skin, like I might float straight off the stage if I didn't find something to anchor myself to.

We soaked in this moment for a little while longer before Madame Germaine promised to post the rest of the cast list by Monday's rehearsal. She told us all to go home and rest over the weekend before pinning me with her wicked eyes.

"Congratulations, Evangeline," she said softly. Pointedly, as if to say that the investor wasn't the only reason I was about to be the lead. "You deserved it."

I followed the other dancers to the exit before the voice spoke again, stopping me. "Evangeline will stay."

The sound of my name from his mouth hit me like a physical thing—like a hand curling around my spine. The spirit of joy and celebration screeched to a halt, everyone eyeing me with either confusion or concern. The room was dead silent.

I looked helplessly at Madame Germaine. She met my gaze, expression unreadable. "You heard the investor," she said. "Everyone else is dismissed."

No one argued. The other dancers filed out of the door, all of them silently wondering what the man hidden in the audience could want with me. To be honest, I was wondering myself.

Mia grabbed my hand and squeezed me once more. "I'll call you later, Eva. Okay?"

Then she, too, was ushered away.

The stage lights dimmed further before the accompanist skittered out the door. The theater was now empty.

My pulse skidded.

Slow footsteps echoed from the audience. A tall figure rose from the shadows, descending the aisle with unhurried confidence. I tried to make out who it was, but he stopped short of the stage, still half-obscured by darkness.

But suddenly the shadows shifted, and I realized I knew him.

I'd know him anywhere.

"Alek," I breathed.

He slowly stepped onto the stage, the light seemingly dimming under the weight of his dangerous aura, fracturing against the crown of his hair. The circles under his eyes were dark, but his irises were darker as they roamed my body, the blue a sharpened hunger like a blade made of midnight.

Weeks apart hadn't dulled him. Every inch of him radiated something predatory. Something that would eat me alive if I let him.

He was temptation give form—his black suit molded to his tall, broad body, tanned skin contoured by sin. He wore a watch that made my eyes bulge out of my head a little, but nothing made my body react more than the way he looked at me like the leash he held himself back with was thinner than a spider's silk, ready to snap.

The thought should have terrified me. I was alone with a man I barely knew. Everyone else was gone. The theater was far too old and outdated to have any sort of cameras or security, which meant that Alek could theoretically do whatever he wanted with me.

But instead of frightening me, my sickened soul was *excited*.

Maybe Mia was right. Maybe the only prince I needed was a prince of darkness.

"Congratulations, solnyshka," he murmured, lips quirking at the corner. "You will make a beautiful Juliet.

"You—" I swallowed. "You're the one who sent me flowers? You're the investor?"

"Yes."

"But..." My words sank in my throat under the weight of my many questions. "How? When?"

He stepped forward, and all I could smell was the musk of his no-doubt expensive cologne, an intoxicating smell that had me forgetting everything but him. "Because I wanted to be here."

"Why?"

He reached forward, cupping my cheek with his large hand and stroking my parted lips with his thumb, eyes turning black at the sight. "Because I saw something I wanted. And I had to have it."

And maybe it was naive of me. Maybe it was my experience showing. But a part of me wondered if he meant *me*. If Alek didn't see the Company, but *me*.

Because I was starting to want him. Not in the distant, dreamy way I'd always imagined wanting someone, but in a way that settled into my bones and refused to leave. Desperately, helplessly, without logic or permission. I didn't care if he was my Prince Charming or something far more dangerous. He was here—real, solid, warm against my body—and that mattered more than any fairytale I'd ever been told.

Standing there with him, feeling his presence wrap around me like something inevitable, I realized I didn't want to keep pretending I could go back to the way things were before we met. I didn't want to walk away again. I didn't want to listen to Jules's rules. I didn't want to be brave or careful or good.

I wanted more out of my life.

And the most frightening part of all was the certainty blooming in my chest: I didn't want a life he was in for only a moment. I wanted to get to know him more, to see his rare smiles and taste his kisses and maybe, if I was lucky, do more...

So despite my lingering fear and apprehension, I looked into Alek's dark eyes and anchored myself in the dark seas. "What did you want?"

"You. Always you, *Evangeline.*" He gave me a pointed look as he emphasized my full name—the one I didn't tell him.

I smiled sheepishly. "Sorry... I technically didn't lie to you. Most people call me Eva. But you never know when someone might be a creep!"

He cocked a brow. "And you thought *I* might be a creep."

"I kind of hope you are a little." I slapped a hand over my mouth, my cheeks already beginning to turn red. Why did I say something so crazy sounding? Did I not want him to *stay*?

But to my surprise, Alek didn't run for the hills like I might have. No, he *laughed*, a low sound that traveled down my spine and settled in between my legs. I'd heard the most beautiful music played by the City Ballet Company's live orchestra, but nothing could compare to the sound of Alek's laugh.

"My, my, Evangeline. Are you saying you're a little freak behind closed doors?"

"I... erm... I-I—"

Alek leaned down and placed a gentle kiss on my lips, one that teased me into wanting more. Whatever butterflies survived my auditions were surely dead by now, having flown themselves into a tornado in my stomach.

Alek smiled against my lips.

God, he was so beautiful when he smiled. It took up his whole face, showing off two deep dimples and a slightly chipped front tooth that I was sure had a unique story. The small imperfection only made him more perfect in my eyes.

I cupped both cheeks with my hands, determined to hold onto that sight for as long as possible.

"Good," he said, kissing the palm of one of my hands. "Because I'm more than a freak for you. I'm fucking feral."

My knees trembled. Did he really mean that?

No, surely not.

I wasn't blind. I knew I was fairly pretty, especially when I took the time to do my hair and a little makeup. But while I could admit that I was fairly attractive, that didn't mean I thought I was in league with *Alek*. He was sex on legs, the most attractive human I could ever imagine. He was beyond a storybook character.

He was a god.

"Y-you are?"

"Yes."

It was shocking how his voice could be so cold yet so warm at the same time. I blushed again, but I still managed to hold his gaze as I said, "You could find out, you know? How much of a freak I am, I mean."

Alek sucked in a sharp breath, a muscle in his jaw twitching. "Fuck, Eva. You're playing a dangerous game right now."

"Maybe I like dangerous."

I honestly wasn't sure, but whatever it was I was doing with Alek, it was clear that I more than liked it based on the reaction in my body. My panties were slowly soaking with every depraved thought my mind conjured, and my heart skipped so many beats that I worried I was going to go to the hospital.

There was a strange feeling building inside of me, a shift of something I'd never felt before, a heat that flooded my veins. I squirmed to try and ease some of it, but Alek merely pulled me closer, his body pushing against me and making it worse.

It was like a string had been coiled inside of me, something tight and awkward yet eased only by him. Every inch of me felt right and wrong at the same time.

Despite some of my... naivety, I wasn't *completely* innocent. I'd watched porn a handful of times, and I'd tried the vibrator Mia gifted me for my twenty-first birthday once before deciding that the size of that thing was terrifying. My hands occasionally ventured to that part of my body whenever I was in the shower. But honestly, I'd never really felt *turned on* before. I'd never had a reason to.

Now, though, I was beyond turned on. I was craving him.

"Eva..." Alek began.

"Maybe I like it—" I stepped forward and ran my hands along the nape of his neck, fingers brushing against the edges of his tattoos. "—when it's with you."

And then I pulled his large, tense body to me and ran my hands along his shoulders before gripping the back of his neck and bringing his lips down to mine.

He was so tall that even on pointe shoes, I had to stretch to reach him, my toes beginning to feel that familiar burn I got whenever I went up on relevé. But any pain was worth it to taste him again, to smell his expensive musk invading my nostrils while his muscles flexed beneath my touch.

Alek wasted no time taking control of our kiss, wrapping one arm around me, his tongue dominating and caressing mine until all I could do was relax into his hold and let him lead me into darkness. My breath *whooshed* out of my lungs until all I could inhale was him.

More. More. More, something inside of me yearned.

Alek seemed to know what I wanted, his hands traveling down my body until they landed on my ass, picking me off the ground. My legs wrapped around his waist, and my fingers tangled into his hair.

I felt myself sinking into him, my nerves relaxing more the longer we were back together. Things between us came naturally, and though a voice in the back of my head insisted that this was probably considered too quick and that Jules would be furious, I couldn't bring myself to care, too drunk off the electrifying feeling in the air, the same one that settled in between my legs.

He pressed himself perfectly against my lower body, eliciting a breathy gasp that I had *never* made before. I couldn't help but arch into him, my hips seeking the contact again. He eagerly complied, thrusting into me, his strong body still managing to hold me steady.

Alek's lips chose that moment to break their contact, trailing themselves down my neck until they reached a sensitive spot that had sparks traveling up and down my body, the place where my neck met my collarbone. I moaned when he bit down on it, the pain making my head dizzy.

Was I crazy?

"You have a birthmark here," Alek mumbled in between kisses. "It's so light I hardly noticed it at first. Where else do you have birthmarks, solnyshka?"

"I guess you'll have to find out."

Did that just come out of me?

Oh God. It did. And I somehow found myself wanting to say a *lot* more to him. It was like the lust-filled haze he put me in brought out something I didn't know existed. Someone alluring and brave, someone completely focused on *him*.

Alek smiled against my neck. "I will."

His breath was warm against my skin. His hands kneaded my ass while I ground into him, my body still wanting more. The theater felt impossibly large and impossibly small all at once, the vast darkness around us pressing in as if reminding us that we were alone.

"God, I can't wait to see you up here."

"You're going to come to the show?"

He pulled away, brows furrowing. "Of course, I am. This theater is mine. The dancers are mine. *You* are mine now, Evangeline. Do you not want me to?"

"Yes!" I said far too quickly before blushing. "I just wasn't sure if you wanted to watch ballet or not. I know some people can find it boring and I—"

But Alek cut me off with a soft kiss. "In all honesty, I *don't* want to watch the ballet. I want to watch you."

"Why don't you come for a private performance then?"

As soon as the words left my lips, I realized I'd said something very wrong. Or perhaps very right...

Alek's hands tightened on my body, and I felt something hard form between us, pushing into the tender part of me that was begging for more.

Oh, I thought, eyes widening when I realized what it was. *Oh.*

I always thought porn stars had unrealistic cocks, that they were exaggerated, maybe even prosthetics.

I was clearly very wrong.

Alek's eyes darkened into twin pits of nights. When he spoke, his voice was gravelly, the sound of it sending bursts of heat to my core. "A private performance?"

The words settled low in my stomach, heavy and electric. "Yeah," I said softly. "No other dancers. No audience. Just you and me."

My fingers curled reflexively in his hair, the urge to move

—to *do something*—buzzing through my veins. I felt hyper-aware of my body, of the thin fabric clinging to me, of the ache still lingering in my muscles from dancing so hard I'd nearly split myself open with want.

Alek tilted his head. "And what would you perform?"

"What would you like to see?"

His smile was slow. Possessive.

"Everything."

My heart hammered so loudly I was sure he could hear it. And I realized—terrified and thrilled in equal measure—that I wanted to show him everything. That I wanted to be cool and daring and sexy for him. That I wanted to bear the parts of me no one else had ever seen.

I disentangled myself from his embrace and stepped back. Keeping my eyes on him, I raised my shaking fingers to the hem of my skirt and slid it down my legs, undoing my pointe shoes as I bent over. A tank top and pantyhose were hardly the most desirable of outfits, but Alek drank me in like I was made of golden nectar. It gave me the courage to slowly slide down my pantyhose until I was standing in just my top and my lacy pink underwear with a little bow on the front.

I bit my lip, insecurities already beginning to rise. What if I looked too childish in front of him? Surely the girls Alek was normally with looked much more *womanly*. And while I liked my cutesy lingerie—always with pink, lace, bows, ruffles, or a combination of them together—I was suddenly feeling far, *far* out of my league.

"Stop," Alek whispered, his pupils blown wide. "You're fucking beautiful."

"I am?"

He nodded slowly, throat bobbing as if he wanted to say more before he rasped, "Very, Evangeline."

My right hand traveled along my inner thigh until I

reached my core. God, I was practically dripping. The fabric was soaked, the smell of lust permeating the air around me.

Alek looked like he wanted to eat me alive, his whole body twitching as if he had to hold himself back from devouring me. Part of me wanted him to, but another part of me wanted to perform for him. I wanted to feel his eyes pressing against the curves of my body while I took pleasure from his longing gaze.

"I don't know what to do," I whispered, because while I'd somewhat touched myself before, I somehow knew that those times—the times in the shower where my hands explored before I got scared and hurriedly got out—were different.

"Has your cunt never been touched, solnyshka?"

I shook my head. "Not really. Teach me how."

"Fuck," he groaned. He looked like a bomb about to detonate, like he wanted me so badly, he was about to explode. "Touch yourself. Feel how wet you are."

Slipping my panties to the side, I dipped a finger into the wetness before slowly dragging it out. Alek let out a shuddering breath, seeming to have a war with himself before he hardened his gaze, gaining control while the passion simmered.

"Now stick your finger inside. Slowly."

I did as he ordered. I plunged a finger inside and moaned loudly, throwing my head back at the sensation. Nothing I'd ever done before had felt half as good as this, as the slow stroke I made while I pretended it was Alek's fingers inside of me instead of mine.

"Eyes on me," he growled, and my head snapped forward as if controlled by invisible strings. At that moment, he was my master. I was helpless to resist his commands—not that I wanted to. I wanted to listen, to make him proud, to be the girl he wanted me to be. Maybe it was some fucked up form of my people pleasing coming back to haunt me.

"Good girl."

I whimpered, my body *really* liking the sound of that.

Alek must have noticed my reaction. "Do you like it when I praise you, Eva?" he whispered, and I nodded, unwilling to open my mouth in case another embarrassing noise left me.

"Slide your finger in and out. Keep your eyes on me."

And maybe it was the commanding tone in his voice, or maybe it was the way he looked at me. Or maybe it was the way I could *feel* my muscles clenching around my fingers, my body slowly losing control to the fire building within me. Whatever the cause, all of my lingering apprehension slowly melted away, leaving behind a primal desire for more.

For Alek.

I began to get more daring, my finger moving in and out without his commands, my thumb even daring to press against my clit. My legs buckled for a second before I regained my balance.

"Look at how beautiful you are when you touch yourself. My pretty, pretty girl," he purred, and I almost fell apart right then and there.

"*Alek,*" I breathed.

"Add another finger."

I stilled my movements for a second, my eyes widening. "*Another?*"

"Yes, another. You have to prepare yourself for my cock, baby."

A thrill shot up my spine at the idea of losing my virginity to him, of his cock being inside of me, our bodies close together. My nipples ached from where they chaffed against my shirt. I wished it was off. That we were naked on the stage floor, Alek already inside of me.

"Eva," he said, his voice deliciously deep, snapping me back to reality. "Another finger. Now."

I obeyed instantly, not wanting to find out what would happen if I didn't. Alek's eyes sharpened with satisfaction as I slipped another finger inside of me, a high-pitched cry escaping me.

It was too much.

It wasn't enough.

I couldn't take it.

I needed more.

"How do you feel?"

"Weird," I panted, twisting and bending my fingers inside of me, the fire inside of me burning and burning and *burning*. I was beginning to lose control of my movements, my movements turning erratic, my vision darkening at the edges.

"How?"

"I don't... I don't know what's happening to me..."

"You're close," he growled under his breath, eyeing me like I was a drop of blood in the middle of the ocean, and he was a starving shark on the edge of a frenzy.

"*Yes.*"

My hips started to thrust into my hand, but it wasn't enough to uncoil the spring within me. Nothing I was doing was enough.

My other hand slid up my body, cupping my breast through my shirt. I began to massage it, to pull and tweak the nipple, but it didn't satisfy me. It climbed higher and higher, the fingers delving into the loosening strands.

"*Alek,*" I whimpered. My lips parted into a soft pout. "I need more."

"What do you need, baby?"

"*You...* Oh God, I need you."

He was in front of me in a second, capturing my wrist and pulling my fingers out of my body with a wet sound that made my cheeks burn. Alek brought my glistening fingers to his mouth and sucked hard, groaning at the taste of me. His eyes closed as he savored it. When he opened them again, his eyes shone with darkness, like something covered in oil.

"You taste so good. So fucking good."

Then, he was pushing his fingers inside of me, cupping my pussy with his hand while his lips descended to my neck. Alek's rhythm was forceful, his fingers much longer than my own. He owned me with every stroke, driving me higher and higher and higher.

"Come for me, Eva," Alek murmured when he could sense me tightening around him. "Fall apart for me. I'll keep you safe."

And when Alek curled his fingers inside of me, I did. The darkness overtook the edges of my vision, everything burning in the wake of the fire.

Alek cursed under his breath, his fingers slowing but never exiting me. He whispered reassurances over and over—how pretty I was, how good I felt around him, how he was going to make me his.

"Mine," he said. "You will be mine, Evangeline Vale."

And maybe I should have told him that that wasn't my real name, but I couldn't bring myself to, not when I was still feeling the shockwaves of everything we just did. So I nodded while the waves subsided until his fingers left me entirely.

I leaned into Alek's strong body, attempting to hide my flaming cheeks against his neck. What had I done? Did I really just throw myself at him, begging him to fingerfuck me? I could feel my dignity leave piece by piece, my pride fully shattered. I was never going to be able to show him my face again.

"Eva," he said, pinching my chin between his fingers and raising it to meet his eyes. But I avoided his gaze, looking everywhere but him. The stage, the velvet curtains, the dying lights. I couldn't bear to see the judgment on his face. Not now, not while I was still feeling the effects of my first real orgasm, my legs feeling like jelly, my eyes wanting to close.

"Look at me."

I tried to shake my head, but he growled. "Eva. Look at me. Now."

Even though I didn't want to, I listened, some part of me knowing that he was in charge here. That I could place control in his hands, and he would take good care of it—and me.

"What's wrong?"

"I mean, I'm a little embarrassed."

I tried to look down, but when his grip tightened, my eyes snapped back to his, some inner part of me knowing I needed to submit to him.

"Good girl," he murmured, stroking my chin. "Now, what are you embarrassed about?"

"I completely lost control back there in front of you. I wanted to be... I don't know. *Sexy*, or something."

"Evangeline. That was incredibly sexy. You are so fucking perfect. Nothing you do could ever be unattractive to me."

"But—"

"You. Are. Fucking. Perfect," he said, eyes boring into me, letting me see the truth written plainly across his face. The honesty in his eyes.

"Alek," I began.

"*No*, baby. You don't seem to understand what I mean, so let me be clear: I *like* you. You falling apart on my fingers was the sexiest fucking thing I've ever seen in my life. I want to see it again many, many times, possibly even tonight if you'll let me. I want to do things for you. I want to bring you flowers each time I take you to dinner, and I want to fuck you with your heels still on after. I want to meet your family, and I want you to meet mine—once I'm certain my mother won't scare you off. I want to pick you up from your dance rehearsals, I want to be in the front row for every show, and I want to make you come after each one. And I want to learn everything about you, including the parts that you think aren't sexy. Got it?"

For a moment, I couldn't breathe. My lips parted on their

own accord, and Alek swiped his thumb across my lower lip while my brain struggled to understand all of his words. It was as if someone had cracked open my chest and poured light straight into me without warning.

My thoughts tangled over each other, every carefully built belief about myself—that I wasn't daring enough, wasn't organized enough, wasn't pretty enough, wasn't perfect enough—fractured under the weight of his gaze. I felt exposed in a way that had nothing to do with my body, like he was seeing past the dancer, past the good girl, past the perfection I chased, straight into the messy, wanting center of me.

And the strangest part was that he liked what he saw.

I could feel my heart slowly beginning to belong to Alek. And I wasn't sure I would ever be able to get it back.

"Got it," I whispered.

"Good. Do you have anywhere to be?"

I thought of Jules, who was no doubt waiting impatiently by the phone, wanting to hear both about the auditions and when to pick me up. I sighed. "Unfortunately. When can I see you again?"

"Whenever you want, baby."

Something warm spread inside of me, beginning in my heart and moving outward. Baby, solnyshka, Eva. I didn't care what he called me as long as he called me his, too.

I smiled. "Okay. I'll text you."

He bent down and placed a quick kiss on my lips, his eyes crinkling in the corners. "Okay, Eva."

Our bodies separated, albeit reluctantly. I slipped my tights on, then my skirt. Alek looked disappointed at my increase in clothing, and to be honest, so was I. But Jules wouldn't have reacted well to me being late, especially if he learned it was because of a man. And I didn't want him to ruin things for Alek and me before they'd even fully started.

Alek jotted his phone number down on a piece of paper,

kissing my hand as he handed it over. Pocketing it, I smiled at him, waving shyly. "Bye, Alek."

"Aleksandr," he said.

"What?"

"My full name is Aleksandr. I figured you should know what you'll be screaming later."

I flushed. "Do you want me to call you Alek or Aleksandr?"

"I want you to call me yours."

God help me, I thought as his hungry eyes followed me all the way to the exit. *I'm in big trouble.*

December 27th

MIA

Get ready, bitch!

We're going out.

EVANGELINE

What?

Whyyyyy?

I just got in my PJs :(

MIA

Well, get out of them. I'll get a cab and pick you up in 30.

EVANGELINE

But I was gonna order pizza. :(

MIA

Eva, NO!

We're celebrating you getting Juliet, and that's final.

EVANGELINE

Jules is gonna say no.

MIA

Eva, I swear to God if you tell your brother.

EVANGELINE

I can't lie to him!

MIA

Then don't talk to him at all. Then, he'll never know, and he won't be a buzzkill. :)

Thirty minutes bitch. :)

EVANGELINE

Fine.

But you owe me dinner.

EVANGELINE
CHAPTER ELEVEN

"Are you sure you want to go *here*?" I asked Mia as the cab pulled up to a dark nightclub whose music I could hear from the vehicle. A simple sign read *OBSIDIAN* in clean letters. Black glass surrounded the edges of the building, but beyond that, it was fairly unassuming. No flashing signs. No neon. Just the quiet confidence of a place that didn't need to beg for attention. It radiated authority, danger, and indulgence on its own.

A velvet rope stretched across the front, guarded by men in tailored black coats who looked less like bouncers and more like sentinels. People lingered nearby anyway—dressed too well, pretending not to stare, clearly hoping to be noticed. A low thrum of bass vibrated through the pavement beneath my feet, felt more than heard, like the building had a pulse.

Warm light spilled from narrow windows high above the street, golden and inviting, hinting at something decadent waiting inside. Expensive cars lined the curb, engines purring softly before disappearing into the night.

Beyond the crowd at the front, a line of people stretched down the sidewalk, curving around the building. They were adorned in sequins, expensive jewelry, leather, and lace. The men could have killed me with a glance. The women seemed worse, like predators in heels. I thought I glimpsed steel beneath a coat, a gun perhaps, though that might have been my active imagination.

This place didn't feel like nightlife. It felt like a hunting ground disguised as a club.

Mia's karaoke bars suddenly seemed tame, like safe little cages compared to this. Those usually consisted of smaller bars with a special on tequila and people singing karaoke badly in the corner. I used to think I hated that, but this didn't look any better.

At least at those other bars, I felt like I somewhat belonged. Here, it was clear that I didn't.

As we stepped out of the car near the front door, I looked down at my outfit and frowned. Mia had helped me get ready after she came over, lending me a pink mini dress that clung to every inch of my skin. The hem was mere millimeters from flashing everybody in the entire city, and the fabric squished what little boobs I had so tightly that they felt like they were in my face. I paired the dress with a leather jacket and matching boots. Mia curled my hair and lined my eyes with thick eyeliner and lots of glitter, though she left my freckles untouched.

Every person in that line was wearing only black, and I suddenly felt out of place in the only color. I felt girly and cute in my outfit with my necklaces and dangly bow earrings, my lipstick matching the dress. But I felt wrong too.

Not to mention, I was freezing because of the cold weather. Half of my body was exposed to the wintry elements. Cold bit into me, sharp as a blade, exposing both my skin and my nerves to the dark night. I shivered, not entirely from the temperature, while Mia looked for a quicker way in.

I opened my mouth to tell her we weren't going to find

one when a slightly accented voice I didn't recognize called out, "Eva?"

A man a few years older than us—close to Jules's age—came bounding over to us, his dirty blond hair flopping into his sky-blue eyes. He was biting back a grin, eyes assessing me standing next to Mia, who moved closer as if to protect me from the stranger. Her glare was a fearsome thing, as was the pepper spray keychain she held in her grip.

"What the fuck are you doing here?" she snapped.

The man held out his hands in surrender, winking at her. "Calm down, princess. I just came over to chat."

"Chat over."

"Mia," I elbowed her softly before holding my hand out to the guy with a small smile. "I'm sorry. Have we met before? You'll have to remind me of your name."

He accepted my outstretched hand, squeezing once before shaking it. "We haven't, but we would have soon anyway." Before I could ask him what he meant, he added, "I'm Nikolai Drakov. Aleksandr's cousin."

Alek's cousin, I realized, my mouth going a little dry. I wasn't prepared to meet any of Alek's friends and family tonight, especially not dressed like *this*.

Wait.

"Is Alek nearby?" I couldn't help but ask, pulse hammering.

I wasn't sure whether I was terrified or craving him—or both. The thought of him here, in a place like this, made my stomach twist with anticipation. Seeing Alek was like getting a hit of a drug. I knew I needed to get away—he practically oozed danger—but I couldn't help but crave more.

Nikolai's grin widened. "I'll ask around. What are you two doing here?"

"What does it look like, dumbass?" Mia grumbled. "Trying to get into a nightclub."

"I apologize for my friend," I said to Nikolai, sending a warning look to Mia. "I'm not sure what's gotten into her tonight. But, yes, I think we were going to go to Obsidian, but I don't feel like waiting in the line in the cold, so I think we'll go somewhere else."

"Eva, no. I've been wanting to go here all week, and you—"

"I can get you guys in," Nikolai said, cutting off the beginnings of Mia's pleas.

She turned to him, eyes narrowed but no longer hateful. Had she met this man before? What was with her random hostility? Mia was normally super welcoming, yet she looked at Nikolai like he was less than dirt on the bottom of her shoe, which I didn't understand because Nikolai had been nothing but polite so far.

I turned to Nikolai. "You can?"

"Yeah. Come with me."

Before we could question him further, Nikolai started walking toward the bouncers at the front, gesturing for us to follow him. I shrugged before stalking after him, my legs wobbling both from the slightly too-tall heels on my boots and from the ache between my legs.

My cheeks heated at the mere reminder of this morning and what Alek and I did together. I hadn't gathered the nerve to text him yet—afraid Jules would somehow sense the betrayal—but I knew I would crack soon.

Especially if I had any amount of liquor in me.

"Masimov," Nikolai shouted to one of the giant men at the front door, gathering their attention. I shrank under their assessing gazes. They were truly terrifying to look at.

"This—" Nikolai pointed at me. "—is Drakov's girl. Evangeline Vale. Got it?"

Drakov's girl. Was that Aleksandr's last name? I supposed it made sense since that was Nikolai's last name and he'd said they were cousins. Still. *Aleksandr Drakov.* The words tasted strange and thrilling in my mouth, like stepping too close to fire and feeling the heat even before touching the flames. My heartbeat raced at the thought of our names spoken together.

I pictured myself doodling the name over and over in my diary like I used to whenever I saw a cute boy when I was younger. I pictured our names said together. *Aleksandr and Evangeline Drakov.*

I liked that. I *really* liked that.

"Remember her face," Nikolai continued. "If she wants in, she gets in. And add Satan's offspring to the list as well, I guess."

"Why you little fucker—" Mia began, but I squeezed her hand to attempt to cut her off.

"Please," I whispered. "Don't fight. Not now."

Mia knew I hated any sort of conflict at all. I didn't see the point in using sharp words to hurt each other. We were all adults. If Mia and Nikolai had an issue with each other, then they could calmly talk about it. No need for insults or name-calling.

It was something I'd been trying to convince my brother of, though instead of witty barbs, he preferred to use the muscles he spent almost every day building and the hothead temper he'd honed over his lifetime. I liked that even less than Mia's sort of warfare and did everything in my power to stop any of his fights before they began.

Mia sighed. "You're right. It's your big night. I'll hold it together."

"Thank you."

"But if he tries anything, I swear to *God*, Eva, I will fuck him up so—"

"Nice, remember?"

"Ugh. Yes." She turned to Nikolai and gave him a saccharine smile. "Thank you, nice asshole, for helping us get inside."

I sighed as she strutted inside. "I'm sorry. She's not like this, normally. I don't know what got into her."

He bit back a grin. "Oh, I do."

He didn't clarify any further, instead gesturing for me to go inside. The two guards at the front of the door gave me a nod of respect, one of them muttering in a thick Russian accent, "Enjoy your time at Obsidian, Miss Vale."

The moment I stepped inside, the world shifted.

The door sealed shut behind us with a muted thud, cutting off the city noise as if it had never existed. All I could hear was the steady pulse of music reverberating in my bones, lining up with the beating of my heart.

Obsidian exhaled around me—dark, rich, predatory. The air was cold, perfumed with liquor and something metallic, expensive, dangerous. Underneath it all, a raw scent lingered. Desire sharpened by the eyes of strangers, the thrill of watching and being watched. Sex.

I gulped. I didn't belong in a place like this.

I followed the tall silhouettes of Nikolai and Mia. The main room was dark, lit only by the occasional flashing light. In the background, I could make out dozens, if not hundreds, of bodies moving in a fluid rhythm, their shadows sliding over one another like ink atop water. Hands rubbing inner thighs, gripping breasts. Mouths poised on necks. Pelvises pressing together.

I wished Alek were there more than ever, not only because I wanted to be like that with him, but because I knew he would keep me safe through it all.

Heads turned as I passed. Conversations paused long enough to make me feel the subtle shift. There was a second-floor balcony where people watched below, drinks in hand, like voyeurs waiting for a show.

I felt like *I* was the show. A siren trapped in an aquarium while people stood by, waiting for me to sing.

Nikolai moved like he owned the currents of the room, unfazed by every stare, every whispered assessment. The crowd parted for him with practiced ease. Every staff member we passed acknowledged him with a nod, their eyes flicking briefly to me before returning to neutral professionalism. My skin prickled. I suddenly felt very aware of my dress, my posture, the way my heels clicked softly against the dark floor. I felt both invisible and overexposed.

I leaned closer to Nikolai, shouting over the music. "Is it always like this?"

He smiled, eyes bright and thrilled. "Only if you matter."

Matter. The word landed in my chest like a challenge. Matter how? And to whom? I imagined their eyes on me like teeth.

Then, I imagined Alek's teeth on me, ripping into my throat, marking me as his. Now, my nerves were lit up, but not for the same reason as before.

"Not perfect," my inner voice hissed, sharp as knives. I tugged at the hem of my dress, aware of every pair of eyes while wishing he were here to keep me from feeling so exposed. *"You will never be good enough for him. Your brother will never accept him. Never."*

Nikolai led us to a booth on the side of the room marked *VIP*, slinging the sign off to the side and holding out his arm to help Mia and me slide into it. The music was lower here, and I breathed a sigh of relief at being away from the prying eyes.

"Have fun tonight, ladies." Nikolai gave me a piercing sky-blue stare. "But not too much fun, okay, Miss Vale?"

I wasn't sure what he meant by that.

Nikolai disappeared into the darkness of the crowd, and I sighed, already regretting saying yes to Mia, though I would never tell her that. How could I when she was clearly so excited to have me here?

The song changed to one I vaguely recognized, a low tune filled with lots of bass and words I could barely hear. "Oh my God! I love this song! Let's go take shots and dance!"

I wanted to tell her that leaving this booth was the *last* thing I wanted to do... but I didn't. I just accepted her outstretched hand and let her lead me to a bar and a night full of bad decisions.

December 27th

EVANGELINE
Hi Alek :)

ALEKSANDR
Hello, pretty girl.

EVANGELINE
You are so sweet. :)
You make me so happy. :)
I'm gonna keep you. :)

ALEKSANDR
Are you okay, Eva?

EVANGELINE
I am MORE than okay!
I was okay like three drinks ago!
But now I'm BETTER!

ALEKSANDR
Where are you, baby? I'll come get you.

EVANGELINE
Umm... I don't know. It's dark.

MISSED CALL FROM ALEKSANDR

EVANGELINE
It's too loud. :(
I can't hear anything. :(
I miss you. :(

ALEKSANDR
Can someone else answer the phone?
Are you with anyone?

MISSED CALL FROM ALEKSANDR

EVANGELINE

Yeah! I'm with Mia!

We're celebrating! :)

But I'd much rather be celebrating with you again. ;)))

I think someone is coming, I gotta go.

Byeeeeee.

MISSED CALL FROM ALEKSANDR
ALEKSANDR

Eva.

MISSED CALL FROM ALEKSANDR

Eva.

Fuck. I'm coming.

ALEKSANDR
CHAPTER TWELVE

"I HAVE THE BEST NEWS FOR YOU, COUSIN," Nikolai said as soon as he strolled into my office at one of the many nightclubs I owned, a shit-eating grin on his face as he plopped into the chair across from me.

"Not now," I growled, hammering my phone against the desk. The call went straight to voicemail. Panic clawed at my chest. *She could be anywhere, exposed. Drunk. Vulnerable. And if anyone touched her—*

I swallowed hard, the wordless threat curling around me like smoke.

I needed to fucking find her. While I trusted Eva to take care of herself, I didn't trust the people in this city. I knew firsthand how dark and cruel the world could be. Liza was not spared its wrath simply because she was a child, and a woman as beautiful as my Evangeline was too much a temptation to ignore.

My mind spun with visions of worst-case scenarios. What if someone tried to take advantage of her? Lead her to their homes and rob her of that innocent light that shone around her? What if the Vallens learned of my growing weakness for her and decided to exploit it while she was vulnerable?

Fuck.

I would put a bullet through the skull of anyone who tried to lay a single fucking finger on her.

I stood from my desk, flinging the paperwork to the side in my haste. Sometimes, I visited my businesses to work and get things done—like tonight, when I'd been trying to look into the outdated infrastructure of the theater, all the electrical work that needed rewiring. It helped to show my face around the place, remind anyone of who they may be crossing. And since I *thought* Eva was safe at her home tonight, I figured I would accomplish some things while the taste of her juices still lingered on my tongue. It was clear that I was going to have to add guards for her—if not guard her myself, because the thought of people watching her for hours made me see red.

"Aren't you going to ask what my news is, Aleksandr?" Nikolai crooned, pretending to twirl his hair like a dumbass.

"No. I'm busy."

"I think you'll want to know it."

"I don't. I need to go."

"Go where?"

"I don't have time for this," I muttered, shouldering past him and opening the door. "I'm going to find Eva. I won't be back."

"Shame you don't want to hear my good news, then. I know exactly where she is."

The turn I made was slow and menacing. The kind of movement that made men reconsider their life choices. Something dark uncurled inside of me, something roaring with possessiveness. *Find Eva. Take Eva. Make her* mine. I was like a dragon with a treasure, determined to hide my golden girl away from the rest of the world.

A flash of fear crossed my cousin's face.

"What did you just say?" I asked, my voice low and cold.

Nikolai gulped. "That I know where she is."

I crossed the room and grabbed him by the collar. Nikolai froze in my grip, but I didn't strangle him.

Yet.

"Where the fuck is she?"

"Relax! I'll tell you." He held up his arms in surrender, breath already quickening. Good. It meant he wasn't going to fuck around like he normally did. "She's here."

"Here?"

"At Obsidian."

"*How?*" The club waitlist was at least a mile long. It was incredibly difficult to get into Obsidian, one of my more luxurious clubs and one of the few that didn't serve as a front to something else. Well, if you didn't include the many business deals made at our VIP tables, where I got a cut for my locational services.

"I spotted her outside with her friend. I brought her inside, told the guards to remember her face. Figured you'd want her here, where she'd be protected, and not at another club. That's what I was coming to tell you: that she's here out on the main dance floor."

I loosened my hold, and Nikolai almost got away before I remembered something else, pulling him right back into my clenched fist. "Wait. You waited to tell me until she had three fucking drinks?"

"Technically, her friend ordered two shots each while I was still nearby, so I only waited for her to have *one* drink—" At my tightening grip, Nikolai sputtered and held his hands up again. "Relax, relax! I came as soon as I could. The crowd is pretty thick tonight, and I didn't even know if you were working. I *tried* to call, but someone ignored me."

I glanced at my phone and cursed when I saw that he was right. Three missed calls and a text asking where I was working tonight sat plainly on my screen, all of them from before Eva started texting me. So he *did* try to contact me.

There would be no violence against my cousin tonight. Shame.

"I'm going to get her," I said, finally letting him go.

Nikolai cleared his throat. "Aren't you forgetting something?"

I sighed at the look on his falsely cherubic face. There was nothing angelic about Nikolai. He could act like a puppy all he wanted, but he was nothing less than a hellhound.

"Thank you," I said through gritted teeth, then adding under my breath, "asshole."

He opened his mouth to curse me back, but I didn't want to hear it, already barreling down the hallway and out into the club to get my girl.

I could feel the music well before I heard it. My office was far enough to thankfully mute most of the noise. Silver and white lights flashed in tune to the raucous noise, and everywhere I looked, people ground into each other, practically fucking in front of me.

"Reaper," a patron nodded at me. I nodded back, recognizing a man who worked for my family.

Making my way to the dance floor, I spotted my girl instantly, wearing the sexiest fucking tight dress, revealing most of her body save for the strips of fabric clinging to her. Her tits were right there, practically begging me to lick and suck them, while her ass shook for the entire world to see. Her brown curls cascaded down her back, and I wanted to wrap my hand around them and pull her to the nearest dark room.

Mine. The word thundered in my skull. *She is mine.*

Eva clutched a drink in one hand while the other roamed up her body and into the air. Mia was next to her, dancing and chatting with another pair of girls. I was thankful to see no men were near her, though they certainly stared. I glared at all of them while I slowly stalked up to her, letting my presence alone serve as a threat.

Because they were intelligent and didn't want to lose their lives to the Reaper, they all looked away.

The blonde girl—one I recognized as Eva's friend from the ballet, Mia—paused as soon as I stepped behind her, mouth gaping while she eyed me up and down. The other two quickly followed suit, but my Eva kept on dancing, clearly unaware of the dark presence behind her.

I looped my arm around her waist, drawing her against me like a predator claiming its prey. She stumbled but righted herself under my steady grip, body stilling as soon as she fell against me, her back to my chest. Eva shivered when my other hand went to her neck, arching her toward me. I couldn't resist touching her, grabbing her, making her breath quicken. Every taste of her fed my beast, and he was starving for more of her.

"Sorry," Mia tried to say, grabbing Eva's arm and failing to pull her from my grasp. "She's already got a man."

"I know," I purred, and another wave of shivers fell down Eva's back at the sound of it. She angled her neck enough for me to bend over and suck on her favorite spot, the one that hadn't yet failed to make her lips part in invitation. "I'm the man."

Though I appreciated Mia keeping an eye out for my interests. I liked her already.

All of their jaws fell to the floor, but I didn't care to witness the rest of their reaction, my eyes too mesmerized by Eva's dilated pupils, her heaving chest, her flushed cheeks. She was a painting of lust, and I wanted to hide the canvas away from the rest of the world.

There was something about the way that her eyes darkened that made her strikingly familiar. Again, a bell rang in the back of my mind, urging me to pay closer attention to her.

"So pretty," I murmured, running my thumb along her bottom lip.

"Hi," she whispered, turning fully so she was facing me. She ran her hands along my torso, biting her lip in a way that made me want to rip it from her teeth and slam my cock inside.

"Hi, solnyshka. I heard you missed me."

She smiled and leaned into me. "I did. You got here quickly."

"I missed you, too."

"How badly?" she purred, standing on her tiptoes to kiss the jaw I clenched to keep from taking her to my office. *She's drunk*, I reminded myself. *You can't fuck her senselessly tonight.*

But God, I wanted to.

I knew I wasn't the picture of morality, but I wasn't going to take her virginity while she was impaired. I was a monster, but not that much of one. Plus, there were too many eyes here. Too many people interested in what was mine.

"I'll show you another time."

She jutted out her lip. Fuck. My cock hardened in my pants, clearly not getting the memo that my shower was going to be cold. Eva was testing what little control I had.

"*Fineeeee*," she whined. "But you owe me."

Yes. Yes, I did.

I leaned forward, my mouth claiming hers in a heated kiss, my lips pressing every ounce of emotion I felt for her. Lust, infatuation, and perhaps something blooming into more. It was a clash of desire that didn't feel satiated. She tasted so goddamn sweet. I needed more. I needed to lift her up and feel her against me, needed to take her over and over—

"Excuse me," her friend said before we could take this any further, drawing Eva's doe-eyed gaze and my glare. I looked down at my girl and found her expression dazed, her lips swollen from our savage kiss. It was a look I very much enjoyed on her.

Mia turned to Eva, brow raised. "*This* is Alek?"

"Yes," Eva said, wrapping an arm around my waist and hugging me in a tight, warm embrace that I didn't hesitate to return. "Alek, this is my friend, Mia, and some girls she knew in high school."

"Nice to meet you," I said, barely nodding in their direction to avoid Eva catching my lie. I wasn't particularly enjoying our meeting when it meant our kiss getting interrupted.

"Eva, when were you going to tell me that Alek is the most fucking attractive person I've ever seen? Oh my God, he ate your entire face off!" Mia tried to come forward and take Eva, but I held onto her tightly.

Like hell they were going to take her away from me. I didn't care who they were—her family, her friends, fucking God himself. She was mine. And *only* mine.

"I told you Alek looks like my Prince Charming," Eva said, voice edging on a whine.

I raised a brow at this. "Your Prince Charming, huh?"

"Yup. You're going to steal me away to your castle, and then we're going to get married and live happily ever after."

I was far from a charming prince, and the mansion I lived in was closer to one fit for modern vampires than for the lovely princess before me, but the knowledge that when Eva thought of her future, she thought of me settled something in my soul. Because I wanted a future with her, too. No matter the cost.

"Sounds good, baby. I'll be your Prince Charming." And her villain, too.

Eva smiled up at me, drunk and glowing and devastatingly beautiful. Mia laughed, clapping a hand over her mouth as her gaze swung between the two of us. "Oh my God. I *love* this for you. Eva, this is... This is insane. I mean, look at him. He's like a god."

Eva ducked her head immediately, fingers tightening in my

suit jacket. It was clear she didn't like all the complimentary attention, but I wouldn't stand for that.

"And look at her," I murmured, fingers lifting her chin up to my eyes before my lips pulled upward. "She's my goddess."

Because she was radiant, yet she didn't seem to know it—not really. She softened herself when she didn't need to, curled herself into small balls like she was afraid of taking up space. But I wanted her to take up space. I wanted her to be proud of who she was, my beautiful, sunshiny princess.

Eva looked up at me, startled, like she hadn't expected me to butt in. Her lips parted, then curved into a small, grateful smile that hit me harder than anything else tonight.

That was when Nikolai appeared at my side like a bad habit I couldn't quit.

"Well," he drawled, eyes flicking to Mia. "If it isn't the blonde menace. Fancy seeing you again."

Mia's entire posture changed. Her smile stayed, but it sharpened—edges drawn tight. Her eyes flashed. "Nikolai. I would *kindly* ask you not to call me that."

"Why not? Would you rather I call you princess?"

"Don't you *dare* call me princess, you stuck-up little—"

I didn't even notice Eva escaping my grip until she was standing between the two of them, arms up to try to get them to act like peaceful adults. And though I knew Mia and Nikolai would never harm her—her friend for obvious reasons, and Nikolai because he enjoyed me not killing him—I didn't like that Eva was ready to sacrifice herself so quickly to keep everyone happy. What other lengths would she be willing to go to? Would she run in front of a bullet if it meant someone else didn't get hit?

Knowing my Eva, the answer was yes, which was why I quickly grabbed her, pulling her back into me while I growled into her soft hair, "You two know each other."

"No," Mia said at the same time Nikolai said, "Oh, yes."

I didn't miss the way Mia's fingers curled into a fist at her side, or the way Nikolai's grin softened a fraction when she looked away.

Interesting.

But I had much more important things to worry about. I looked down at Eva and noticed her eyes darting across the room, breaths quickening. I cupped her cheek and noted how heated her skin felt underneath my palm. "Want to get some air, solnyshka?"

Eva nodded immediately. She turned to Mia—who was in the midst of telling Nikolai a very colorful array of words—and said, "I'll be right back."

Mia whirled to face her before pinning her glare at me.

And I glared right fucking back.

"You're still coming home with me, right?" In other words: *Are you going to his house?* I wished the answer was yes, but I also knew my gentlemanly morals could only last so long. If I got Eva into my bed, there would be no tearing me away from her. Especially if she kept looking at me with that pouty mouth, asking if I fucking *missed her.*

"Yeah," Eva said, much to my disappointment, though it was for the best.

I took her drink from her as I led her through the club, grimacing when I took a sip. "What the fuck is this?"

Eva shrugged. "I don't know."

"You *don't know*?" Who the fuck was giving her random drinks? I would fucking kill them, I would—

"Well, I ordered an amaretto sour, but I think they just gave me what the other girls were ordering. I don't think I'll get it again. It's not very good, but it's okay. I'm taking sips."

Before she could say anything more, I grabbed her hand and pulled her with me to the bar, gesturing to the bartender, one of our newer employees, Dariy.

"Yes, Reaper?" he asked, polishing a glass.

I slammed the cup onto the bar hard enough to make the glass crack. Dariy looked at me with wide eyes, his fear growing before I made a single threat. "When our customers order a drink, serve them the correct one."

He heard the *or else* plainly lining my words. "Got it," Dariy whispered before his eyes looked at Eva.

I snapped my fingers. "Don't look at her. Look at me. This girl receives better service than you would give even me. Now make her fucking drink."

"An amaretto sour, please," Eva said in her soft, sweet voice. Always an angel, my girl.

When Dariy left to make her drink in a frantic rush, she turned to me, lips pulling down in a frown. "You didn't have to be mean to him. And you *really* didn't need to do that. I was fine with the drink I had."

"No, you weren't."

"No," she began, "but I'm all right with drinking something I don't like to make someone's job easier."

"His job is to make the thing you ask for. If you didn't get what you asked for, he didn't do his job." I stepped into her, inhaling her sweet scent of vanilla and sugar. My favorite combination. "It's okay to ask for what you want, Evangeline. Demand it, even."

She wrinkled her nose. "I won't be doing that."

"Then I will do it for you."

A moment later, the bartender passed her the drink, and Eva took a careful sip before nodding.

"Better?" I asked.

"Much."

I placed my arm on her back, savoring the feeling of her skin under mine, before I realized the skin was slightly raised. Goosebumps. Eva had *goosebumps*.

The club was kept cool on purpose because of the number of people who danced and moved, sweating themselves into a fervor. Plus, liquor always made them warmer. But Eva, who was standing on the edge of the dance floor and barely sipping her drink, was probably freezing. She was built for warmth and sunlight, not dark rooms blasting air conditioning.

"You're cold," I said.

She blinked, surprised, then shook her head immediately. "No, I'm fine."

But I was becoming familiar with the taste of her lies.

I reached out, my hands brushing against her arms. She shivered, skin cool beneath my touch. "Eva," I said, voice deepening. "Are you cold?"

She sighed, caught. "I... Well, I lent my jacket to Mia. She was freezing in here, so I figured—"

"You figured that you'd give her yours?"

Of course, she had.

Something ugly twisted in my chest. Eva was always giving pieces of herself away, like they were expendable, like she came second to everyone else in the room when she should have been at the forefront of everyone else's mind like she was for me. Yet they took and took and took from her, uncaring of how much of her was left.

Well, I wouldn't let her become hollow. I would make sure she was whole and cared for every day of her life.

I shrugged out of my suit jacket before she could protest and draped it over her shoulders, settling it firmly on her body. My jacket swallowed her, dark fabric against soft skin, my scent clinging to her instantly. And fuck me, my cock hardened at the sight of her in my clothes.

Eva looked up at me, lips parting. "Alek, you don't have to—"

"I want to," I cut in calmly. "And you're going to let me."

She stilled, fingers curling into the lapels. A war was going on behind her eyes, and I was afraid she'd make herself the casualty.

"There's nothing wrong with being kind," I said quietly, cupping her face and kissing her forehead. "But you don't have to sacrifice yourself for everyone. Anyone who deserves you won't ask that of you."

Her throat bobbed as she swallowed. Eva considered my words before turning to me, her brown eyes shining. "I'll remember that," she whispered.

I hoped, for the world's sake, she would.

I took her hand again, leading her away from the bar and into a long hallway that led to my office. The music dulled behind us, replaced by low lighting and shadowed walls. I didn't notice before, but the air was heavier here, charged with something. Like my growing want for her was permeating the atmosphere.

My office door appeared at the end of the hallway, door slightly ajar, inviting us in. To be honest, I wasn't sure why I invited her back here. Maybe I was tired of watching her spirit dim the longer our friends fought.

Or maybe I just needed her alone again before I fucked her in front of everyone, because God, she grew more beautiful with each passing moment.

Eva turned toward me. "I like your jacket, Alek."

"I like it on you," I said, voice low. "But I'd like it much better off."

That was all it took.

We crashed against each other, a frantic mess of lips and tongues and teeth. I barely had enough time to place my hand against the back of Eva's head before I slammed her into the wall, lifting her body so our cores were aligned. Her hands roamed all over my body while she melted into me, lips parting for mine to claim them.

It was hot. Messy. Hungry.

Eva made a soft sound that went straight to my cock, her fingers fisting in my jacket like she was about to combust. I kissed her harder, slower, letting her feel exactly how much I wanted her—how little restraint I had left.

"Alek," she breathed.

I pulled back enough to look at her, pupils blown wide, lips swollen and pink. I wanted to memorize the picture of her coming undone, commit it to memory so hard that when I died, the image would still be burning the backs of my eyelids.

My hips fought not to buck into her as I carried her down the hall straight to my office door. I couldn't keep my hands off of her—her hair, her ass, even her tits, which I managed to squeeze with one hand as I nudged the door open with my body.

"I want to taste you," Eva moaned, leaning into me further.

"You are tasting me."

"No, I—" She made a whimpering noise in the back of her throat before wriggling out of my arms. Before I could ask her what she was doing, why she was no longer kissing me, Eva dropped to her knees, hands fumbling at my trousers, before she unzipped my cock and freed it.

She stared at my throbbing cock, mouth agape as she studied the veins snaking down the shaft. A bead of precum was already at the tip, a side effect of our earlier kisses.

"Eva, you really don't have to— *Fuck*!" A deep moan vibrated my chest as Eva slowly took me into her warm, wet mouth. She coughed around the length, face turning red, before I said, "Breathe, Eva. In and out through your nose. You can take it, beautiful."

She did as I commanded, and her submission had me hardening even more. The sight of her on her knees, my cock in between her pink lips, her eyes dark with desire and wide with fear, made me want to come all over her.

A part of me wanted to fuck her, use her mouth like it was my toy, and fill her with my seed until she was choking on it.

She would like it, too, my Eva, always giving, always knowing when to take.

"Use your hand to grip the other end. Squeeze as you suck. That's it. Such a good fucking girl."

I wrapped her hair around my fingers, doing my best not to pull it and make her cry. That would come later. For now, I would take it slow. I would teach her what to do and break her into my kind of lovemaking.

Slowly, I began to thrust into her mouth while she sucked around me, her tongue running all along my shaft. She gagged when I hit the back of her throat, and a whimper slipped out in between thrusts when I did it again. "Relax, Eva. You're going to let me fuck this hole of yours, and when you're ready, I'll fuck your pretty pussy."

"*Mm*," she moaned, squeezing her thighs together. Eva loved to be praised, which worked well since I loved to praise her.

My thrusts picked up speed thanks to my grip on her hair. Eva was no longer trying to keep up with my movements. She let me fuck her face, her arousal practically soaking the air. She looked at me with unrestrained desire, and I wanted to capture that look and keep it forever, a reminder to the world that only I could make her like this.

Eva's hand traveled down her body before pulling up her skirt, her hands finding her pussy. She was probably fucking drenched. I wasn't sure where to look—at my cock going in and out of her mouth, at her eyes flooding with delicious tears as she choked on it, or at her finger beginning to slip in and out of her cunt.

"Are you horny, baby? Does your body like the feeling of choking on my cock? It knows it belongs to me. You're fucking mine, Eva. Every inch of you, every one of your tight little holes. *Mine.*"

Eva tried to respond, but the only thing that came out was

drool and more tears. She looked so fucking erotic like that, her good girl image coming completely undone as my darkness crashed against it, shattering her innocence. I couldn't wait to see how she looked when my cock was fully inside her, thrusting in and out of that tight cunt I felt earlier.

Her moans got even louder, her fingers turning more erratic, pumping in and out and in and out. I tried to match the rhythm, but my control was shredded at that point. Both of us were on the edge of an orgasm, but I would be damned if my pleasure came before hers.

"Come for me, pretty girl," I growled. "*Now.*"

And then her moans turned into cries of pure ecstasy, her mouth tightening around my cock.

"Fuck, Eva!" I groaned, thrusting into her mouth one more time until my cock tightened and my cum shot into the back of her throat in violent spurts. Eva choked on it before swallowing it, even going as far as to lick a stray drop on her lips. "Good girl. My good girl."

"I like it when you call me that," she said as she pulled her fingers out of her pussy.

"Good," I said, grabbing her fingers and putting them in my mouth. "Because I like calling you it."

I lifted her to her feet before setting her onto my desk and kissing her deeply, my hand sinking into her hair, and my tongue delving into her mouth. I groaned at the taste of my cum on her lips, salty mixed with her sweet lip gloss.

Eva moaned into my mouth before pulling back, her eyes dazed from her orgasm. "I'd better get back."

"Or you could stay with me."

"And risk my brother finding out and going ballistic?" She huffed. "Unfortunately, he's going to be difficult about... this."

"'This?'"

"You know." Eva gestured back and forth wildly before her brows furrowed. "This!"

I smirked. "I don't know, Eva. What do you mean?"

"Whatever is going on here! I don't know, are we friends?"

"Fuck no," I growled, pulling her back into me. My cock was already hard again, and I pressed it into her, letting her feel what she did to me. "Does this feel like I want to be *friends?*"

"N-no," she whispered.

"No. You are not just my friend, Evangeline. You are *mine.*"

Her breath hitched. "Y-yours?"

"Is that all right?"

She nodded once before her face split into a huge grin. "Yeah. Yeah, that's all right."

And though the beast inside of me was ecstatic at her words—at finally calling this beautiful girl mine—another part of me stirred, too. A part that I thought died long ago when Liza did. The part of me that was capable of caring for another person, that had feelings and other weaknesses.

My little sun was thawing my icy heart.

And I knew it wouldn't be long before I melted for her.

December 28th

MIA

How was the date???

EVANGELINE

Ugh, it was so good.

Alek is literally perfect. 😍

MIA

What did you guys do? I need the deets!!

Want to come over and tell me them over a bottle of wine?

EVANGELINE

I wish, but Jules is acting crazy lately.

Something about a business rival acting weirdly...

I don't know, he's making me stay here tonight.

MIA

BUZZKILL.

Tell me all about it.

The date, not the buzzkill.

EVANGELINE

Well, he picked me up in a suit and a car worth more than all of my college tuition. AND he gave me another bouquet of pink flowers even though the last one is still overtaking my entire kitchen counter.

And then he took me to this fancy steakhouse.

MIA
And dessert???

EVANGELINE
We didn't have any.

MIA
Girl, you have the biggest sweet tooth of anyone I know.

I don't believe that for a second.

EVANGELINE
Well, HE had dessert. I didn't.

MIA
?

OHHHHHH.

EVANGELINE
CHAPTER THIRTEEN

ONE WEEK AFTER ALEK'S AND MY NIGHT AT THE club, my kitchen was overflowing with pink flowers of all shades and sizes. They were never as loud or overwhelming as Alek's first bouquet, though I knew that was because he wanted to get my attention after weeks apart.

I was beginning to learn things like that—how Alek thought. We texted constantly and saw each other almost every day after Jules dropped me back home after rehearsals. Alek couldn't even wait twenty-four hours after one of the best days of my life to ask me on a date, taking me to a nice restaurant that night before showing me how it felt to be consumed by a villain.

And now I knew he sent me flowers because he simply didn't want to go long without seeing me, which was good because I liked how he clung to me. How he continued to give me articles of clothing, refusing to take the scarf back. How he was always asking me if I wanted to go to dinner, the movies, or for a walk around the park.

And though I'd never gone to his house —because I knew once we did, we'd take that final step together—he'd come to mine often, sometimes to cuddle me while we watched trashy television, sometimes to make me feel things I'd never felt before.

Tonight would be our first night without seeing each other. The thought brought a frown to my face as I stretched on my kitchen counter the morning before my second rehearsal as Juliet. I'd had to quit my job at the cafe due to my new role, which would have really stressed me out had my salary not increased with our new investor.

I had Alek to thank for that. And I was too grateful to protest it much.

My sudden unemployment should have meant my brother eased up on me, but he'd only tightened the reins. Jules had been insistent that his business rival was up to something nefarious, and he didn't want to risk me getting hurt.

"Trust me, Evangeline. This guy is bad news. I need you home, safe," Jules had said. *"Our families have too much bad blood for you to get in the crossfire."*

I would have argued with him more—because I seriously doubted a businessman cared about me in my little apartment —but Alek had also said he had to work, kissing my forehead as he told me to enjoy time with my brother. So while I still thought Jules was being a little overdramatic, I was looking forward to the *Romeo + Juliet* movie night he promised me.

Our city was split in half, ruled by empires built on fear and fire. One strike, one misstep, and someone ended up in a hospital—or worse. Even a simple trip across town could turn into a battle, and I was reminded that my life, small as it seemed, was always tangled in the war.

Our family was one half, owning several businesses from hotels and restaurants, to shipping and transportation, to things I was sure I didn't even know about. My parents used to manage all of this until Jules became of age and took control of them with all his might. They never offered any positions to me, but I wasn't sure I would have taken them anyway. I liked dancing, and I didn't want to take my sights off my career at the Company.

But no one ever told me much about the other family. Jules refused to even speak their names, but I pieced together enough from conversations and actions over the years. Our families had been at war for as long as I could remember. One would do something to sabotage the other, and they'd retaliate. Back and forth, back and forth, sometimes ending in people getting hurt. A few years ago, the other family sabotaged a gala held at one of our hotels. Four people had to go to the hospital. I was thankfully at ballet practice instead of attending, but Jules's reaction to it was absolutely ballistic. He even made me stay home from school for weeks, acting like seventeen was way too young to be roaming the city.

And for a long time, a part of me wondered if the feud was why my parents were always sending me off to things like boarding school or lessons. If they wanted me so far away from any potential danger that they were willing to sacrifice our relationship together.

But another part of me knew I'd drive myself crazy if I kept thinking about that and other "*What ifs*?" So I'd stopped asking myself that long ago.

I wished, though, that Jules trusted me enough not to get myself hurt over a little business interaction. He acted like they would kill me the first chance they got, which seemed a little far-fetched. What would the other family ever want to do with me?

Smiling at my array of flowers, I grabbed my bag and waited for Jules to arrive to take me to rehearsal. Alek gave endlessly. Pink ranunculus one morning. Peonies the next. White roses with soft blush tips that looked like they'd been painted on by hand. They might have been too much for anyone else, but I craved it.

No. I craved *him*. Every flower, every note, was a reminder that he was always watching, always near, always claiming me as *his*.

What could I say? Princess treatment felt good.

The sound of a car horn jolted me from my thoughts, and I jogged down the apartment stairs, waving at my neighbor, who always smelled a little too much like beer. Jules's sleek red sports car idled at the curb, and I slid inside, kissing my brother on the cheek. "Hi, Jules."

"Hi, Annie. Got everything you need for tonight?"

I held up my bag. "Yup. And I'm gonna make you buy me so much candy."

My brother rolled his eyes as he pulled into the street. "I would expect nothing less."

On the way there, I checked my messages and smiled when I saw one waiting for me from Alek.

> ALEKSANDR
>
> Good morning, solnyshka. Have fun at rehearsal. Call me later?

I shot off a quick response before shoving my phone in my bag, not wanting to risk Jules seeing it. I still wasn't sure how my brother would react to the news that I not only had a boyfriend, but had gotten one without even mentioning Alek to him once.

Yes, boyfriend. Because the other night, when we were cuddling on my couch underneath my pink fuzzy blanket, I'd made the mistake of saying I wasn't sure if Alek was my boyfriend, which I felt like was fair considering he only ever called me "his" and not anything *normal* like girlfriend.

Needless to say, Alek decided to punish me with his tongue by not letting me come for what felt like hours. By the time he did, I was a sobbing mess, apologizing over and over and over while he kissed my tears away.

"Say you're my girlfriend, and you can come, baby," he'd

murmured against my neck. And when I promptly obeyed, Alek had made me see stars.

Jules glanced over to me, his brown eyes a mix between concerned and confused. "You're quiet today."

"Yeah?"

"You're never quiet, Evangeline."

I gaped at him. "Yes, I am!"

My brother gave me a pointed look. "No, you're not. You used to talk to your bedroom door for fun."

"Because you never wanted to play with me!"

At the time, I was always so hurt that my brother would hardly ever play with me. Now, as an adult, I was surprised he did at all. Playing ballerina dress-up and acting out princess stories with a six-year-old was probably excruciating for a thirteen-year-old boy.

"Maybe I never wanted to play with you because you talked too much," he teased before pulling to the side in front of the theater. "Same time as yesterday?"

"Yup. Bye, Jules!"

The studio was bustling with dancers who had to be there earlier to work on some of the corps de ballet scenes. That used to be me—moving through the choreography as a unit, Mia always by my side. Dancing on my own would take some getting used to.

"That's because you don't belong here," the voice inside of me whispered. The new spotlight, the rehearsals, the excitement with Alek—all of it stirred a storm in my head.

The break in my routine, the new environment, all of my overstimulation from Alek—though amazing—was making the voice stronger. I thrived best when I knew where to go, what to do, and who to be. Routines. Rules. Anything to silence the buzzing.

Now, I had to work twice as hard to get out of bed some mornings, tragedy after tragedy replaying in my head.

What if I wasn't fit to be the lead?

What if I embarrassed myself and the other dancers?

What if I hurt myself like Elsie did?

What if I took the spot away from someone else who truly wanted it?

What if Madame Germaine only chose me because of Alek's suggestion?

What if my brother found out about Alek and me?

What if Jules didn't accept him as my boyfriend?

What if this empty feeling—the one that insisted I was never doing anything right—never went away?

I ignored all of those questions and the dozens that followed, shoving them into the box deep inside my heart with all of the other emotions I couldn't deal with. That was my life: constantly trying to please everyone but myself. Even the little voice in my head.

"Evangeline," Madame Germaine said as I began to warm up. "I hope you worked on your épaulements last night."

"Yes, ma'am, I did." I stayed at the studio for an extra hour trying to get my shoulders to turn just right. It was a small thing in ballet—not even a full move—but Madame Germaine didn't become director of the Company by ignoring the small things.

"Good. You'll be working on the balcony pas de deux with Raphael today."

I tried not to frown. It wasn't that I didn't want to do the balcony pas de deux—because I did. It was one of the most romantic dances in my humble opinion, at least. Though it wasn't as technically difficult as other pas de deux from ballets like *The Sleeping Beauty* or *Cinderella*, there was something about it that tugged at my heartstrings whenever I had the privilege of watching it. So much yearning captured in such simple movements that I couldn't help but cry at their families keeping them apart. Juliet's innocence and hesitation,

Romeo's pleas and obsession, all of it coming together for true love. I was honored to be the one to perform that for our Company, and I hoped that I would do it justice.

But there was something about it that I was struggling with.

The kiss.

At the end of the balcony scene, Romeo would pull Juliet into a slow, passionate kiss full of all the longing they couldn't say aloud. I'd always dreamt of performing the ballet with my Prince Charming. I *hadn't* dreamt of him being out in the audience, watching it all happen.

In my heart, I knew Alek wouldn't take the news well. He was very possessive of me, guarding my heart as if someone could ever have the chance of stealing it. It didn't matter that Raphael was in a very committed relationship with a violinist in the orchestra. All Alek would know was that someone was kissing what belonged to him.

My legs clenched at the thought of his reaction, which was why I hadn't figured out a way to tell him. I shivered before diving into the balcony scene with Raphael, listening intently as the choreographer directed us while Madame Germaine corrected every little thing. We moved through the scene a few times before the director called for some of the fight scenes, dismissing me for the day.

Mia came over as I was lacing up my shoes, texting both Jules and Alek that I was done early. "You looked really good today," she said. "I already noticed a difference from your practice, and Madame Germaine hardly had any notes for you."

"Yet," I huffed, looking at myself in the mirror, fixing my slightly askew ribbon.

"Eva, it's day two. You're not going to be perfect this soon. You know it takes time."

I did, but that didn't mean I accepted it. I shrugged, but before I could give more of a rebuttal, we were interrupted by a man walking into the studio with a large bouquet of pink gardenias. I knew instantly who they were for, though I still waited for him to call my name.

The other dancers affectionately rolled their eyes, teasing me under their breath. Mia had let it slip yesterday that I had a new boyfriend, and they all enjoyed making me turn bright red, apparently. I signed for the flowers, thanking the driver, before bringing them back to my bag.

"Another bouquet?" Mia asked as I fiddled with the card.

I smiled. "He gives them to me every day."

The card had the same hurried handwriting as all of the others, this time torn from a piece of paper that had a crest of a dragon on it. It was such a small thing, but the fact that Alek took the time to write a note with all of my flowers, no matter when or where he was, made all the difference. He was always doing thoughtful things like that, remembering everything I told him, asking how my rehearsals were going, bringing my favorite candies to the movies, always getting the door, and picking up the bill.

Sometimes I felt like I wasn't giving him enough back, but Alek always insisted that I was doing plenty by just being his, whispering to me that all he ever wanted from me was a kiss, which I happily provided. And though my insecurities sometimes rose to fight, Alek would always reassure me, quieting the OCD side of me that tried to argue with him.

"You're glowing," Mia said. "I mean that in a slightly alarming way."

I giggled. "That's because I'm happy."

"Does he ever leave you alone?"

"I'm sure if I told him to, he would, but..."

"But..." Mia began with a knowing smile.

"But I don't want him to. I like spending time with him, and I think he likes spending time with me, too."

She pretended to gasp, elbowing me until I laughed. "Who

are you, and what have you done with my unconfident friend?"

I shrugged, but I couldn't hide the blush on my cheeks. "I don't know. He's so caring and considerate, and I've never met anyone who makes me feel like this. Like I'm enough as I am."

"Good," Mia said, her grin widening. "You deserve to feel like that, because you *are* enough. Even with your sugar-rotted teeth."

"I have *two* cavities!"

"Yeah, and it's a miracle you don't have more. I truly don't know how you fit into your costumes with the amount of sour gummy worms you consume."

I rolled my eyes, and Mia hugged me, spotting an incoming text from Jules saying that he was close. She turned to me, one eyebrow raised. "You honestly think your brother will accept him?"

That made my pulse quicken—not with fear, exactly, but anticipation. "He'll love Alek," I said far more confidently than I felt. "Once he meets him. Jules just needs to see that I'm safe and I'm happy."

"Uh-huh." Mia studied me for a long moment. "You really believe that."

"Of course I do."

Why wouldn't I? Jules would have to come around eventually. I couldn't go my entire life completely alone. My brother worried because he loved me.

And Alek...

Alek was *good*. He was gentle and kind and loving. He made me feel like I was the most precious thing on Earth. And, yes, he sometimes had a dark side that I glimpsed whenever he thought there was a threat to me—like when one of my neighbors approached me as I was letting him into my building. But I knew that despite some of his darkness, his soul was made of light, and that was all that mattered.

I said my goodbyes to Mia and grabbed my flowers before going out to meet Jules, mumbling something about another dancer gifting them to me to congratulate me on getting the role—some excuse I had no idea how he believed. He helped me get them into the car before rubbing my shoulder and asking me how rehearsal was. And for a moment, everything felt okay.

Until I looked into my brother's eyes and knew, for a split second, how Juliet must have felt, knowing her family would say no to Romeo but hoping they would say yes anyway.

January 3rd

MOTHER

Aleksandr Andreyevich Drakov.

What is this your cousin tells me about a date?

Are you going out with a girl?

You have never gone out with a nice girl, Aleksandr, and now that you finally have, you have not brought her home to meet your mother.

Are you trying to break my heart, my darling?

Bring the girl for dinner soon!! I want to meet my future daughter-in-law and get her ideas for the wedding.

Have you two discussed nursery themes? I'll need to ask your grandmother to start the quilt soon. You know how she struggles with her hands.

Have you visited your grandmother, Aleksandr? Are you taking the girl there?

I expect to meet my grandchildren soon, Aleksandr. And maybe ask her if she has a nice friend for Nikolai. That boy needs a leash.

Have fun at work, my darling. We'll chat soon :)

ALEKSANDR

Fuck.

ALEKSANDR
CHAPTER FOURTEEN

I PRESSED BULLETS INTO THE MAGAZINE OF MY favorite pistol when Nikolai barged in, draped in a belt of weapons like a wannabe warlord. For once in his life, the smirk was gone. "The Vallens are moving their shipment to the North Docks."

"Tonight?"

"Yup. Same crew as planned. Trying to throw you off, I guess."

I smiled, sharp and cold. Sometimes, he was just *so predictable.* Men like Julian Vallen never failed to underestimate the power of men like me—a mistake that would cost them.

Julian Vallen was head of the scum of the Earth known as the Vallen family. Though he was my prize, I knew I had to take out the rest of the organization before reaching him. His parents were off traveling the world, which made them regrettably too much of a hassle to target. For now. And the daughter, Anne-something, was somewhere off at school. I was hesitant to involve a woman and a child who seemed to have no true ties to her family's darker dealings. So, unless she decided to stick her neck where it didn't belong, I would leave her alone.

Julian, though... I would break him piece by piece, watch him beg before he even thought to breathe.

"Prepare the rest of the men. I guess we're going north," I said, adjusting my suit jacket as he slipped out of my office.

It wasn't necessary to dress so cleanly for a night like tonight, but I figured I should look decent. After all, my face was going to be the last several men saw tonight. Might as well give them something nice to look at.

Plus, black hid the bloodstains well.

I was about to head out the door when my phone buzzed from atop my warehouse desk. The picture on it made me smile. It was a selfie Evangeline took from the front seat of my car as we were on our way to our first date. She looked stunning in her satin pink dress and fluffy white shawl. A true prima.

"Hi, baby," I said, holding the phone up to my ear. "How was your rehearsal?"

It would have been over a few hours ago, but I knew she was staying with her brother tonight, which helped me breathe a little easier as I walked into a danger zone. Knowing she was somewhere supervised and protected, away from any potential Vallen retaliation, made my beast somewhat relax.

But only somewhat. I knew that I was the only one who could truly protect her.

"It was good," she said, breathless in that way she got when she was excited. "We worked on the balcony pas de deux."

I leaned back, letting the world fade. Her voice—always soft and careful—made the edges of my rage dull. Everything about her reminded me that she was a delicate thing in a brutal world. And I would be the one keeping that perfection alive.

"And how was that?"

"Good! Rapha thankfully has had some experience as the male lead, so he's been giving me tips, which I *really* need."

I gritted my jaw, hating the fact that another man got to touch her intimately, even if it was for show. But I knew how important this role was to Evangeline, so I kept my mouth shut, vowing to destroy the man if he ever hurt her or made her uncomfortable.

"I'm sure you're even more wonderful than you think, solnyshka."

Nikolai walked into the room, spotting me on the phone. He rolled his eyes before tapping his watch and mouthing, "*Time to go.*"

Eva giggled, one of my favorite sounds she made. That and her soft moans as she came around my fingers and tongue. And soon, my cock.

"You always say that."

"Because it's always true."

There was a pause, the faint sound of her moving around her brother's home. I pictured her curling into her bed, lining the blankets just right, smoothing back her pillows. Making her small, precise order in a world that had never given her enough of it.

"I got your flowers. They were perfect."

"You deserve perfect, Eva."

"Did you know gardenias are supposed to mean secret love?"

"I do now," I replied. I didn't know flowers meant anything at all, honestly. I just saw them and thought of her, of the little smile she got whenever I gifted her anything.

She hummed, pleased. "I wish you could've been there today. Watching rehearsal, I mean."

I was, I thought, hidden behind one of the curtains,

unable to stay away from her all day. But aloud, I said, "Maybe I can come sometime soon."

"That would be great!" Eva paused before saying, "You sound tired."

"I've... I've had a long day." I hated lying to her, but she didn't need to know I wasn't tired. I was simply thinking through all our logistics one more time before I walked in and introduced several men to the angel of death.

"Oh," Eva said quickly, her voice tightening. "I can let you go. I just wanted to hear your voice."

I softened without meaning to. It was automatic with her, the way my body responded. The way the sharp edges dulled. "Eva. You can call me anytime."

Her breath caught. "Okay."

Glancing at my watch, I cursed under my breath. "I've gotta tie up some work things, baby, but I'll text you."

"Sounds good. I've got to shower anyway."

Fuck.

It was crazy how two little words could make me so fucking hard. *Eva. Shower.* That wasn't something we'd tried yet, but it was on my very long list of places I wanted to consume Eva. The vision of her with her hands pressed against my tiles and her wet hair wrapped around my fist while I thrust into her from behind made my balls tighten.

"Send me a picture."

"Sorry, you're working, so I can't," she said, and I could hear the grin through the phone.

That little minx.

She loved to toy with me—until her punishment came back to bite her in the ass, usually in the form of edging because I loved listening to her beg me to let her come.

"Eva. Picture."

"Sorry, what?"

"Eva—"

"I can hardly hear you, Alek. Bad signal or something."

"*Eva*," I growled.

"Bye, Alek."

The hanging up sound echoed in my ears as I stared at my phone, no longer seeing my girlfriend's picture lighting up the screen like she should have been.

"You done pretending to be human?" Nikolai asked, raising an eyebrow.

I glared but said nothing. I picked up my gun from my desk, checking the weight of it, its familiar comfort settling into my palm.

Nikolai drove us to the North Dock, his stupid pop music playing too loudly. Normally, I would have turned it off and insisted on silence, but I was too focused on the mission tonight to care about his terrible singing.

We were finally moving forward on my plan for vengeance against the Vallens, slowly destroying their foundation brick by brick until the whole family fell. My family had been trying to take them down for decades, but we also had to elevate our own status, which meant not enough focus went to our enemies. That all changed when I took over from my father several years ago.

We had a long way to go—killing higher-ups, finding out where Vallen *actually* lived (not that stupid fucking fake apartment he tried to throw us off with), and destroying their connections. But tonight, we were sabotaging one of their important shipments, placing seeds of doubt between them and their supplier.

Whose men were compromised? Who was at fault? How many were dead? These were the questions I wanted Julian Vallen to ask himself tonight when he went to bed. And one more, too.

When was Aleksandr Drakov going to strike next?

The city passed by in streaks of light and shadow. The noise coming out of Nikolai's mouth was grating, and before I could smack him upside the head, my phone buzzed with a text.

> **EVANGELINE**
> Have a fun night at work! 🤍
>
> Oh, and…
>
> *EVANGELINE SENT 1 PHOTO*

"Fuck," I muttered, teeth clenched, trying not to crush my phone in my hand. I resisted the urge to adjust my rapidly growing hard-on right in front of my cousin. She was so fucking sexy it was unreal.

It was a simple picture: Eva in a towel that pushed up her breasts, her wet hair crawling down her spine, her pussy barely out of view from the camera. But it was the teasing nature of it —the fact that I *knew* what was under that towel, yet she hid it anyway—that made me fucking desperate for more.

Mine. Mine. Mine.

Eva was lucky she was at her brother's, because I would have turned this car around and climbed through her window to see under that towel myself. Right now, my control was thin at best.

> **ALEKSANDR**
> Such a good girl.

"Dude, focus," Nikolai grumbled under his breath. "You can flirt with your girl later."

The warehouse in the North Docks was easy enough to breach. The car in front of us had five of my men inside—this was a small operation that probably didn't need Nikolai and me at all if it weren't for our pride—and they'd gone ahead and killed what few guards Vallen had. The arrogant fuckers probably didn't think we'd figure out their little plan. They had no idea how deep my claws ran in this city, how far my beast had gone to avenge my little sister.

They would learn. Far too late.

It was over too quickly for my tastes. My men entered first, taking out any extraneous Vallen guards with a few quick, well-aimed shots. Their blood slowly stained the concrete floor, their lifeless eyes fixed on the ceiling. I waved at their supplier to leave, wanting someone to spread the word amongst his people. After all, how could trust be broken if this were a slaughterhouse?

Julian Vallen needed to know that he had a fucking rat. *My* rat.

I walked up to the Vallen man, the one who was the head of tonight's operation. He'd been with the Vallens for at least twenty years, according to my research.

He'd be valuable.

"Fucking Drakovs," he snarled while Nikolai pinned him to the ground, bloodlust evident in my cousin's eyes. "I knew you would find a way to get your greasy paws everywhere."

"Oh, you were thinking about me?" I purred, nudging his cheek with my boot before bending down, grabbing my switchblade from my pocket.

"Never."

I ran the blade down his cheek, the monster in me humming in satisfaction at the bead of blood that formed beneath my touch. Such a pretty sight, this violence. Almost as pretty as my girl.

"I'm going to have fun with you."

The man spat, the disgusting liquid getting on my lapels. "I will never tell you anything."

"Such sweet lies from such a sour man," I whispered, carving the blade even deeper when I pressed into his skin.

"You will scream my name before this is all over. And your cries will be music to my ears."

By the time we left, the man was already singing. I smiled.

Because it wouldn't be long until every goddamn Vallen in the city would sound the same. I would destroy them.

Every last one.

January 10th

ALEKSANDR

How was rehearsal?

EVANGELINE

Amazing!!!

I think I'm improving a lot. This was the first day I actually felt like I deserve the role.

ALEKSANDR

Of course you deserve it, solnyshka. No one works harder than you, and even I could see your natural talent.

I'm very proud to call you mine.

EVANGELINE

Awe! You're so sweet!!

ALEKSANDR

Can I pick you up in an hour? I know it's sooner than we planned, but I missed you.

EVANGELINE

You saw me last night, silly.

ALEKSANDR

I know. I'm replaying it over and over in my mind.

EVANGELINE

;)

Yeah, an hour works. Just let me get ready and then we can go.

ALEKSANDR

The time cannot pass soon enough.

What are you wearing?

For the date, but also, if you want to show me what you're wearing underneath, I wouldn't mind.

Are you all right? Haven't heard from you in a little bit…

If you're in the shower, show me.

Eva?

MISSED CALL FROM ALEKSANDR

Baby, I'm starting to get worried.

MISSED CALL FROM ALEKSANDR

Please tell me you're all right.

Eva.

MISSED CALL FROM ALEKSANDR
MISSED CALL FROM ALEKSANDR
MISSED CALL FROM ALEKSANDR

EVANGELINE
CHAPTER FIFTEEN

THERE WAS A MOMENT SOMEWHERE BETWEEN WHEN I stood at my counter, my hand poised to apply my mascara, and when I fell to my bathroom floor. And that moment was when I realized I no longer felt like a person. Like I was a space where a person had once been.

The apartment was still. *Too* still.

The kind that presses in on you, making you hyperaware of your own existence and yet completely unsure if you're actually here or if you're just watching yourself move. I knew my body was doing things—breathing, blinking, existing—but I wasn't attached to it anymore. I was observing it from far away, like it belonged to someone else who had left the room and forgotten to come back.

My phone lay on the counter, and I knew I should have called someone. My therapist. My brother. Mia. Charlotte, who I knew dealt with mental health issues of her own and would probably never judge me in the least. Maybe I should have called Alek.

But I couldn't bring myself to touch the cursed device.

A terrible, heavy certainty settled itself deep in my stomach. I was a black hole of pain and suffering, of feeling unsure of when the universe's punishments would drop on me. Anyone I'd ever loved would suffer from knowing me, from being pulled into the gravity of a beast that slowly fed on me. It was better to let myself succumb to the void than to drag them there with me.

I thought I was getting better. God, I thought this feeling would be *gone*. Medication, therapy, getting my dream role—all of that was supposed to actually help me. My life was improving with each day, and I thought my illness was too.

Clearly I was wrong.

I could feel Death hovering behind my shoulders, its fingers grazing the backs of my arms, settling into my skin, waiting for me to do something wrong. And everything was wrong. Every choice. Every movement. Every thought. My existence felt like a trigger.

My throat tightened, my body carving a space in itself for the fear to live and grow. I couldn't tell if my heart was racing because I was anxious or because something was genuinely wrong with me—if this attack would be the one to finally kill me.

I pressed my forehead to the cool tile floor, wrapping my arms around myself while my thoughts blurred into each other, stacking and looping, folding inward like a collapsing star.

What if I was violent and didn't know it?

What if I was going to hurt someone I loved?

What if my thoughts meant something about who I really was?

What if this wasn't illness at all? What if this was me?

That was the cruelest part. The not knowing. The constant interrogation. Which thoughts were mine? Which ones were intruders wearing my voice? Where did I end, and the sickness begin?

I counted the tiles on the floor. The cracks in the ceiling.

The hitches in my breath. Not to calm myself, but because if I didn't, I knew something bad might happen.

One... Two... Three...

Wrong. Again.

One... Two... Three... Four...

Wrong. Always *wrong*.

The void crept in slowly, thick and suffocating. It wasn't loud. It wasn't violent. Yet it swallowed me alive until only the emptiness inside of me echoed. Like if I leaned into it just a little more, I might disappear completely.

My thoughts circled endlessly, chewing on themselves, my mind consumed by a relentless wave of anxiety that had no clear shape and no exit. I was imprisoned, judged by my own soul, sentenced without a trial. I kneeled inside of myself and confessed to crimes I didn't commit, my mind a weapon I couldn't disarm.

My thoughts might one day destroy someone I loved. I had a predator in my own skull, clawing at me from the inside.

I hated everything.

I hated my mind.

I hated this illness.

I hated how violent it felt, how it made me feel dangerous, broken, unlovable.

I hated *me*. Terrible, imperfect me.

I thought of Alek then, and it nearly crushed me. How could he not hate me, too? Loving me would be like tying something solid and asking him to stand in the ocean. It only ever ended in emptiness and pain, because one day, the tide would rise, and I would pull him under without meaning to.

Something heavy banged in the distance, but I barely heard it through my shallow breaths. It was a loud noise, furious and sudden. The sound of darkness and determination made real. But I knew it wasn't real. Nothing ever was.

A few moments later, it came again.

Harder.

My body flinched before my thoughts caught up. My heart slammed painfully against my ribs, each beat loud and wrong. For one horrifying moment, I wondered if this was it. If I'd waited too long, and my indecision had finally turned fatal.

I heard the sound of wood hitting the floor. Was that my front door?

"Eva!" his voice cut through the fog, raw and unrestrained. That sound—my name, spoken like that—cracked something open inside me.

The sound of thudding footsteps vibrated the floor as he called out my name, but I didn't move. I couldn't. My limbs felt locked in place, heavy and unresponsive, like they belonged to a statue instead of a person.

"Eva," he breathed, crossing the bathroom in seconds, dropping to his knees in front of me. "Fuck, Eva..."

All of a sudden, a pair of blue eyes so dark they looked almost black filled my vision. They reached me through the fog, low and real and unmistakable. He cut through the void like a hand reaching down into icy water and pulling me from the depths.

Alek's expression was furious yet lined with terror. His eyes scanned my body while his hands hovered, unsure where to touch first. I longed to reach out and smooth the lines on his handsome yet twisted face.

"Are you hurt?" His voice was rough, edged with something close to panic. "Did someone come here? Did they touch you?"

I shook my head weakly, the motion barely perceptible.

"No," I whispered, my voice thin and distant. "I just..."

He scanned the room again, jaw clenched, body coiled like a weapon, already planning retaliation against enemies that didn't exist.

When he looked back at me, really looked, something shifted. The fight drained out of him all at once. He saw it then—not blood or bruises, not signs of a struggle, but the vacancy in my eyes, the way my body had folded inward, the tremor running through me like a fault line.

He exhaled, long and shaky, like he'd been holding his breath since the moment I stopped answering.

"Tell me something real," I finally rasped. "Please... I need something not inside my head."

Alek hesitated, chewing on his lip for a few moments before softly saying, "I was twelve when my sister died in my arms. Liza was eight. It was a car accident, but a purposeful one. I don't think she was supposed to be the casualty. I think I was. My world has always been a dangerous one, but until then, I lived in ignorance. That day, I looked Death in the eyes and made a vow that I would become his master. And I have. I am the Reaper. It does not bring Liza back, but... it helps."

I blinked a few times, his words pulling me from the fog a little. He was *twelve*. He was just a child, yet he took on such a burden. I understood, then, why Alek could sometimes be so cold. Why he would do anything to make me his. Because in Alek's mind, ownership meant control. It meant safety.

I looked up at him, at the thin line of his lips, the worry in his brow. "I was in a car accident once. I was only four, so I don't remember it much, but I remember it being my fault. I distracted the driver, screaming when I saw an ice cream shop. It was stupid, but I suppose I paid for it. I was injured pretty badly." I lifted some of my curtain bangs and showed him the long, thin white scar. "My life changed so much after that. My parents became distant, and my brother stopped being my friend and turned into my protector. I started wearing things like bows and ribbons, so I had something other than the scar to look at when I stared into the mirror. And a voice appeared in my head. A mean voice. A *cruel* one that wouldn't let me forget how much I ruined things for my family."

A choked sob escaped me as I remembered that lonely little girl with only her thoughts for company. And those thoughts were not kind.

"I'm broken," I whispered.

"You're not broken, solnyshka. That little girl did *nothing* wrong. And her scar? It makes her so fucking beautiful."

I shook my head, unable to speak, my throat locked tight.

"Can I touch you?" Alek asked. I nodded in response, and he softened himself deliberately, reining in whatever violence had brought him through the door. His movements became careful, measured, as he reached forward, deliberate and unyielding, pulling my trembling body into his lap as if he could physically shield me from every invisible threat in the world.

I nuzzled my face into his neck, breathing in the scent of his cologne. Alek's chest was warm, his heartbeat slowing. His arms around me were firm, grounding me in his body, silently telling me he would never let me go, no matter how heavy I became.

"I thought something happened to you," he murmured into my hair. "When you didn't answer... I was so worried, baby."

"I'm sorry," I said, because everything was my fault. I wasn't enough. I wasn't perfect.

"You don't have to be sorry, Eva. You don't have to explain yourself. You don't have to do anything but be here."

I went still in his arms, my breath catching—not from fear this time, but from the sudden, overwhelming realization that no one had ever said that to me before. Not really.

I had spent my whole life performing existence correctly. Being good. Being manageable. Being quiet enough, strong enough, grateful enough to take up space, to one day earn my parents' attention.

And here Alek was, holding me like I deserved all of it and more.

"I don't know how to stop it," I whispered after a long moment. My voice felt scraped raw, like it had clawed its way out of my chest. "My brain. It tells me things. Awful things. That I'm dangerous. That I ruin people. That everyone will one day leave me because they'll realize that loving me is a mistake."

His arms tightened around me, and I felt his heart thump against me. "Look at me," Alek said.

I hesitated, then lifted my head. His face was close now, eyes dark and intent, but no longer wild. They were focused entirely on me.

His thumb brushed against my cheek, catching a tear I hadn't realized had fallen. The tender movement made something in my chest ache.

"I am not ruined. I am not frightened away. I am not leaving," he whispered. "I never will, Eva. You are mine. Nothing can keep you from me. Not even you."

The words hit me so hard my breath stuttered. I shook my head, tears blurring my vision. "You don't understand. This doesn't go away. It might get quieter sometimes, but it always comes back."

"Then it will come back," he said simply, his accent coating the edges of the words. "And I will still be here."

There was no hesitation in his voice. No doubt.

Something in me gave way then—not fear, not panic, but a surrender so deep it felt like stepping off a ledge and discovering air could hold you.

"You will?" I breathed. "You won't eventually hate me?"

"I don't know how to hate you, solnyshka. I don't think I ever could." Alek paused before adding, "You think that this illness makes you a monster. But I am a *real* monster, baby. And my demons will not stop until yours are driven away."

He leaned in slowly, giving me time to pull away.

I didn't.

His lips brushed against mine before they pressed into me. The kiss wasn't demanding or hungry, but soft. Tender. One that felt like a promise instead of a claim. A gentle undoing of all the knots inside of me, one by one, until every thread wrapped around my heart and tethered me to him. I was no longer hollow but full. So full of warm and fuzzy emotions, all aimed directly at the man taking my breath away.

I realized, then, why every great love story always revolved around a true love's kiss. Because the things I was feeling for him were worth fighting villains, succumbing to spells, eating poisonous apples, and sacrificing everything.

I melted into him, my hands coming up to clutch at his coat while he held my cheeks steady. Alek's tongue pressed into me before he groaned in the back of his throat. He tasted like mint and vodka and darkness, but also like daydreams and happy endings. He tasted like he was *mine*.

I knew then with quiet certainty: I was falling for Aleksandr Drakov. Or maybe I had fallen already.

Maybe I was too far gone.

When he pulled back, he stayed close, his breath warm against my lips.

"Alek," I said softly, my voice trembling.

"Yes."

"Can we... Can we go to your place?" I didn't want to be alone in the space where I had almost disappeared. I wanted to go somewhere where I could be surrounded by him. And...

And I wanted to feel him inside of me. Fully. Driving away all of my darkness.

Alek heard the meaning behind my words, the ones I hadn't asked because I knew once I walked through his front door, I would be leaving my virginity behind. It was a silent promise between us, a code we'd written together.

His gaze turned hungry, though he tried to rein himself back, blinking a few times, his eyes getting bluer with each one. "Of course. We don't have to do anything if you don't want to. I can make up a guest room for you, and—"

But I silenced him with another kiss.

"I want everything," I mumbled.

Alek swallowed. "Then you shall have it."

January 10th

MISSED CALL FROM MIA
MIA

Girl... I have crazy tea for you... Girls night stat!!!

WAIT

You and Alek have another date tonight, right???

How's it going???

Send me pics of your outfit!!

Did he pick you up in a sexy car or something?

OMG did he bring you more flowers?

Are you in love yet?

I'm assuming you're not answering because you're madly in love and are planning your wedding.

I better be the maid of honor, you bitch.

You're fucking, aren't you? 😏

EVANGELINE

Mia!!! STOP!!!

MIA

You definitely are.

Use protection!!! I'm not ready to be an aunt yet!

EVANGELINE

MIA!!!!!

ALEKSANDR
CHAPTER SIXTEEN

THE DRIVE BACK TO MY HOUSE PASSED BY IN A BLUR. All I could remember was my leg bouncing every time we hit a stoplight and my hand gripping her thigh, ready to tear into her.

No, I told myself. *Gentle. Gentle. GENTLE.*

But I didn't want to be gentle with her. I wanted to eat her alive.

I wanted to hear her screams as they shook the very walls of my mansion. I could almost taste the fear, and it only made my need grow sharper, hungrier.

I'd never been so close to losing control, to pulling the car over and hauling her to my lap, letting her moans fill the small car while I held her head to keep it from slamming into the roof. I kept reminding myself that she was a virgin, that if she decided she wanted to fuck me tonight, I needed to be careful. I needed to keep up the Prince Charming pretense.

But the thoughts I was having about her while we drove through the city were nothing less than villainous.

The skyscrapers passed by in a blur. I normally didn't drive myself—preferring to work from the backseat of my car while my driver took me everywhere—but tonight, I was in such a rush to reach her that I didn't wait, speeding across the city fast enough that I would have been pulled over if my family didn't fund half of the police force in the city.

Before long, we reached the outskirts of the city where my mansion overlooked the water. The neighborhood was flanked by iron fences and tall hedges, the perfect place for a family who needed privacy. I built this home when I'd begun to inherit the empire from my father. Lately, I'd tended to reside in my family's townhouse in the heart of the city, where I would be closer to Eva if she needed me. But when she asked me to bring her home, this was the only one I thought of.

It was far from Vallen territory, from them trying to use her to exact vengeance for my activities over the past week. And it was heavily guarded only by men who had proven they would die for me.

The mansion loomed at the end of the long driveway, a dark monolith of stone and black glass. Every line was sharp and deliberate. From this distance, it looked untouchable, impervious. Exactly as it was meant to be.

The road was flanked by sculpted trees. Beyond them lay the many acres of gardens. I could already envision Eva out there, planting as many pink flowers as she wanted before lounging by my pool, a glass of pink lemonade in her hand while she watched the ducks swim across the lake.

It surprised me as we neared the door to find all of my visions consisting of her and me in this home together. In what was mine becoming ours.

Marble steps led up to an arched double door, black with iron studs, flanked by lanterns that cast warm light over the façade. I parked my car in the circular drive and helped Eva out of the seat, tugging her body to me and holding her tight.

Eva let out a shaky breath, her pulse fluttering against her neck. Everything in me roared to wrap my hand around it and squeeze until her face was a pretty shade of pink, begging me to paint her with my cum. As much as I wanted to worship her, to make her feel things she'd never felt before, a part of me wanted to make her hurt too. Make her *scream*.

I knew she would like it. My Eva was meant for me, and I'd always preferred a little pain with my pleasure.

In addition to being a submissive, my girlfriend was proving to be a little masochist. She had to be one to wear those ballet shoes of hers, the ones that squeezed and morphed her feet into new shapes to hold her body while leaping and bounding across the stage.

If she could handle that, what else could I give her?

I debated reaching forward and wrapping my hand around her pretty little neck to find out, but I didn't. It was hard enough to hold myself back as it was. If I touched her right now, I wouldn't be able to stop.

Crowding her against the car, I leaned in as far as my control would let me. And the sight of her below me, all fucking submissive, her ribbon looping through the hair I wanted to pull while she was bent over, made something inside of me vibrate with the need for more.

I leaned into her, my tongue darting out to taste her neck. Inhaling her warm vanilla scent, I forced myself to calm down.

Control

"Eva, I want to fuck you. I want to bury myself so deeply inside of you that I feel you when I fall asleep. I want to watch your eyes roll back in your head, and I want to greedily inhale your cum on my tongue. But if you're not ready for that, I will tuck you into bed and go take a long, cold shower. Nothing between us will change. I promise."

"Alek," she whispered, lips parted and begging to take my cock. "I want all of that, too."

Fuck being in control. I wanted her. *Now.*

Eva let out a shaky breath as my tongue traveled down to her collarbone, to that sensitive spot I already knew she loved to be bitten on. "Tell me how much you want it, baby," I rasped before biting onto her.

"*Ah!* I... uh..."

"*Tell me,* Eva," I said, this time biting harder as I picked her up and carried her through the front door, waving away any staff member who came to greet us.

I pressed her into the nearest wall. She squirmed against me, her hips subtly rocking into mine, and nothing pleased me more than feeling her pulse increase with fear. I wondered what her eyes would look like when they were wide and afraid. Would she beg me to stop?

Would she beg me to keep going?

"Does my needy girl want me to take care of her now?"

"*Yes.*" She bit her lip, and I couldn't help but thrust a little into her at the sight of her so damn willing for me already.

Fuck. I could feel the heat of her through my pants.

"And how do you want me to take care of you?"

Eva gulped before softly saying, "Any way you want, sir."

A gasp escaped her lips when I harshly gripped her waist before carrying her through my home like a man possessed. I could feel her erratic breaths through her dress, whose strap I shoved down so I could bite her shoulder hard enough to leave a mark.

We reached my bedroom in record time, and I threw Eva onto the black silk sheets. She hardly had enough time to recoup before I was on top of her, settling between her legs while my hand fisted her hair. Eva arched her body into me, and I took the chance to thrust my hips into hers, running my other hand all along her sexy curves.

"Such a good girl you are. Submitting to me so *easily.*"

Eva moaned, lifting her hips. The sound went straight to my cock, and I rocked into her, hitting her clit while my lips trailed her jawline.

"Do you like hearing me tell you what a good girl you are?"

But Eva didn't answer. Instead, she curled her toes and clutched the bedsheets.

I slipped my hand down and pulled her dress up. Fuck, she was already soaked. The sight of her pussy glistening through her thin underwear—the little bow wrapping her up like a presence—awoke the demon inside of me. Every part of me was ready to take her. To make her mine.

"Should I take off this sexy little dress?" I asked, and my hands started to make my words come true, undoing the zipper at her back and slowly peeling her dress off, releasing her tits. They were so pretty, perfectly round yet small enough to fit in my mouth.

"Should I squeeze these perfect nipples?" I palmed one of them, savoring its weight in my palm. But I let my hand continue to travel until it found its favorite place between her thighs.

"Should I play with your clit? Or should I—"

I swiped a finger inside of her, feeling her warm and wet pussy clench around me. Eva's hips buckled, and a heady breath slipped past her lips.

I leaned into her, nipping at her ear as I whispered, "Or should I fuck this pussy until you can't stand tomorrow?"

"Anything," Eva said with a slight whine in her voice. "I want anything. Don't hold back."

Fuck.

Fuck, fuck, *fuck*.

She didn't know what she was asking for. She didn't know the beast she would be unleashing, the pain I would make her feel. She didn't know what she—

"Alek, *please*."

And the wire inside of me that was pulled taut—the thin shred of my composure that held a monster back—snapped.

"Begging already? My, my, aren't we needy?"

"*Yes.*"

I let out a growl before I slammed her legs apart, ripping her panties off. Eva gasped at the cold air, but the sound was soon replaced by her moan as I stuck my face forward and licked. She was so wet that my tongue slipped in easily, drinking her juices while I committed the taste to memory. Her cunt was so fucking delicious, every taste so sweet.

Eva's hands flew to my hair, holding me in place while I consumed her like a man starving. Her walls clenched around my tongue, and I knew she was close to the first of many orgasms tonight.

My tongue licked along her slit before my mouth latched onto her clit and sucked. *Hard.* Eva cried out in pleasure, her body twisting and turning in my hold. I held her stomach in place and forced her to remain still. To let me control her pleasure.

"Look at me," I mumbled against her folds. But Eva didn't listen, squeezing her eyes tightly and turning her head. "Eva. *Look at me.*"

She must have heard the dominance in my tone, because her eyes flew open, chocolate brown gazing as I drove her higher and higher.

"Good girl." And then I rewarded her by taking two of my fingers and slipping them deep inside of her.

"Oh, Alek, yes!"

I continued my rhythm, alternating between licking and biting her core and fucking it with my fingers. Her pussy clenched around me, practically begging me to drive into it until it was covered in my cum.

"Alek, please... I need more..." she pleaded, pulling at my hair but not taking her eyes off me.

"Such a good fucking girl," I said, curling my hand inside of her and reveling at the way her cheeks flushed and her usually-perfect hair became a mess.

Her nails scraped at my temple, and the pain brought forth a groan that vibrated her folds, making her breath even more erratic. I claimed those sounds, forcing them out of her, marking her as mine with every stroke of my tongue. Every inch of her belonged to me, and I would remind her of that until she couldn't think without remembering this night.

Only I could make her feel like this. Only I would ever know how beautiful she was as she was falling apart. And only I would ever put her back together.

"Please, Alek, I want you inside of me. *Please.*"

My cock pressed against my zipper, straining to reach her. She was so empty, my Eva. She needed me to fill her up, to show her how pleasurable darkness could be.

"I will be, baby. Soon. But first, I want you to come on my tongue."

Eva's body trembled, her hips rocking up to meet my quick movements. She was close. I could feel it.

I could *taste* it.

Her eyes became glassy, unfocused. "Alek... Alek, I—"

But she was cut off by the sound of her own orgasm rippling through her, her moans cut off mid-sound like everything inside of her was trembling. I hummed as the sweet taste of her cum filled my senses, my favorite flavor in the world. I wanted to wake up with the taste of her pleasure in my mouth every morning for the rest of my life.

"That... that was amazing," she sighed, still looking at me like a good fucking girl.

I hummed, my lips pulling into a smirk. "Did you think I was done with you?"

Her eyes widened, the lust still fully present in the chocolate depths.

Eva's gaze flicked to my tattoos, which I was beginning to learn she really liked if the way her irises darkened was any indication. My whole torso was covered with them, and with the way I'd slightly unbuttoned my black shirt today, they were more in view.

And my little minx *liked it*.

She undressed me with her eyes before saying, "You're not?"

I shook my head, and her knees trembled a moment later. "No, solnyshka. I'm not. I plan on fucking you until you're begging me to stop, and your legs are shaking from trying to hold in my cum. I want to watch it leak down your thighs while your eyes roll back in your head again and again. I want to choke you and slap you and make you so goddamn red that no one will mistake who you belong to."

And though she looked frightened, she still breathed out, "Then do it."

I unzipped my trousers and freed my cock. A bead of precum coated the tip. Eva licked her lips at the sight of it, my girl not frightened even at the sight of pain.

She lifted her hips as if to entice me to move quicker. Her wet pussy pressed against my cock, and she gasped. "I need you. *Now*."

My hand shot out to grab her throat. I squeezed, savoring the feeling of her life under my hand. Such a heady feeling, power. "Did I say you could move?" I growled.

She whimpered. "No, sir."

"So then don't. Fucking. Move. Just take what I give you like a good girl."

With one of my hands, I grabbed her hips and held her steady. With the other, I cupped her breast, pulling and tweaking the nipple until it hardened under my touch. I did the same to the other one until her entire body burned for me.

"Alek, please—"

Eva didn't have time to brace herself before I thrust deep inside of her, stretching her to the point of fullness, groaning as her body tightened around me, yet welcomed me eagerly.

She cried out in both pain and pleasure, hands flying to my back, her nails digging into the skin. Soon after, I felt something warm and wet cover my cock.

Fuck. It was her blood.

It took everything in me not to pound into her at that realization, my demons practically singing at the fact that she was finally, officially *mine* and only *mine*.

A tear crawled down her cheek, landing on her full bottom lip. Seeing it shouldn't have pleased me as much as it did, but I always did enjoy the sight of suffering. Especially on someone so fucking beautiful.

My hand moved down to her clit, rubbing it and making her wetter. I knew this hurt her, but she was strong enough to handle it.

"You can take it, baby," I murmured, pressing my lips to her back while I slightly rocked, letting her get used to the feeling of being stretched. "You were made for me. You can handle it."

She closed her eyes, inhaling deeply.

"Look at me, Eva."

Her eyes fluttered open, chocolate meeting mine with steady resolve. *That's my girl.*

"Don't look away. Look at me. Tell me if you want me to stop."

She nodded, inhaling one more time. "I don't want you to stop."

I gave her a second to change her mind, but she only seemed to become more determined, her hands pressing hard into my back as if to move me herself. I withdrew my length only to slowly push it back in even further.

She hissed, but this time, I didn't stop, continuing to move in and out of her while my hands roamed her body. "You feel so good. So good, pretty girl. You're so fucking *perfect*, Evangeline."

I looked down at her determined expression and almost smiled. "Who do you belong to?"

"Y-you."

"That's right," I said, stroking her cheek where another tear had escaped. "You're mine. You can take all of me. You're doing so well. *Fuck*, Eva. You're so fucking tight."

A hint of a moan lined the breath she let out when I thrust again, feeling myself bottom out into her. "Is that a good thing?" she asked.

"It's fucking incredible."

When her face finally slackened, all hints of her wincing gone, I increased my rhythm, going faster and faster and faster until I was slamming into her. Eva's body rocked, but she held onto my body even when I could tell the pain was assaulting her from every angle.

In and out, I pounded into her soaking pussy while her moans and my grunts filled the air.

I leaned forward, shifting our angle slightly. Inch by rock-hard inch, I drove into her like an animal. Our skin slapped together, my balls hitting her with force, and I could feel myself becoming more beast than man. A primal thing that cared only about fucking *my* woman.

Soon, every one of Eva's breaths was either a whimper or a moan, the little sounds driving me even more wild. I loved how fucking vocal she was, how she let the pleasure consume her completely. I committed the music to my memory, vowing to replay it over and over in my head until I died.

When Eva bit her lip, I snarled and reached forward, gripping her jaw so tightly she gasped. My fingers ripped her bottom lip free. "Don't you *ever* hold back those pretty little sounds from me. I want to hear you scream my name so everyone knows who is making you feel like this."

"*A-Alek*," she whimpered.

I grabbed onto her chin and forced her to look me in the eye, to look at her reflection in the dark void of my irises. "Look at how pretty you look when I fuck you. Look how beautiful you are when you fall apart for me."

Eva tried to shake her head. Her pretty curls were falling apart against my pillow, her bottom lip was bright red from biting it, mascara was crawling down her cheeks, and her eyes were red from unshed tears. But she'd never looked more incredible than in this moment.

The moment she became mine.

"You're so fucking beautiful, baby," I whispered, letting my cock punctuate each word. "So beautiful. So *mine*."

"Yours," she shuddered before her lips parted, eyes rolling in the back of her head. The orgasm took control of her body. Eva succumbed to it, hands white from where her nails carved into my back while her pussy clamped around me.

A noise of pure ecstasy escaped her. "Alek!"

"Eva," I groaned before losing myself too, my cock pulsing inside of her, spilling my cum into her, marking her as mine. The thought of it mixing with her virgin blood, of it coating her pussy while she walked around, was enough to make me hard again.

But I couldn't. She would be sore after today, and if I took it too far now, I could break her. She might have liked it rough now, but my world still needed easing into.

I pulled out of her, almost moaning at the sight of all our fluids on my cock. Unwilling to wipe any of it away, I put it back into my pants before unbuttoning my shirt. I shrugged off the dark fabric before taking the sleeve and cleaning her as best as I could, wiping away some of the blood stains but leaving my seed to dry there. I was a possessive man, and I wasn't willing to wipe away any of my marks, which was also why I used my favorite shirt instead of a washcloth.

I wanted to walk around this city with traces of her still on me.

If I wasn't before, I was now obsessed with my little ballerina. The little echoes of her I'd had so far weren't nearly enough. I needed to consume Eva until every breath carried her essence. I wanted us to be so intertwined that when death finally came to claim us, the worms would feast on my heart and taste her there.

Eva fell slack against the bed, her body molding into my soft mattress. I stood, muscles flexing, before I carried her to the bathroom. Eva groaned as I set her onto her unsteady legs.

"Come on, baby," I urged her. "You need to go to the bathroom."

"Why?" she whined.

"Would you like a UTI?"

"No... I want to go to sleep."

I chuckled before kissing her head. "So go to the bathroom while I grab us a couple of things. Then, you can sleep all you want as long as I'm holding you."

She leaned forward and kissed me softly, sweetly. "Can you get me a snack, please?"

"What do you think I'm getting, solnyshka?" I grinned. "I've got some of your favorites stocked in the kitchen."

Eva raised a brow. "You have sour gummy worms?"

At my nod, she asked me why, and I replied with a cheeky wink, "Because I knew it was only a matter of time before you came here. And I take care of what's mine."

I hurried to the kitchen and grabbed some snacks, water, aloe for the bite marks I left on her neck, and some pain medicine in case she was sore in the morning. Eva was already in bed by the time I came back, her smile drowsy and her arms open, waiting for me. It didn't take long for me to gather her into my arms while she shoved a few neon, battery-acid flavored candies into her mouth, yawning a few times before curling into my chest, the smile lingering on her face while she fell asleep.

And to my surprise, I found myself smiling back as the darkness pulled me under.

January 11th

NIKOLAI

Have you two boned yet? :)

ALEKSANDR

Shut the fuck up, Nikolai.

EVANGELINE
CHAPTER SEVENTEEN

When I woke up the next morning, I expected it to be cold. It was the middle of winter, and my apartment's heater was almost always struggling to keep it above freezing.

And yet when I stirred from my dream-filled sleep to the dim sunlight of morning, I was *warm*. It felt like a warm blanket had been draped over my body, curling around my back. I sighed happily and snuggled in deeper.

Only to find that my blanket wasn't soft fabric but the hard, toned skin of a sleeping man.

My eyes shot open as memories from the previous night flooded my mind. The tender spot between my legs throbbed in a dull ache, and my bladder burned with the need to pee.

Alek was sleeping with his arms wrapped tightly around my waist. My body was tucked into his very muscular chest, and our legs tangled together beneath the luxurious sheets. A tanned arm pressed into my stomach, making my desire to go to the bathroom much worse.

I angled my head to find Alek's mouth slightly opened, his hair strewn messily across the pillow. He was quite cute in the mornings, though, to be fair, he was cute all of the time. But there was this softness about him that didn't exist when he was awake, a light limning his darkness. I wished I could run my hands along his face, savoring the smooth lines. But considering he was pinning me in place, that wasn't going to happen.

"Eva," Alek mumbled before beginning to lightly snore.

Oh my god. That is adorable.

I wanted to wake up like this every day—his body cuddling mine, my name on his lips, my pussy sore from our lovemaking. My heart was so full from the overflowing tenderness. I'd only known him for a little over a month, yet I wanted him for a lifetime.

Was I going crazy? Or was I falling in love?

I smiled to myself and snuggled deeper into the spooning position, reveling in the way his arm seemed to subconsciously tighten around me in his sleep like he couldn't get enough of me.

Well, until I needed to pee. Like *right now*.

I attempted to wriggle out of his grip, but it was no use. Alek was six and a half feet of pure muscle. His arms were *jacked*, the veins bulging at the surface even in the throes of sleep. In another life, he might have been a world-famous athlete or a knight of the realm.

But in this life, he was mine.

Still, Alek was strong, even when unconscious, which normally would have turned me on, but now frustrated me endlessly. I tried to lift him off of me, but he didn't even budge an inch.

I cannot be that weak, I thought, though I kept proving myself wrong the more I tried.

"Alek," I hissed, but he continued to snore. "Alek!"

Nothing.

I huffed with annoyance *until* an idea popped into my head, one that made the corners of my lips turn upward.

I shimmied up, so I was face-to-face with him before laying

a soft kiss on his lips. *There. That'll interrupt his snoring and wake him—*

Except I wasn't planning on Alek suddenly shifting us, so I was underneath him, my face pressed into the pillows while his mouth hungrily devoured my neck.

"Mmm," he moaned in between kisses. The sound made shivers tingle down my spine as a familiar warmth returned to my body.

I didn't even realize my body was moving against his until I felt him move back, his hard member grinding into my ass. I arched into him, gasping for air while he harshly bit at me, the pain overloading all of my senses.

"Good morning, solnyshka. This is quite a way to wake up."

I moaned while he thrust into me, teasing me ruthlessly. At some point in the night, he must have dressed me in a t-shirt, slipping into boxers that didn't conceal his length. And since my panties were somewhere across the room, I was currently drenching his bed, my thighs becoming slick with want. But I was too turned on to be embarrassed. And anyway, Alek probably liked it, knowing him.

His cock nudged at my entrance. A thin layer of fabric was the only thing keeping him from slipping into me again. Despite my earlier soreness, I craved feeling him fill me up, his cock thrusting inside of me while his mouth bit me everywhere he could.

God, it felt so *good*. *He* felt so good. The feelings Alek brought out of me made me wild, turning my brain into a pile of mush that only wanted more.

"A-Alek."

He chuckled. The sound was hoarse from sleep, and yet it was somehow sexier. The vibrations of it traveled down my spine to my dripping pussy. "Yes, Eva? Is there something I can help you with?" he teased while his hands traveled up to my aching breasts.

"I need you. Right now," I breathed. I needed to be filled. I needed to feel him inside of me again. Once wasn't enough.

Alek grabbed onto my wrists with his hands and held them above my head. He left my body for a second before returning with a tie and a smirk. Before I could ask what that was for, Alek wrapped the tie around my wrists and bound me to his headboard. I tried to pull back, but the tie kept me in place. I wriggled my fingers, but Alek had done his job well. I couldn't move.

A whimper slipped past my lips as I realized I was completely trapped. I was at Alek's mercy, and that thought both thrilled and exhilarated me.

"You're going to take what I give you like a good girl, huh, Eva?" Alek cooed into my ear, biting the lobe and eliciting another gasp. He grabbed my hips and propped them up with a pillow, making my back naturally arch. The position felt unnatural at first, but I settled into it, accepting my fate. Wishing I could look into his eyes, but being all the more excited at the possibilities to come, at the sound of fabric rustling, yet not knowing when he would enter me.

"Y-yes."

"You're going to let me smack that ass while I take care of you?" He rocked into my core, and I felt his bare cock brush against my folds.

I moaned, my legs buckling. The tie was the only thing keeping me in place, the only thing preventing me from rocking my hips backward so he would finally be inside of me. "Yes, sir."

"Fuck, I love that."

And then he was pushing into me, this position unlocking a whole new feeling inside of me. I cried out in ecstasy, my fingers clenching around the headboard. He was seated so deeply inside of me that when he thrust, I felt it in my stomach. Thanks to my birth control pills that Jules miraculously let me get to manage my cycle, I was able to feel every part of him against every part of me.

"Your pussy feels so good, baby," Alek groaned, thrusting even deeper.

One of his hands dug into my hair and wrenched my neck upward. My body was bent and twisted so much I hardly felt like a person, yet I loved it. The way he took control of me, dominating me, *owning* me, made me so dizzy I could hardly see.

And when Alek's hand landed on my ass with a loud *crack*, I almost hurled off the edge of something new and frightening.

"Alek!" I cried, though I wasn't sure if it was from horror or pleasure. My cheek throbbed with the stinging of his slap, yet a part of me almost liked it. It was another way he was owning me, showing me who I belonged to, rutting me like an animal.

"I'm going to mark every inch of that beautiful body," Alek said, punctuating his words with a harsh bite to my neck and a pinch to my nipple that made my knees buckle. "Everyone is going to look at my pretty girl on the stage and know you're fucking *mine*."

"Yours," I tried to say, though I was pretty sure it sounded more like *armphg*.

Alek chuckled. "I love it when you make those little fucking noises. Let me hear them. Let the whole damn house hear them."

And then he was going faster and faster, one hand alternating between slapping and rubbing my ass while the other pinched my nipples. His thrusts were brutal, pushing me up the bed until I was forced to use the headboard to brace myself. His tie rubbed at my wrists, and the assaulting feeling over every sensation drove me closer and closer.

"A-Alek, I can't... It's t-too much..."

My brain was beginning to go fuzzy. My toes curled, and my hands flexed involuntarily. Any sense of control I had was destroyed by Alek and the dangerous dance we did together.

"Yes, you fucking can, Eva, and you *will*. You're going to come all over my cock, and then I'm going to clean you up and hold you in my arms and kiss all of my marks better. And we're going to do this every damn day and night for the rest of our lives, because I'm yours and you're mine and *nothing* will change that."

"Oh my *God*, Alek—"

He kissed my spine before reaching forward and pulling my chin back to look into his eyes.

Midnight oceans.

Maybe it was seeing his eyes, the tender feelings in them, despite the violent undercurrent of his movements. Maybe it was the way he quickened his pace, hitting spots inside of me that made me see stars. Or maybe it was the way he whispered, "Come for me, solnyshka. Fall apart against me."

And I did. I let the darkness consume me until my brain was nothing but mush. My body tingled from the zaps of pleasure while Alek groaned and came inside me in hot spurts of cum, making me come even harder.

When I came to, blinking off the orgasm, Alek was taking a washcloth and cleaning between my thighs, kissing the quivering muscles as he did so. He gathered me into his arms and carried me to the bathroom, turning on the water to the most luxurious bath I had ever seen. Like the rest of his house, it was modern yet classy in a way, marble with black veins, all sleek lines.

With dazed eyes, I looked around the giant bathroom—at the matching marble shower, the expensive cologne on the counter, the bedroom beyond—and realized Alek was more than just rich.

He was a billionaire.

Alek stepped into the tub and settled me on top of his lap. The water was warm, but it felt burning against my aching skin, tender from our lovemaking.

He grabbed a container of soap and squirted some onto his hands, lathering it before running his hands all along my body. I couldn't help but notice the way he pointedly avoided cleaning my pussy.

"My cum stays in you," he murmured into my ear, kissing my flaming cheeks.

Then, he massaged shampoo into my scalp and conditioner into my ends, taking great care to pull apart any tangles caused by his rough hands. I sniffed the air and frowned. "Is that my shampoo?"

"Yes, solnyshka."

"Why did you get that? How did you know the right one?"

How are you always so perfect?

Alek grabbed my chin and pulled my face to meet his. Our lips met in a gentle kiss, his tongue slowly entering me before eating me from the inside out. My breath hitched, his softness surprising me.

"Because," he whispered, "I know your mind well enough to know that you're thinking of all the reasons you can't stay here with me. And I want you to run out of them."

My lips parted, heart thundering in my chest. And before I knew it, we were kissing again, and Alek was pulling me to face him, and his cock was burying inside of me, and everything was right with the world.

I realized I *was* falling. Hurtling toward something unknown, something terrifying, something that had the power to kill me, to shatter my fragile heart. I had fallen in love with Aleksandr Drakov.

But I trusted him to catch me.

January 12th

JULES

What are you up to tonight, Annie? Want to come over for dinner?

MISSED CALL FROM JULES

You're not at rehearsal, are you? I didn't drive you.

Are you at work? You told me you quit your job.

MISSED CALL FROM JULES

Evangeline, where are you? I came by, and you weren't at home.

MISSED CALL FROM JULES

Are you at Mia's?

MISSED CALL FROM JULES
MISSED CALL FROM JULES
MISSED CALL FROM JULES

Evangeline, answer me.

MISSED CALL FROM JULES
MISSED CALL FROM JULES
MISSED CALL FROM JULES
MISSED CALL FROM JULES

Evangeline.

EVANGELINE

CHAPTER EIGHTEEN

A STEADY, BUZZING SOUND WOKE ME FROM A LAZY nap back in Alek's bed. Both of us passed out after we'd managed to drag ourselves from the bath. My body was sore and spent, ready to rest for the entire weekend. Which, thankfully, I could do, because I didn't have rehearsals for a couple of days.

Groaning, I rolled on my side and tried to bury my head into the pillow. Alek followed behind me, wrapping his whole body around me and placing sleepy kisses on my naked shoulder. I smiled, arching my body into his like a cat.

I wasn't sure I could go another round, but if he asked me, I wouldn't turn him down. Alek must have been thinking the same thing, because his hand started to slide down my body to my waiting thighs.

"I can't get enough of you, solnyshka. I am addicted," Alek said, his accent thickening as his voice roughened.

Sometimes, when his emotions clouded his head, it did that. Alek once told me that both of his parents had heavy accents, and he'd inherited a mixture of the two, though he admitted his skewed more toward his father's because he grew up surrounded more by the Russian side of his family. His grandfather was the one who brought the Drakovs here to the city, though Alek said they visited Russia frequently. His mother, on the other hand, emigrated from Italy when she was very young.

According to Alek, his family was very close-knit. He was forced to go to multiple dinners a month with his mother, who kept insisting on meeting me, to my utter glee, and Nikolai was almost always glued to his side. The Drakovs were fiercely protective of one another, a trait Alek had clearly inherited, as he'd insisted many times that he would do anything for me.

Even die for me.

It was that protectiveness, that possessiveness, I thought of as Alek's hands spread my thighs apart and—

Bzzzt. Bzzzt.

I abruptly sat up, my mind awake enough to recognize that sound. "Crap," I hissed under my breath, my hands searching everywhere for my phone. I jumped off the bed and began to search through the disarray on the floor, finally finding it in my purse.

Ten missed calls.

I had *ten* missed calls from my older brother.

"Crap, crap, crap," I said before I clicked the green button, raising my phone to my ear with a wide smile. "Hi, Jules—"

"Where are you, Evangeline?" he seethed into the phone. I knew him well enough to know that his fury was barely contained. If he were a cartoon character, there would be steam coming out of his ears.

Alek's eyes darkened as he stood from the bed and slowly stalked over to me, his posture stiff like a predator. Apparently, his wrath was at the surface, too.

His hand shot out to grab my throat, blue eyes almost black with fury. The morning—*crap*, it was afternoon, I realized—sunlight fell across his body, illuminating the dark tattoos on his naked torso. My mouth watered at the sight of them, my hands running over his sculpted chest.

"Jules?" he snarled lowly. His hand tightened around my neck, not in a painful or frightening way but in one that made heat travel down my body. "You're *mine*."

"*My brother*," I mouthed, because apparently in all the stories about my older brother, I'd failed to ever say his name.

Alek relaxed, but only barely. He nodded once before pulling me back onto the bed with him, settling me on his lap, rocking up with his hips. We were still naked from earlier, which meant that his cock was rubbing against my sore pussy. I instantly became wet, my whole body tightening when his tip slipped inside of me.

I gasped, covering up the sound with a rushed question. "What are you up to?"

"'What am I up to?' *What am I up to*? I'm over here fucking worried about you, Evangeline! I've called you ten damn times and no answer! TEN TIMES, EVANGELINE!" he roared through the phone. I had to pull away to keep from getting a headache.

Alek—who had previously been teasing my slit with his hard shaft, his eyes so hungry that they were almost black—gritted his jaw.

"Like hell someone is going to speak to you like that," he said with so much wrath that it made me shiver, my core warming at the darkness in his tone.

There is definitely something wrong with you, Eva. You're on the phone with your brother, *and you're getting turned on.*

Though anyone who heard Alek's voice at that moment would have been horny, too. He sounded like a god of sex.

I held up my hand and gave Alek a look that I hoped said, *trust me*. His face turned cold, but he nodded, and that was enough for me.

"Who the fuck was that?" Jules screamed.

Despite how it might have appeared, my brother could be really sweet sometimes. He was the most thoughtful person I'd ever met—well, maybe second-most now—always going to my shows, supporting my dreams, thinking about me when I most needed it. But Jules was sometimes a stubborn bulldozer, while I had the tendency to be... easily bulldozed. It was a combination that didn't go well together.

I knew he meant well. He wanted to protect me in a world he thought was unsafe.

I just wished his form of protection didn't feel so restricting.

"It's the TV, Jules, calm down."

"You don't have a TV."

"It's Mia's," I said, trying to calm my racing heartbeat while Alek kissed down my body with a smirk that promised mischief. "I'm at her place. And before you ask, she came and got me, I didn't take the metro, and I didn't answer because I was taking a nap. You know, resting? Like you've been wanting me to do?"

It frightened me how easy it was becoming to lie to him. Once upon a time, Jules and I told each other everything. We were best friends because we were the only people we had. Jules didn't trust anyone very much because he worried they would backstab him, and I was kept so sheltered that I couldn't make friends even if I wanted to.

Yet despite the betrayal in my heart, I didn't want to stop. The lies were the only thing letting me still see Alek.

Alek nudged my legs open. He reached forward, hands sliding up my thighs. I tried to flash him a warning look, but it was right when his finger brushed across my clit. All my breath left my lungs as Alek dipped one finger to me before pulling it out slowly, agonizingly, and bringing it up to his lips.

He stuck his finger in his mouth and sucked, opening it

enough for me to watch the way his tongue swirled around my juices, greedily inhaling each drop.

My breath stuttered. I wanted him. I wanted *more* with him. I wasn't sure I could ever get enough of Alek.

"—are you even fucking listening to me, Evangeline?"

"Yes, yes, I'm sorry. You cut out."

I tried to shoo Alek away, but he smirked at me, his lips still moist with my juices. Then, he ran his finger along my slit, gathering more of my wetness. I watched, enraptured, as he brought it to his cock before pumping himself up and down, using me to lubricate himself.

My mouth watered at the sight. I wanted him in my mouth again, in my pussy, getting his cum all over my aching body.

I reached for his cock, needing to touch him, but he swatted my hands away, his eyes teasing me as if to say, *That's what you get for trying to push me away earlier.*

Pouting, I leaned back and enjoyed the sight of him stroking himself. Alek's eyes darkened as they roamed over my body, lingering on my stiff nipples and drenched core. My skin was littered with bite marks and subtle bruises from his hands. I liked the sight of them—how they made me remember his tattooed, veiny forearms holding me close as he pushed into me.

"Evangeline," Jules began, tone warning.

"It really is! I can't control a bad signal, and I figured you didn't want me to leave her apartment alone." The pause told me how much he believed me, so I quickly added, "You know I answer your calls as soon as I see them. I know the rules."

"Fine," he bit out before his voice softened. "I was calling to see if you wanted to come over for dinner. I feel like it's been a long time since I've seen you."

Alek's pace quickened, and I licked my lips, needing this

phone call to be over with so I could feel him again. He gritted his jaw, mouthing, "*Like what you see, baby?*"

"Yes," I breathed. Then, I blinked before saying, "I mean, yes, Jules, dinner tonight would be great. You can pick me up from Mia's closer to dinnertime?"

"Sounds good."

Alek winked.

"Very, very good," I murmured. "Hey, Jules, I might go hop in the shower, but I'll see you later."

"Okay, Ann—"

I hung up on him immediately, planning on blaming the bad signal if he asked me about it later. I wasted no time seating myself on my cock, sighing with relief when we finally rejoined.

Alek thrust upward, his mouth already finding my neck while his hands settled on both of my breasts. "Such a naughty girl trying to keep me away from these. How should I punish you?"

"You could fuck me."

"Mmm, but I think you'd like that too much."

"Then *ruin me, Alek*." I looked at him, my eyes hooded, and my lashes fluttering closed. I leaned into him, letting my lips brush against his. "Fuck me like I'm yours."

Alek snapped.

He pounded into me from below, hitting that sweet spot over and over again with brutal thrusts. I tried to gasp, but the sound was cut off by his hand grabbing my throat and squeezing until I saw stars. The word *stop* balanced on my tongue. I knew he would do it if I asked, but I didn't want him to stop. He controlled the very air I breathed, whether I could gasp or moan or scream out for more. And handing over that control—my *life*—was terrifying.

But I trusted him enough to take care of me. Alek would never hurt me. Everything he did was to make me feel pleasure.

And in a world where every one of my decisions had the potential to send me into catastrophe, it was so freeing to trust someone like that. To have them take away the buzzing and leave me in my silence.

"Mine," Alek growled, biting my neck. "You are fucking *mine*, Evangeline."

"I'm yours. All yours."

"Forever. You're mine forever, baby."

I had a split second to decide what to say next. "Come with me to dinner then," I murmured, rocking my hips back and forth, becoming more and more comfortable with having sex now that we'd done it a few times. "Get my brother's permission, and we can have our forever."

"I don't need permission for you to be mine."

"You do if you want us to ever get married in the future. My brother's opinion means a lot to me."

Alek groaned. "Fine. But only if I get to come inside you at least three times before."

I grinned. "You'd better get started, then."

January 12th

EVANGELINE
Hey, can I come over?

MIA
Yes, OMG!!!!

I miss you!!!

EVANGELINE
I miss you too!! Twenty-four hours is too long. :(

MIA
Totally agree.

Everything okay though?

Tired of getting dicked down by Mr. Perfect?

EVANGELINE
I actually need your help with something…

Alek is coming over for dinner with Jules tonight. 😬

MIA
I'M SCREAMING!

Evie, this is huge!!! You two are SERIOUS, huh?

EVANGELINE
Yeah…

MIA
I'm surprised Mr. Buzzkill agreed to meet him.

EVANGELINE
About that…

MIA

OMG.

Eva, you didn't.

EVANGELINE

I did...

EVANGELINE
CHAPTER NINETEEN

I HADN'T BEEN ABLE TO SIT STILL EVER SINCE ALEK dropped me off at Mia's apartment, kissing my cheek and vowing to see me later. The dark look in his eyes made me shiver, and I had to peel myself from his grasp. I wasn't sure my body could take another round with him, not to mention I had limited time to get ready before Jules came to pick me up.

Half an hour later, Mia was applying glitter on my eyelids with a small smile to herself. "We're going to make you look so damn angelic that Jules *has* to hear you out. I want him to ask himself if this sweet face would ever be irresponsible."

I wasn't sure about her strategy, but I liked glitter, so I wasn't going to argue.

"So what's your tea?" I asked a few minutes later when she was curling my hair. I didn't necessarily need her help getting ready for a simple dinner with my brother, but Mia had a secret passion for beauty. She once told me that in another life, she might have been a hairdresser or makeup artist instead of a ballerina. I encouraged her to follow wherever her heart led her, but she had just shrugged before saying that helping me get beautified before each show and night out scratched her itch.

Mia sighed dramatically. "You will *not* believe this. Guess who—"

"Hey, Mia, can you take me to the pharmacy to get my meds?" a smooth, quiet voice asked from the doorway. I turned only to shriek in surprise, jumping up and wrapping Charlotte, Mia's younger sister and my college friend, in a hug.

"Charlotte! What are you doing here?" I exclaimed, hugging her tightly.

She was so thin that it felt like holding bones. I pulled back, worried, my eyes darting between her and her sister's tight smile.

"Charlotte has decided to drop out of school," Mia said through clenched teeth. "And since she refuses to tell our parents about her decision—because she knows it's a stupid one—guess who has a roommate? That's right! Me! Only instead of a normal roommate, this one sleeps on my couch, eats all my food, and doesn't pay rent."

"And she doesn't complain about it at all," Charlotte said dryly, her eyes almost rolling.

Unlike her older sister, Charlotte was the definition of a closed book. She never smiled when she danced, never betrayed her emotions on her face, never let anyone know what she was feeling. Where Mia was a raging waterfall—full of mist and rainbows and splashes in your face—Charlotte was a river, one whose depths were invisible, not realizing it was deep until you were drowning in the current.

I loved her, but sometimes she worried me.

But I knew that Charlotte would talk about things whenever she was ready. And I would be there for her through it all, no matter what.

Charlotte looked around the room with her pale gray eyes, her expression unchanged. She pushed a strand of long, black hair out of her face and said, "I'm deferring my enrollment. I'm not dropping out. I just need some space for a while."

"What are you going to do?" I asked, trying to keep my voice supportive.

She shrugged before walking out of the bathroom. Mia and I watched her go, both of us wearing identical frowns. "Is she all right?" I whispered as soon as I was certain she was out of earshot.

"I don't know. Probably not," Mia said. Her gray eyes, identical to her sister's, failed to contain her worry. "You know what the university director has said. Charlotte is the best dancer the program has *ever* had... a program that is over a century old. Charlotte used to love dancing. It was the only thing we could ever get her to talk about. But now, she's here, sleeping on my couch and only speaking when she needs something. So, no, I don't think she's okay, but if I know my sister, it's best to let her come to us. If we push her too hard right now, she'll completely shut down. Whatever it is, she'll tell us when she's ready. I hope."

My frown deepened. I supposed Charlotte's story was one for another day, though I would keep her tucked in the back of my mind until then.

Mia plastered a fake smile on her face. I knew because I wore the same one often. "No more talk of upsetting stuff. Sit back down. I need to get you ready for war."

I PLAYED WITH THE HEM OF MY PINK SKIRT AS I SAT down on the leather sofa in my brother's living room. The air smelled like polished wood, and the scent had taken up a permanent residence in my nose. It was so cold and sterile that I kept wrinkling my nose, wishing he would light a candle or something. But that would make the room cozy, and Jules's house was anything but that.

The smell of wood, the feeling of it pressing around me,

was familiar. This was the home I grew up in until my parents passed it to Jules to enjoy being empty nesters around the world. Mahogany carvings lined the walls and ceiling, reminding me of a jail cell. This place was suffocating. It was never my home, never someplace I wanted to go. All it did was remind me of being alone.

That wasn't to say my brother hadn't tried to make it nicer. He'd attempted to liven up the place with mismatched throw pillows and redid my bedroom to make it pink, even going as far as to string bows along the canopy bed and hang twinkling string lights from the ceilings.

But it felt like putting makeup on a monster. There was something dark beneath the bones of this house. Something that made my skin crawl.

Maybe that was just the echoes of my childhood making me nervous.

My brother handed me a fluffy pink blanket, and I used it to cover my goosebump-riddled legs. He cocked a brow. "You didn't have to wear a dress to dinner. It's just going to be us. Elsie couldn't make it."

Which was true, but I'd wanted to look cute for Alek. The pink sweater dress was fairly cozy, with little bows on the bell sleeves to match the one Mia put in my hair and the kitten heels that hung off my feet. It was nicer than I normally looked to see Jules, but I didn't feel too out of place since he still wore a green button-down from work, the sleeves rolled up to his forearms to reveal a tattoo of three interconnected Celtic knots that he got when he was sixteen.

"Speaking of that," I began, my voice trembling, and my face already contorting into a wince. "I have something to tell you..."

Jules whipped to face me, eyes turning black. He clenched his jaw as he yanked me up from the couch and began to inspect me for injuries. "What's wrong? Did someone try to hurt you? Is there someone I need to take care of?"

I pushed his hands off. Well, I tried to. Jules still kept a tight grip on my bicep, and I was too weak to actually push him off. But he did take a step back after I said, "No. Nothing like that."

"Well, what is it, Evangeline?"

I frowned because he was using my full name. He was being serious. More than he normally was, at least.

"There's someone I wanted to come to dinner tonight."

If I thought Jules's expression was dark before, it was *murderous* now. Behind his dark eyes, there was a thunderstorm. I worried he would break his jaw with how hard he was clenching it.

"Evangeline Vale. You'd better say that this 'someone' is a new girl you met at the ballet."

I bit my lip before shaking my head with the look of a sullen child who had been scolded.

"*Fuck*. A boy?" Jules looked like he was one wrong word away from going on a rampage. There was a reason I hadn't said Alek's name yet—so Jules wouldn't do something stupid like trying to kill him.

"Yes," I whispered.

"No. No way," Jules said, shaking his head vehemently. "Not a chance, Evangeline. You're not going to date anyone for a *long* time. Maybe never. I don't care if this man is Jesus fucking Christ himself. You are not seeing him anymore."

My lips parted, eyes stinging with tears that began to blur my vision. "That's not fair! You have Elsie. How come you can date, and I can't?"

"Elsie and I are *not* dating, and even if we were, it's because I'm..." But he trailed off.

And it hurt. Because I knew exactly what he was going to say.

Because I'm me. Because you're you. Because you're weak. Because you're not strong enough. You never have been.

I ripped my arm from his grasp and took a few steps backward. My whole body trembled. For once, I didn't feel the need to mend the cracks I had created. The urge to apologize, to make myself small again, didn't appear. Even my voice was silent.

I took a few deep breaths before I said in a shaking voice. "I'm twenty-one years old, Jules. I have hardly any friends. I haven't been out of state since I was four. And I've never dated anyone. I'm kept in a cage while you have the freedom to do anything you want. You lock me up and dangle the key in front of me like it's *nothing*. And now, when I've finally met someone who makes me feel free for the first time in my life, you want to take that away from me? You want me to give it up because *you* aren't ready, even though I am? How does that seem fair?"

His face fell. "Annie, I—"

"Don't call me that. I don't want to hear any more from you," I whispered, my voice cracking at the end as I did the one thing I never thought I would do.

I began to build a wall between us. The only family I had left. My brother. My closest friend. The one person I trusted to be there for me no matter what. The one person I'd *never* kept anything from.

But if he forced me to pick between him and Alek, I was beginning to think he wouldn't like the choice I would make.

A lone tear fell down my cheek, and I hurriedly wiped it away. I began to stalk out of the room only for a hand to grab my own and pull me back. I refused to look at my brother, even while he tried to wrap his arms around me in a tight hug.

"Annie, please. Listen to me."

Sighing, I turned to face him. Jules was looking at me, his brown eyes filled with concern. All of the anger was gone.

That was the thing about having a hotheaded older brother. Yes, he lost his temper sometimes, but he gained control back quickly.

"I'm listening," I muttered.

"I will meet the boy," Jules said in a tight voice that showed how truly painful it was for him to say it.

My hopeful heart skipped a beat. "Really?"

"Really. I can't promise that I'll like him, but if he's nice and he treats you well, then—"

Jules broke off when I threw my arms around his neck and squeezed him tightly, cutting off the circulation to his head. "Thank you, Jules! Thank you, thank you, thank you!"

He chuckled and hugged me back, picking me up off the ground as he spun me around. "You're welcome, Annie. I will *try*. But that's all I can promise."

"That's more than enough," I said, squeezing his hand.

I could hardly contain the excitement radiating through my pores. What if this went really, really well? What if Alek and Jules became friends? What if our relationship could be *real*?

Somewhere deep in my chest, a strange, fluttering feeling bloomed—like standing on the edge of something enormous, something inevitable. I told myself it was excitement. Romeo and Juliet finally getting their happy ending.

After all, what could go wrong with a simple dinner?

I had no idea I was standing at the precipice of something major, smiling like a girl who forgot the *real* ending to *Romeo and Juliet*.

A girl who forgot it was a tragedy.

January 12th

EVANGELINE

HE SAID YES!!!!

You can come over anytime! :)

ALEKSANDR

That's great, baby.

I'll be there soon.

ALEKSANDR
CHAPTER TWENTY

"Hello, my pretty girl," I whispered as I grabbed onto Eva's waist and pulled her flush to my body before my lips found her neck. It took everything in me not to bite her again, but I was trying to contain myself. Her brother probably wouldn't like watching me fuck her against my car, nor would he like seeing her neck riddled with my marks.

Normally, I didn't give a fuck what other people thought of me. If I wanted to make my girlfriend scream, I would. If I wanted to paint her with bruises like a fucking Picasso, I would.

But I knew how much this meant to Eva. She still yearned for happily ever afters, for moments where the crowd cheered as the prince kissed his true love.

I didn't believe in that shit. Happy endings were taken, not earned. And I would take and take and take until I got mine.

But, again, *Eva*. She cared about those things. She believed in them. And I would suppress my monstrous nature if it made her smile. I would cut out my own heart if she asked it of me—as long as she continued to be mine.

"Hi, Alek," she said, her voice soft and musical.

I groaned. "Solnyshka, you know what saying my name does to me."

I turned and pressed her into the dark metal, letting her feel my already-hard cock. Eva gasped, neck already arching in submission. She was a natural, bending to my will with just one look. I fucking loved it. She knew her place was with me—underneath me, against me, by my side. I would do anything to keep her there.

Pulling away, I forced myself to look anywhere but her soft, glossy lips, the way they parted like her tongue needed to be fucked as much as her pussy did. My eyes traveled down her body, to her pretty pink dress that slightly flared at her hips, inviting me to grab onto her thighs and pick her up.

The shoes. Look at her shoes. There's nothing too sexy about those.

But I was wrong, because everything about Eva was fucking intoxicating. Her shoes were cute little heels, and while I didn't care about them at all, I looked at her bare ankles and pictured running my lips up her leg until I reached her core. She would be so wet, my Eva, her pussy already aching for me, needing me to stretch and fill her—

Focus. Meeting the fucking brother.

"I missed you," I rasped, because no words seemed to explain how long the afternoon had felt without her. Hence my insufferable clinginess.

"It's only been a few hours."

"A few too many." I nipped at her neck and almost fell to my knees at the taste of her, at the feeling of her pulse jumping beneath my teeth. "Fuck. I need to taste you."

Eva blushed. She looked back and forth, making sure no one was around to see. But, thankfully, Eva's brother lived in a rich fucking neighborhood. Not as rich as mine, but not everyone could be on my level.

It was an older part of the city, the houses all made out of faded brick and stone. A place made of generational wealth, of the people who watched the world change without doing anything about it themselves.

I could never be like that, could never be satisfied with my place in the world. I would always want more until the beast in me was finally satisfied. Since I couldn't chain my girlfriend to my side and bring my sister back from the dead, I never would. So I would continue to take and take from this infernal hellhole until nothing could threaten what was mine again.

Lifting Eva's skirt so my hands could slide up, I groaned when I realized my innocent little girlfriend wasn't wearing fucking underwear.

"No underwear?" I growled as my finger dipped into her perfect, pink pussy. She was practically dripping for me, her little curls soaked and waiting for me.

"I... um..." Eva shook her head. "I couldn't. The dress would show the lines."

"You really are fucking perfect."

She furrowed her brows, but I paid it no mind, thrusting my fingers into her before shoving them into my mouth, moaning at the sweet taste. Her body tightened, lips parting. *She is divine.*

But when I went to unzip my trousers, Eva put her hand on mine, stopping me. I gritted my teeth. "I need to fuck you."

"Not now, Alek. My brother could see."

"So let him see. He'll learn that you're mine."

"Later, Alek." At my dark look, Eva sighed and kissed me gently. "You know I want to feel you inside of me. But I can't risk Jules seeing us and going ballistic. I promise we can later, okay?"

I groaned and adjusted my hard-on. "Fine. But you're paying for it later."

Eva smiled. "Looking forward to it. Are you ready to meet my brother now?"

"I guess," I said, voice rougher than intended, because I would have much rather pulled her into the backseat of my car and recreated this morning over and over. I planned to make good on those failed wishes many times later.

I had no idea she wouldn't keep her promise.

The house loomed larger the closer we got. Brick pillars flanked the entrance, worn smooth with age. Cold light spilled from the tall windows, curtains swaying with staff eyeing us with curiosity. The light from the lanterns flanking the entrance did nothing to soften the place. If anything, it made the shadow sharper.

Eva slowed at the door, turning to face me one last time. Her eyes searched mine—not fearful, not uncertain, just... hopeful. Trusting.

That look landed somewhere deep in my chest.

She took my hand, lacing her fingers through mine like it was the most natural thing in the world. Like she had no idea of her ability to completely undo the heir and de facto leader of the most powerful mob in the city with a single look and the absence of a little fabric. Eva squeezed my hand once as if meant to reassure me. But I could tell from the way she bit her lip that it was she who needed reassurance.

"Hey," I said, gripping her chin and bringing her dark eyes to meet mine. "Everything will be fine."

"I know. Jules promised to be on his best behavior, and he even said he'll let us get settled at the dinner table for a few minutes before the interrogation begins. I'm sure it'll be great." A stormcloud of worries thundered behind her eyes, and the annoyance in me softened.

I brushed my thumb along her jaw, every touch reverent. "I'll behave," I told her quietly. "For you."

Her lips curved into a smile meant only for me. "That's all I ask."

She leaned in, pressing a quick kiss to my mouth—

sweet, restrained, nothing like what we both wanted. Yet it was still a temptation, because Eva was sin wrapped in sweetness.

My girl smiled at me. Then she opened the door.

Cold air rushed out to greet us, thick with the scent of polished wood and something sharper beneath it. Oil, maybe, or even blood. Something that soaked into the walls over decades and never quite left.

I stepped inside after Eva, immediately aware of how quiet the house was. Not peaceful, but hushed. Like something was holding its breath, studying me, gauging whether I was predator or prey.

I straightened my posture and glared into the darkness, shuffling closer to Eva, who led me through the home, occasionally commenting on different aspects of the house.

There was wood everywhere. Dark mahogany floors, dark walls adorned with crown molding, a sweeping staircase that curved upward like a spine. Everything was pristine and expensive and utterly *lifeless*. There were no photographs. No art that didn't look like it was purchased at an auction house. No sign of clutter or warmth. No, there were only objects chosen because they were old, rare, and worth more than most of the people in the city earned in their lifetime.

It was money without taste. Wealth without joy. Immaculate in the way that mausoleums were.

I fucking hated it.

Eva's hand slipped from mine as she continued through the home. I fell behind her, noticing the way her shoulders rounded a fraction, and her steps faltered as if unsure. The lightness she carried around with her everywhere she went dimmed, like someone had turned down the flame on one of those old-timey gas lanterns the moment she entered.

My solnyshka shrank.

The sight of it made my jaw tighten. What kind of fucking

childhood did she have to feel like she didn't belong in her own family's home?

Eva had occasionally told me stories from when she was a kid, though most of them were happy memories involving her brother playing with her. She rarely spoke of her parents, and when she did, it was with an air of detachment—like she was talking about a distant cousin or something. My Eva was never unkind, but it was as if she barely knew them.

I didn't realize how true that was until I looked around this house she claimed she grew up in, unable to find a sign of her anywhere.

There were no photos of a little girl with her brown hair tied in pigtails adorned with pink ribbons. No crooked drawings framed with pride. No evidence that a little girl had ever laughed or cried or grown up here. If I hadn't known better, I would've assumed this house had been occupied exclusively by ghosts and men who didn't believe in tenderness.

I imagined Eva small in these halls—too quiet, too careful, learning early how not to take up space. Thinking that she had to earn her love from people who refused to give it to her.

Something ugly arose within me. This wasn't a home. This was a breeding ground for all the demons I'd been trying to eradicate within her.

Without thinking, I pulled Eva back to my side and kissed her. My tongue dove into her, and my hands curled around her waist, reminding her that I was here. "I'm so proud to call you mine," I rasped against her lips.

Eva pulled back, her eyes shining. "W-What?"

"You're amazing, Evangeline. And I will spend the rest of my miserable life showing you how much."

I meant every word. I made a mental note to fill my home with photos of her, maybe even some of us together. Fuck, I would plan a whole damn shoot if that would continue to bring back some of the lightness she'd lost in here. I would dedicate wings of my mansion to her—a ballet studio, a library, a movie room, whatever the fuck she wanted—and I would make sure that every time she stepped inside, she would know it was *hers*. That as much as she was mine, I was hers too.

Eva smiled, a soft smile but a real one. Her cheeks turned a lovely shade of pink that matched her dress. "Thank you."

And my heart tightened. Because for the first time, Eva accepted my compliment. She didn't throw it away, didn't try to argue it.

She continued to lead me through the house, her steps now much lighter and her hand back in mine. Eva didn't bother to explain more of the house, and I didn't ask her because I didn't need to hear it.

I'd seen places like this before. Houses built to impress rivals and intimidate allies. Fortresses masquerading as estates. This was the kind of home families like the Vallens prized—filled with old power, the walls practically oozing the blood of the families they stepped on to get there. The sort that believed the city belonged to them simply because it always had.

And maybe it did once upon a time.

But that was before my grandfather came in like a fucking wrecking ball and rewrote the rules. He watched the Vallens kill his brother for getting in the way, and he let his anger fuel an empire.

At first, the Vallens didn't care about some scum beneath them. Until we became a fucking threat. But by then, it was too late. The power was transferred to my father, and now, my father was slowly handing it over to me. Three generations of Drakov men hungry for vengeance. For my great-uncle and for Liza.

The day they perished was the day I would finally know peace.

I had never seen the Vallen home—the rats were good at keeping it hidden—but I imagined it looked like this, all arrogance built into the architecture. Old money always looked the same when it rotted.

I shoved my thoughts away as Eva started walking down a hallway. She glanced back at me, offering a small, nervous smile.

"The dining room is down here," she said softly.

I followed, cataloging every exit out of habit, every shadow, every creak of the floor beneath my shoes. The hallway stretched long and narrow, portraits of unfamiliar men staring down at us with flat, unimpressed eyes. I saw traits of my Eva in all of them, in the freckles painted on their faces, in the darkness of their eyes.

But as we got to the newer portraits, I frowned. Something about them, about the stern set of their thin lips and the harshness of their jaws, looked incredibly familiar. Like I'd *seen* these people before, if not in person, then in photographs.

I tried to find the most recent picture, hoping to see her father, but before I could, Eva cleared her throat. Her hands were hovering over the handle of the door for half a second before she opened it and led me inside.

The room was massive. A long table carved from dark wood dominated the space, already set with pristine silverware and linens folded with surgical precision. A chandelier hung overhead, casting light that felt more interrogative than warm.

Eva took a seat next to the head of the table, and I followed suit behind her, pulling out her chair before sitting to her left. The room was empty, thankfully, though that didn't settle the awareness prickling in the back of my head. Whatever storm was coming, the air already tasted like its lightning.

She turned to me, giving me one of those wretched, false smiles I abhorred. I didn't want her to hide her emotions from me. Every part of her was *mine*—including the parts she didn't think were good enough. "Our cook is pretty good, but if you don't like what she's made, you can tell me, and she'll make something else. And if Jules ever asks you something too personal, you can make a signal or something. I'm pretty good at changing the subject, but sometimes he can be a pain. And if you want to leave, just let me know, and I'll—"

"Eva," I said, tearing her from her ramblings. My lips brushed against hers, and she smiled, though it wasn't real.

I scowled. "Don't hide your true feelings from me, Eva."

"What do you—"

I pulled her face to mine sharply, and Eva gasped, her hands reaching out to grab the lapels of my suit. I was wearing the shirt that I cleaned her up with yesterday because, yes, I couldn't resist the urge to wear her juices on me like a badge of honor.

I was a sick fuck for her.

"Don't lie to me," I murmured, my voice dark. It was taking everything in me not to bend her over the table and thrust into her from behind, to force her face to reveal something real. "If you aren't happy, don't pretend to be. I want the real Evangeline Vale. Not some pretense."

But instead of looking reassured like I thought she would, Eva's face fell.

"Alek, about that..." she began, but I didn't get to hear what she said. Because next, the door opened.

And all hell fucking broke loose.

January 12th

NIKOLAI

Ayeeeee good luck meeting the in-laws.

If she has any hot cousins or something let me know.

Thought I could get in with blondie, but that kitty has claws, and this face is too pretty to be scratched.

ALEKSANDR

What the fuck are you talking about?

EVANGELINE
CHAPTER TWENTY-ONE

RIGHT THERE. THE WORDS WERE *RIGHT THERE* ON the tip of my tongue, ready to spill from my lips. *Alek, you should know: my name is Evangeline Vale. But it wasn't always.*

It was one of the many things that changed after the accident. My wound still had all of its stitches when my mother dragged me to the courthouse and signed paperwork to change my name. Anything to distance themselves from me. Anything to finally rid themselves of me.

And for a long time, I was devastated.

I felt like I wasn't a part of my own family, an outsider who lived beyond the walls they'd built. It took me years to realize that my family was the people I chose, not the ones who shared my last name. My family was Jules and Mia. Maybe Charlotte. And, if tonight went well, Alek.

I was getting ready to tell Alek about my name when the door to the dining room opened. I knew instinctively by the dark and imposing presence that it was my big brother. A nervous smile took over my face as I prepared for the two most important men in my life to meet.

My brother stepped into the room.

And immediately pulled out his gun.

I screamed at the sight of such a vulgar weapon pointed in my direction. A strong hand gripped my arm and wrenched me behind their body. All the air escaped my lungs when I saw that Alek had pulled me behind him, his body shielding mine while he had another gun pointed at my brother. I might have screamed again, though I wasn't sure. My blood was thundering in my ears, too thick for me to tell.

What's happening? Why do they have guns? Why are they aiming them at each other?

My hands instinctively wrapped around Alek, my soul craving some form of comfort. His body was hard, tension radiating from every pore. I couldn't see his face, but what I did see reminded me of the Angel of Death. Shadows lined his handsome expression, and his eyes were pitch black. I shuddered at the sight of his thin, determined lips, at the fury in the gaze aimed at Jules.

"What's going on?" I whimpered, clutching Alek even tighter.

"Stay behind me, solnyshka," Alek growled. "I'll keep you safe from this fucking bastard."

"Annie, get the fuck over here." I peeked out from behind Alek's back to find Jules standing in a similar expression, his eyes promising wrath if I didn't follow the quiet order. Wrath not for me, but for Alek.

Oh my God. They're going to kill each other.

Alek didn't take his eyes off Jules, though I felt his attention flicker to me. "Annie?"

"It's a childhood nickname," I explained. "Only my family calls me that. I don't really know why. I guess because Ev-*an*-geline."

His jaw tightened. "Let me guess: *you're* Annie Vallen?"

I frowned. "I mean, kind of? That was what I was trying to tell you. My name used to be Evangeline Vallen, but my parents changed it when I was four."

"Seventeen damn years ago," he hissed. Alek narrowed his eyes at Jules and clicked his gun. I didn't know a whole lot about weapons, but I knew that wasn't a good sign. "Julian Vallen. Such a *pleasure* meeting you in the flesh."

Jules did the same thing with his gun, and my breath quickened. "Aleksandr Drakov. I wish I could say the same, but you're holding my baby sister hostage. If you harm one hair on her head, you and your entire fucking family will burn."

"I would *never* hurt, Evangeline, you bloody—"

"*Wait*," I said, my head spinning as I tried to put together all the puzzle pieces floating around me. But they all felt out of reach. My heart quickened from the stress, and my vision temporarily blurred. I could feel the voice in the back of my head growing louder, meaner, hungrier for my pain.

"*You did this. You caused this. You ruin everything. You're not perfect.*"

Then, it started to play the most horrible visions I'd ever had. Sometimes, my mind latched onto terrible things—me accidentally stabbing myself, me setting buildings on fire, me running over someone in a car. But never had my mind tortured me like this.

Alek shooting Jules.

Jules shooting Alek.

Blood.

So.

Much.

Blood.

Staining the walls. My hands. My soul. Blood everywhere until I was surrounded by the taste and feel of death.

I blinked a few times, shoving it all into the overflowing box inside of me, and turned my attention back to the present, hoping that the anxiety of this all would be enough to keep me from breaking down.

My eyes swung back and forth between Jules and Alek. "You two know each other?"

"No," Jules said at the same time Alek said, "Yes."

I had deja vu of another night, a much happier night with Alek, Mia, and Nikolai. Oh, how I wished to go back there, to a time when I was naive enough to think everything would go well. "Well, which is it?"

"Would you like to tell her, or shall I?" Alek said with a cold, cruel smirk. I hardly recognized the man I was falling in love with in it, could hardly see the tenderness I knew lurked beneath. But despite his icy gaze, Alek's body was gentle where he gripped me. Whatever anger he had wasn't aimed toward me.

"No," Jules hissed.

"Tell me what?"

The two said nothing.

"Alek. *Please.* Tell me what?"

His body softened a fraction of an inch, and it was enough to give me hope that my Alek was still there, that he hadn't lost himself to whatever darkness had claimed him. "Your brother is the leader of one of the most powerful mob families in the city."

I staggered back, my heart jumping to my throat. I swallowed. "W-what?"

"And the boy you're hiding behind," Jules began, "is the heir to the other."

For a moment, the room spun. I hadn't realized I collapsed to the floor until both Alek and Jules were hovering over me, apparently having forgotten their feud for a moment.

Trust me, Evangeline. This guy is bad news. I need you home, safe. Our families have too much bad blood for you to get in the crossfire.

The Drakovs.

They were the other family. The rivals. The empire.

"Breathe, baby," Alek whispered, pulling me to his chest and stroking my hair. "I've got you. You're safe."

I hadn't even realized I was hyperventilating until the moment when my breath calmed.

A mob. I was a *mafia princess,* and I'd had no idea because my family had kept me so far away from it all. Was this why they changed my name? Sent me away to school and lessons? Refused to acknowledge me as their daughter? Was it their twisted way of trying to keep me safe from this violent world? A world where men like Alek would have attacked me?

No. Alek and I hadn't been together for long, but I knew he wouldn't do that. Alek would do anything to keep me safe.

I was sure of it.

"Don't fucking touch her," Jules said, trying to grab my arm.

But I held onto Alek, part of me convinced that if I let go, Jules would kill him. I had always thought Jules might murder the first guy I brought home, but that was a joke. I never dreamed it would be *real*, that my big brother was the type of person to attack people so viciously without a second thought.

I was twelve when my sister died in my arms. Liza was eight. It was a car accident, but a purposeful one. I don't think she was supposed to be the casualty. I think I was.

A broken sob slipped past my lips. I looked first at Alek, then at Jules. "The car accident your sister died in," I whispered. "That was seventeen years ago."

I watched as Alek shuttered away his emotions, stifled his grief and pain, shoving both in a box just like I did with mine. "I know, solnyshka. The thought has crossed my mind already."

"I was in the other car." My lower lip trembled. "It was my fault. I killed your sister."

Alek cupped my cheek. And though I could tell the next

words pained him to say, he murmured, "It's not your fault, Evangeline. You were a child."

"So was Liza."

"I don't blame you." Alek swallowed. "Truly. I don't. It... It is hard to think about. But my sister would have forgiven you in an instant. I know she would have, so I do too. And I wouldn't change anything that happened. Because my life, though filled with darkness, has led me to you and your light."

I opened my mouth to say something, but was interrupted by a scoffing sound. It was Jules. "You can't tell me you believe this shit, Annie."

"W-What?"

Jules stood, aiming his gun at Alek once more. Alek followed suit, this time holding me to his body, his heart steady from where I pressed into his side. Maybe I should have been more worried about the two weapons, but all I could think about was Alek. I needed to hold him, to touch him, and remind myself of his words.

I wouldn't change anything that happened. Because my life, though filled with darkness, has led me to you and your light.

I was his light in the darkness. And, in a way, he was mine, too.

"I consider myself to be a reasonable man. Maybe not a *likable* man, but a reasonable one. And since I promised my sister I'd behave, I will let you walk out of here uninjured. As long as you vow to never come back."

"Jules!" I gasped.

"No," Alek said. "I'm not leaving Eva."

"You will leave here one way or another." Jules clicked his gun again. "Dead or alive, Reaper. Your choice."

"No!" I cried out, holding Alek tighter, burying myself in his familiar scent, in the feeling of his suit jacket against my silent tears. "Jules, you can't do this. I... I love him."

Alek stiffened for a moment before his hand found my

waist and squeezed once. It wasn't exactly a declaration of love back, but I didn't want one right now. All I wanted was for Alek to be okay, for us to be together like a normal couple.

I was beginning to think normal wasn't possible as far as Aleksandr Drakov was concerned.

Jules scoffed. "Do you truly believe he loves you back? Are you that gullible, Annie?"

I flinched, and Jules noticed it immediately, guilt flooding his face. But the first one to react was Alek, who grabbed my waist and tucked me into him before firing his gun. I screamed as a bullet shattered a vase right next to Jules.

"If you fucking talk to her like that any more," Alek said darkly, "I will not hesitate to shoot again. And I won't fucking miss."

"Alek, no," I said, but my reply was weak, my heart still wounded. I looked at Jules, feeling my eyes fill with tears again, blurring my vision. "You promised. You promised me you would try, Jules. You *promised*."

"Not him. You can date whoever you want, Annie, but not him."

Normally, I might have gaped at Jules. Anyone I wanted was a freedom I'd never been granted before.

But Jules didn't understand. The only one I wanted was Alek.

I shook my head. "No. I want Alek. No one else."

Alek's grip on me tightened. He bent down to kiss my forehead, but I knew his eyes were still locked on Jules. His lips curved against my temple. He was no doubt smirking victoriously at my brother. "And you shall have only me, solnyshka."

"Annie, he doesn't want you for the right reasons. I've been watching him for a long time, much longer than I've cared to. He doesn't think of storybook endings like that—doesn't care about marriage or families. Aleksandr Drakov doesn't care about anyone. Not the strippers he sticks his dick into, not his underlings, not his family, and not you. This is another one of his fucking games to get ahead, and I will not let you be a part of them."

If Jules thought that would finally make me run to him, he was sorely mistaken.

I stepped back, clutching my heart as if that would keep it from feeling like it was bleeding out onto the floor. A tear fell down my cheek, landing on my trembling lip. I tasted salt and devastation. The main ingredient in a recipe for a broken heart.

"Is that really the only reason you think someone would want me?" I asked, my voice cracking. "For revenge?"

"No, no, Annie, I—" He made to move toward me, but Alek held up his gun as a reminder.

With the hand not holding the weapon, Alek lifted my chin and placed a gentle kiss on my lips. His tongue swept across my skin, licking all the tears away. Then, he turned his head toward Jules, keeping his lips still on mine as he said, "She's mine, Vallen. You can't change that."

"Like hell, she—"

"Eva is mine," Alek said slowly, "in every fucking sense of the word."

My cheeks immediately flushed, and Jules's eyes flashed with burning rage. "You fucking asshole. You fucked my baby sister. You're *DEAD!*"

The next moment, all of my senses seemed to be moving in slow motion.

Sound: The booming echo of a bullet firing from a chamber as Jules roared, "*DRAKOV!*" with the fury of a century of darkness. A moment later, it was the sound of Alek desperately shouting, "*NO!*" just as a distant scream left my lips. Then, the clattering of chairs as everyone ran.

Touch: The feeling of Alek's body tensing, moving, shifting, pulling me with him. But I fought him, running to cover him, to protect him like he was trying to do for me. Then, pain. Endless, fiery *pain*.

Smell: The bitter, iron tang of blood. A stark contrast to the sterile smell of the wood. It permeated my nostrils, burying itself in there long after I left.

Taste: The lingering salt on my tongue before blood filled it from where I bit my tongue as my body collapsed.

And, finally, *sight:* Crimson staining my pretty dress, running down my arm, dripping onto the floor. A cruel sight. A dangerous one, a sight brought upon by a shot meant to kill. Only it wasn't Alek's blood.

It was mine.

January 12th

MIA

Good luck with the dinner, babes!!!

I can't wait to hear all about it!!!

…

Okay… it's been a few hours…. Did it go well?????

ALEKSANDR
CHAPTER TWENTY-TWO

THE SECOND-WORST DAY OF MY LIFE WAS THE DAY I held my sister as she died in my arms. One moment, she was sitting next to me, giggling about something funny she'd seen in one of the shows I refused to watch with her. Then, a car slammed into the side, and I came face-to-face with Death for the first time. I'd clutched her to my chest as blood ran down her temples and screamed, "No! You can't have her! No!"

That was when I learned the world didn't care what I wanted. There was no fate to grant me mercy, no God to listen to my prayers. So I changed. I became the thing that God would fear, the one that would *make* him listen.

And for seventeen years, my life worked well like that. I was never afraid when I walked into a warzone, never scared that I would meet Death again.

Until tonight. When the worst day of my life began.

I felt like an idiot for not realizing it sooner. Not realizing that I recognized Evangeline, not because she was the woman of my dreams, but because she was the younger sister of my greatest enemy. She'd left school a year early to join the ballet, so while I thought that Anne-something Vallen was at school, the *real* Vallen daughter, Evangeline Vale, was dancing in the

Company, blissfully unaware of the danger her family had brought her into.

They'd tried to distance themselves after Liza's death, probably worrying that the accident would bring on retaliation against their youngest. It was a fucked up form of protection, though a part of me understood that. Because I was all kinds of fucked up things for my Eva.

Maybe this all would have been easier if I hadn't understood the Vallens a little bit. If I blamed her for Liza's death. But how could I? She was a fucking child, four years old. So maybe there was no one to bring to justice for Liza. Maybe some things truly were a matter of fate's cruel timing.

Things like finding out my girlfriend shared the blood of the family I'd sworn to destroy.

Despite all the obstacles, for a moment, I thought that we would work it out. Julian hadn't shot me on the spot, and Eva was finally finding the backbone I'd been pushing her to form. I naively thought that our relationship would survive the dinner, that I wouldn't lose her.

I hadn't realized I could lose her another way.

My arrogance had gotten in the way, the beast inside of me urging me to taunt Julian, to make him hurt, to force him to realize that I wasn't fucking going anywhere. I smugly looked him in the eye and all but told him I fucked his baby sister.

And I knew, looking into his eyes, that Julian saw red. He let his fury control him, let that fire build deep within him.

But that was the thing: fire was scorching.

"You fucking asshole. You fucked my baby sister. You're *DEAD*!" Julian had yelled. And at that moment, I didn't doubt it.

Julian raised his gun. And the next few seconds had seemed so slow yet so fast at the same time. Like I was underwater, watching the fish swim past me while helplessly drowning beside them. I wasn't used to such a feeling, wasn't used to having my control wrenched from me.

I fucking hated it.

I stiffened my body and prepared for pain, trying my best to shove Evangeline out of the way. I would have died sooner than I'd risk that bullet coming anywhere near her.

But as the metal swiftly traveled through the air, I suddenly found myself being shoved out of the way. I fell onto the ground with an *oomph,* my body clanging against the sturdy dining room chairs. I cursed as my head hit against the ground, black dots bursting at the edge of my vision.

And when I looked up, there was Eva. My angel, my little sun. My everything.

Beginning to bleed.

It was so small that I barely noticed the little dot of red appearing at her shoulder. Then it grew, and her pink dress slowly turned red along her arm.

Eva raised her shaking fingers to the wound and pulled them back, her breath shuddering as she stared at the gore. She looked at me with wide, helpless eyes.

Then she collapsed.

I dove across the floor, my hands catching her before she hit the ground. The thud she made would haunt me for the rest of my life. I was certain I'd have nightmares about it, about the little whimper she made when her eyes turned to her wound.

"Alek," she cried, her frail body curling into me. Tears streamed like twin waterfalls down her cheeks, and I felt my heart breaking more and more with each one.

"I'm here, baby." I grabbed her head and placed it in my lap, stroking her soft curls and examining the wound. Thankfully, the wound was a shallow one. As long as she went to the hospital soon, she would be fine.

But that didn't mean the sight of blood on her delicate body didn't rip me to shreds.

If I had any questions on whether Evangeline was a part of a ploy from Julian to attack me, they were answered now. She took a bullet that surely would have hit me in the heart, saving my life, not caring if that meant losing hers.

Why? I wondered as I wiped away her tears. *Why did you push me out of the way? Why did you get yourself hurt over me? Why?*

"Alek, it hurts," she whimpered.

"I know, baby. I'm going to take you to the hospital, and they're going to make it better. Okay?"

She nodded her head, though the movement seemed to cost her greatly. "Okay."

"I'll be with you the whole time."

"No, you fucking won't be," Julian—who I honestly had forgotten was there—growled.

With a snap of his fingers, I was yanked backward by two men who were closer in size to a tank than to a normal human being. They held my arms behind my back and began to tie me up with a rope that rubbed my skin raw. I fought with everything I fought them with everything I had—elbows, shoulders, teeth—but I was off balance, dizzy, and too far from her.

Way too fucking far.

"Don't hurt him," Eva cried weakly, her voice barely more than a breath. She pushed herself onto her good arm, her face pale, her lips tinged blue. Blood still welled from her shoulder, soaking through the fabric no matter how hard she pressed her fingers against it. Soon, she fell back to the ground, her body not used to the pain of our world.

Julian went to her side and picked her up, cradling her to his body. That should have been me. How *dare* he try to keep me from her? She was bleeding. *She needed me.*

His face was cold when he looked at me, but it softened

with guilt whenever his eyes darted to Eva. His eyes said so many emotions he wouldn't dare show in front of me. The realization of what he had done. The horror as her face continued to pale. The soul-crushing shame.

"Jules... please—" Eva began.

"He'll be fine, Evangeline." He looked down at her and kissed her forehead. "Let's get you to the hospital."

"I'm coming with you," I said, straining against the men holding me until the cords burned my skin raw.

"No, you're not. You'll never see her again." He looked down at Eva and said with a hard voice, "This ends tonight."

"No," Eva whispered, arms straining to reach me. "No, Jules, you can't. This is my fault. I stepped in front of him. Please let him come, I—"

"I said *no*, Evangeline."

"But... But I love him." Her voice broke, and something in my chest broke with it.

The men tried to drag me back, but I fought with everything I had. The beast of darkness roared inside of me. They could not keep the Reaper contained for long. "Eva! Eva, look at me!"

Her eyes found mine instantly. Even like this—hurt, shaking, terrified—she still listened to me. Still trusted me. *Good girl.*

"You're mine. Do you remember what I told you in your bathroom?"

You are mine. Nothing can keep you from me.

Eva nodded, and I forced the next words past the invisible iron fist wrapped around my throat. The one made entirely of fear. "I meant it," I said.

"Okay," she whispered, smiling like she didn't believe a single word. That fake fucking smile of hers.

"Eva, I—"

"Get rid of him," Jules snarled. One of the men slammed a

fist into my ribs, knocking the air from my lungs. The familiar taste of blood came flooding into my mouth. I coughed some onto the precious Vallen dining room table.

"Alek," Eva sobbed. "*Alek.*"

She weakly reached for me, and I tried one more time to get to her. I yanked against the ropes again, skin tearing this time. I didn't care. I would have ripped my own arms off if it meant getting to her.

"I will fucking find you, Eva," I vowed darkly. "That's not a promise. That's a *threat*."

Because, as they dragged me away from her—away from the blood, away from her broken little sobs, away from the life I had almost believed I could keep—I knew one thing with clarity:

This was no longer a generational war between families.

This was a war over Evangeline.

And I would burn this world before I let it take her from me.

January 12th

ALEKSANDR

Prepare for war on Julian Vallen.

I want him gone. Dead or alive. Whatever gets him away from Evangeline.

NIKOLAI

So...

I take it the dinner went well.

Why are we going to war again, boss?

ALEKSANDR

Because he's trying to keep me from her.

And he will pay.

EVANGELINE
CHAPTER TWENTY-THREE

The drive back from the hospital was completely silent. It wasn't the peaceful kind of quiet. It was the kind that pressed in on my ears until I could hear my heartbeat, sharp and uneven, echoing through my skull. The kind that felt like a punishment.

Jules drove back to his house with both hands on the steering wheel, his knuckles white, and his jaw locked so tight I thought his teeth might crack.

He hadn't said a word since we left the hospital. Not when the nurse helped me into the backseat. Not when I hissed softly as the movement pulled at my shoulder. Not even when I whispered his name, testing the air between us like I used to when we were children, and I'd broken something important.

But his eyes said everything. He was disappointed with me. And there was nothing I could do to make this situation better.

I sat rigidly upright, my back pressed against the cold leather. I felt like a prisoner in the backseat. Jules's eyes occasionally glanced back in the mirror as if he expected me to jump out of the moving car. Maybe if my arm wasn't hurting so much, I would have.

The doctor said the pain would follow me for weeks. A deep bruise had already started to form where the wound was stitched together, and I'd been given medication to last me through the worst of it. Thick, white bandages were placed over the hole where the bullet had gone cleanly through my body, though they were already starting to bloom a faint shade of pink from all of my movement.

The doctor had said I was lucky. That my surgery to repair the minor tissue was simple, and that I would be able to return to normal life in a few weeks once I was discharged in the morning. But he didn't know that there *was* no normal life for me. Not anymore.

I'd cracked my world open and shattered all the pieces. So despite my doctor's words, I'd spent the past night in the hospital feeling very, very unlucky.

My injured arm was strapped tight against my body in a sling that felt more like a shackle than medical equipment. Every bump in the road sent a sharp, white-hot reminder through my shoulder, the pain blooming and curling down my arm like fire. But I didn't react, because everything hurt me.

It hurt to breathe. To think. To live. Without Alek there to comfort me, my life was filled with pain.

I stared at my lap, at the hand that had held his only a day ago. My dress had been changed at the hospital, the other one cut away with surgical precision. One of Julian's guards—a freaking *guard*—had brought me a new outfit. The pink was gone, replaced with gray sweatpants and an oversized hoodie that smelled faintly of antiseptic and plastic packaging. The sweatshirt, of course, was black.

It seemed fitting. No more pink, no more ribbons, nothing. Because I knew my life was about to not be mine anymore.

I swallowed hard through the realization.

Alek's face kept flashing whenever I closed my eyes. The sound of his voice as he vowed to find me echoed in my ears. I couldn't get over the way his hands had shaken as he held me, like he was afraid I'd disappear if he loosened his grip even a fraction. Like I was already halfway gone. Like maybe, just maybe, he loved me too.

My heart ached worse than my shoulder.

This is it, I thought numbly as the city passed me by. *This is the end.*

The end of sweet kisses and burning tension. The end of whispered promises about a future that wasn't to come. The end of feeling like I was finally somebody worth knowing, somebody worth fighting for.

Because I knew that Alek would want nothing to do with me after this. Why would he? I was a total mess. I was his enemy's sister, the girl responsible for the wreck that killed his sister. I was not worth all of this trouble, all of this heartache and pain. I was—

"*Not perfect,*" a voice in me whispered.

Julian cleared his throat, and the sound made me flinch, jostling my arm. He looked back at me, eyes hard. "I've already taken your phone. You will not receive it back until I am certain you will not try to contact him."

"Jules—"

"No."

The word landed like a slammed door. Maybe even a coffin lid. There would truly be no more messages from Alek, no more smiling at my screen as he listed all the ways he thought I was beautiful.

My whole life. Gone.

"You're not leaving the house," Jules said flatly. "For two weeks, you will remain in your room, resting your shoulder. If I think you are good enough to return to rehearsals, you may go and watch, but I will be aware of all rehearsal start times, and I expect you back at the car no less than a minute after they end."

My stomach dropped. He was treating me like a child. And worse, he was laying down all these rules while refusing to look at me. "Jules," I whispered brokenly.

"You will not see anyone without my express permission. Mia will not be coming over until I'm certain she had nothing to do with this—which, knowing your nosy friend, she did. And you sure as hell won't see him ever again."

"But—"

"No," he snapped. I bit down on the inside of my cheek until my mouth filled with blood, a dull echo of what had happened last night.

Jules smoothed back his hair and took a deep breath. "He's dangerous, Evangeline. You're lucky you're alive. He could have used you to get an advantage over me. He could have killed you for vengeance. Do you really want to be with someone who would use you like that?"

But I said nothing. My heart had run out of words.

I stared out the window at the blur of streetlights passing by, my reflection ghosted over the glass. I looked smaller like this. My body had folded in on itself, and my soul had disappeared from my eyes. I looked like a shell of the old Evangeline, the stupid girl who believed Romeo and Juliet might one day find a way to be together. The girl who believed in fairytale endings and charming princes falling in love with the wrong girl.

I should have known. My life was too far from those books to ever be true.

"Evangeline, answer me."

I said nothing.

"Evangeline. Please. I only want what's best for you. I'm not trying to be an asshole."

I said nothing.

"Annie. It will be all right. He is just a boy. There will be others."

I said nothing. Alek was not just a boy. He would always be so much more.

Jules looked through the mirror, and for the first time, his disappointment and anger left his brown eyes. There was only worry in its place, his heart slowly winning out over the fire of his emotions. But mine had become hollow, leaving behind a black hole where the sun once was.

"Annie," Jules whispered one more time. "I'm sorry."

I said nothing.

The house came into view too quickly—the looming brick, the iron gates already opening like a mouth ready to swallow me whole. I felt something inside my chest cave in as we pulled into the driveway.

Home.

I'd never felt further from it in my life.

As Julian parked, he finally turned around to look at me. Really look at me. His eyes flicked to the sling, the bandages, the faint tremor in my hands. Something dark crossed his face. Guilt, maybe. Or anger, redirected inward.

"This is for your own good," he said.

And again, I said nothing.

I followed him inside to my bedroom, which felt like a prison cell. My brother tried to tuck me under the pink comforter, but I shrugged off his arm and tossed the blanket on the floor, curling into a ball on top of the sheet. I didn't want warmth that wasn't from Alek. I didn't want anything but sleep.

I was tired. I was so, so tired of this. Of being the helpless baby sister. Of being the girl with the broken mind. Of not being strong enough to fight for my love with Alek.

That thought made my eyes sting with another onslaught

of tears, my heart splintering even more—knowing that if I was good enough, maybe we could have been together.

And that hurt me worse than the bullet ever could.

January 14th

MIA

Soooo, you weren't at rehearsal today??? Is everything okay? Are you sick???

January 15th

MIA

Eva!!!! Again?? You must be dying, you NEVER miss rehearsal. What's going on???

January 17th

MISSED CALL FROM MIA
MIA

Girl, it's noon. There's no way you're still too tired to answer. Call me back!! I want details on your dinner with Jules!!

January 19th

MIA

Okay… why aren't you answering? Are you mad at me?

January 21st

MISSED CALL FROM MIA
MISSED CALL FROM MIA

MIA

Eva, oh my god, are you missing??

MISSED CALL FROM MIA

Text me if you need help!! I'm getting worried here...

January 23rd

MIA

Just talked to Elsie... she said you're not coming for a while???

MISSED CALL FROM MIA

UH... WHAT?!?!?! Call me ASAP

EVANGELINE
CHAPTER TWENTY-FOUR

Water splashed in the bathtub as Elsie poured a cup down my back, rinsing the frothy shampoo. My arms hung limply by my side, my skin a mixture of purple and blue from the bruise that spread like a sunbeam through my shoulder.

But I felt nothing.

Elsie hummed to herself as she continued to rinse me, squeezing a dollop of conditioner and smoothing it onto the ends of my hair. She'd been staying with us for almost two weeks. Jules had called her in to help me because he knew I would be uncomfortable with him helping me bathe—both from the "being naked in front of your brother" aspect and because every time he saw my wound, he would cry and apologize profusely until I walked away. And at first, I couldn't get my stitches wet so I couldn't do it myself. Now, my arm was so sore I couldn't lift it very much, so Elsie remained like a doting sister.

Jules probably knew that if I wasn't forced to get out of bed by her, I probably wouldn't have.

He'd gotten frustrated when I continued not speaking to him, so Elsie was his form of reinforcement. She was the one who came into my dark room and forced me to eat. She was the one who helped me get dressed and bathed, the one who brushed my hair as she reassured me that Madame Germaine hadn't given away my role despite how unconvinced I was that it was true.

"You should have been Juliet," I whispered, my voice raw from almost two weeks without use.

"I'm glad I wasn't," Elsie lilted. A strawberry blonde curl twisted down her face, and she blew it away with a huff. "I think it's about time to hang up my ballet shoes."

I leaned against the side of the tub and raised my eyebrows in an expression that said, *Really?*

She nodded. "I think I've been ready to say goodbye to it for a while. I've already told Madame Germaine that this is my last show. So I'm glad you're Juliet. I get to see that the Company is being left in very capable hands."

I cleared my throat, trying to push down the shock I felt. The Company had been Elsie's entire life for eleven years. She was seventeen when she auditioned and was accepted, working her way up the ranks within a few years. Elsie had been the company's principal for almost eight years now, having been cast when she was only twenty.

But while she was still so young, even in ballet years, I couldn't help but notice the way she sometimes limped on her ankle, rubbing it whenever she thought no one was looking. Maybe her injury pained her more than she wanted to admit. Maybe Elsie needed to find something that didn't make her suffer.

"What are you going to do?" I asked, and for the first time since our conversation had started, Elsie smiled. It was a soft look, a sweet one.

Elsie Farrow was the perfect girl next door. No wonder my brother loved her—though, as far as I knew, he still had yet to admit it. But anyone with eyes could see that those two were soulmates. Elsie was the only person capable of turning my brother into a tender man. Even I wasn't enough to soften some of his stubbornness.

"I wish I could move out of the city. I'm not sure yet, though," Elsie said, pulling the plug on the bath and grabbing my towel.

I might have been embarrassed at having Elsie see me so naked and vulnerable, but she'd been the closest thing I'd ever had to a sister since she came into my life when I was six, a thirteen-year-old girl who scowled at my brother for his inability to work on their group project together. In a few weeks, something had changed between them, and they became friends as they got older, which meant Elsie kept coming over, and Jules kept hoping she would come back.

"Where?"

"I think if I had the courage, I'd give small-town life a try." She shrugged. "Get away from everything here. Maybe open a bakery."

My eyebrows raised, though I said nothing. Elsie was a terrible cook—and I knew that because for the past couple of weeks, she'd been making things to try and cheer me up. I shuddered at the memory of the crumbling cookie she'd fed me. They were probably one of the worst things I'd ever eaten.

"Do me a favor?" Elsie asked, and I nodded. "Please don't tell your brother. I'm waiting for the right moment, and right now, he's under so much stress because..."

She trailed off, but I knew what she was going to say.

Because of you. He's under so much stress because of you.

My shoulders slouched, and my throat dried up. There was nothing more I wanted to say, so I nodded again at Elsie and let her help me dry off with the fluffy pink towel Jules had bought me. It was as if he thought that flooding the house with pink would somehow make me change my mind about wanting to escape. There were random pillows on the leather couches, blankets everywhere, pictures of him and me strewn across the mantel.

But while a part of me appreciated the effort he was going to in order to make the home more comfortable for me, a larger part of me thought that he couldn't just slap a pink Band-Aid on a broken heart to fix it.

Because my heart *was* broken. Without Alek there to fix it, I worried it always would be.

Elsie helped me get dressed in a pair of soft, pink pajamas, brushing my hair for me before kissing me on the side of the head and tucking me into bed like an overcautious older sister. She was just like Jules in that way, treating me like a porcelain doll they were convinced would break at every misplaced breath. Too fragile to even move.

I sat on the edge of the guest bed—my bed, technically, though it didn't quite feel like mine—and folded my socks into a perfect rectangle for the third time that morning. They were already folded, but my hands kept moving anyway, smoothing edges, aligning seams, trying to make something in my life behave.

"*Not perfect,*" the voice in the back of my head hissed. I wasn't sure if it was talking about my clothes or me.

The silence pressed in around me, broken only by the tick of a grandfather clock down the hall. I had nothing to keep me entertained, nothing but redoing my laundry over and over again, hoping it would make the voice go away. Jules gave me a television remote, but I couldn't bring myself to turn it on. And any books I read just spun around in my head, the words jumbling together until they formed only one word:

Alek.

He was there in everything, everything. Every thought, every moment, every quiet moment.

All of it.

Alek.

I wished I could have called him. I wished I could hear his smooth voice crawling down my spine, reassuring me that everything would be all right. But Jules had yet to give me my phone back, so all I had was this unbearable quiet and an emptiness where my love had once gone.

It can't be all bad, I tried to tell myself. *Think of the positives.*

But the only positive I could come up with was that I was *positively* sure Alek was gone, and that he wasn't coming back. That he probably thought I wasn't worth all of this trouble, not when I'd done nothing to fight for him like he had for me. He might have promised to find me, but promises were easily broken under the wrong circumstances, and everything about this was wrong indeed.

I needed to accept it. Maybe we weren't meant to be. Love was fragile, and fragile things always broke.

A soft knock rapped gently at the door. "Eva? Can I come in?"

I don't know why you ask. You'll do whatever you want anyway, I thought, though I said nothing.

Jules stepped inside, tall and broad, dressed casually but still somehow intimidating. My brother didn't know how to take up less space. It was something he and Alek had in common.

I curled up on the bed, turning away as soon as he took a step toward me. And maybe I was being unjust toward him. After all, he was my older brother, in charge of protecting me ever since we were kids. But Jules was convinced the world was too dangerous a place for me for whatever reason, and he was also convinced the only way to fix that was to hide me away from it.

But I didn't *want* to be hidden. Not from the world, not from my friends, and not from love.

Not from Alek.

Why could he not put aside his stupid grudge? Why did I have to bear all the injuries from all the Drakov and Vallen emotional wounds?

Why couldn't life be a fairytale?

"Cook is making your favorite for lunch. And Elsie is going to try to make you some brownies—box mix, so I'm not sure she can mess those up. But I wouldn't bet on them tasting good anyway."

I'm not hungry, I thought.

His jaw tightened, though his eyes remained soft. "You can't stay like this, Annie. You've been here for days, and you've barely smiled. You haven't said a word to me. You don't seem to care about anything. I've apologized so many times. I wish I could take it back. I wish you were never near those weapons. But I'm not sorry for keeping you away from him. Clearly, when he's around, you get hurt. And seeing you get hurt *kills me.*"

Some of my resolve to stay angry at him cracked. I was disappointed in his decision to keep me from my normal life, from rehearsals, from *Alek*. But I knew his heart was in the right place. He was worried about my recovery, and I knew he was worried that Alek would use me to hurt him. I just wished I could prove to him that what Alek and I had was genuine, that Alek truly had no idea I was the sister of his enemy.

But maybe what Alek and I had wasn't real. Because the man I knew would have let nothing stop him from getting to me, and all I'd known for the past two weeks was silence and a sense of hope that died more with each passing day.

Jules studied me for a long moment, his expression softening. "You know I'm not trying to cage you, right?"

My throat burned when I swallowed, and still, I said nothing.

Jules sighed. "I'll leave you alone, Evangeline. But I'm here for you, okay? This will all work out. Soon, you won't even remember his name."

I highly doubted that.

He slipped out of the room with a promise to come back in a second, probably to force me to eat whatever Cook had made.

After his footsteps faded in the hall, I lay back on the bed and stared at the ceiling again, counting the additional strings of lights he'd added. Then, I counted my breath. Then, the seconds that passed. Until, finally, I began to count all the ways it felt like everything was slipping through my fingers.

Alek's face rose unbidden in my mind. His lips slightly swollen from our kisses, his eyes dark as he drank me in. His voice as he groaned my name, his fingers digging into my thigh, his body making me feel things no one ever had. The last image that settled in my mind was the way he looked at me —like I was something precious. Something worth keeping.

Maybe it was over between us. Maybe this was my life now —safe, contained, perfectly arranged, and quietly breaking apart.

I turned onto my side and hugged a pillow to my chest, the weight of the house settling around me until I fell into a restless sleep and dreamed of him.

January 26th

MISSED CALL FROM MIA
MIA

> That's it. I'm coming over.

> I don't know WHY you're not answering me, but you can't ignore me forever. We're besties, bitch.

> Jules just called me, and I'm coming over. Be there soon!! xx

EVANGELINE
CHAPTER TWENTY-FIVE

A FEW HOURS LATER, MIA SHOWED UP LIKE A glitter bomb with heels. Her golden blonde hair was straightened, looking as cutting as her narrowed eyes, which took in the room like she was examining a prison cell.

In a way, she kind of was.

I'd cracked my eyes open mid-nap to the sound of a voice shouting down the hall, "Evangeline Vale, if I don't see you in the next ten seconds, I'm committing a felony."

I swore, for a second, my heart actually stuttered.

I jumped out of bed, rushing to my bedroom door as Mia swung it open, wearing oversized sunglasses, fierce black knee-high boots, and a sequin mini skirt that hinted at her slight party-girl nature. Her hip was cocked, and she aimed a glare back at Jules, who stood sullenly behind her, lips twisted like he'd tasted something sour. In less than a minute, my best friend managed to look like she owned the place.

"Mia?" I breathed, part of me unconvinced that I hadn't dreamed her here. It'd been over two weeks since we'd called, texted, or seen each other, which was forever in girl years.

Mia looked up, grinning like she'd found buried treasure,

and ripped her sunglasses off. "There she is. God, you look like a Victorian ghost. Is there no self-tanner in this castle?"

I laughed for the first time in days, the sound bursting out of me before I could stop it. Jules, who still hadn't taken that aggrieved look off his face, softened a little, his eyes darting to me. "You're okay with company?"

"Of course she is," Mia scoffed. "I'm her *best friend*."

I smiled softly and nodded. Jules let out a relieved breath, eyes flicking between us, clearly running through worst-case scenarios at lightning speed. "Stay on the property. I'll be around if you need anything. And please, Renford, don't break anything."

Mia saluted. "Yes, Daddy Warbucks."

The moment Jules disappeared down the hall, she grabbed my wrists and dragged me across the room. "Okay, you are not spending another second moping in this mausoleum."

"I wasn't moping," I protested weakly.

"You're surrounded by knick-knacks dustier than my great-grandma's ashes, and you're not watching any reality TV," she shot back. "You're definitely moping, and that stops now."

"I *really* can't leave the property, Mia. I don't want to make him angrier."

"I know. We won't leave, but we're going to make this place a hell of a lot less depressing."

Mia turned my room into chaos in under three minutes. She threw the wispy pink curtains open and began to blast pop music from her phone. My neatly folded clothes were dumped onto the floor, and all my blankets were shoved into their place on the bed. She turned on the twinkling lights and shoved me onto the bed before getting onto her phone and furiously typing on it.

"We're doing a girl's day," she declared. "That means face

masks, bad movies, sugar, and gossip. You look like you haven't eaten or made a bad decision in days."

"That's because I haven't."

She paused, bright eyes flying up from her screen, studying me more carefully now. "Okay. The decision thing, I get, because you don't have a bad bone in your body. But the eating thing?"

I bit my lip and nodded. "I mean, I've eaten *some*."

Like once a day. My body just didn't want any more. It didn't want *anything* but Alek. Not even food.

"So something's wrong-wrong."

I swallowed and didn't answer.

Mia waited a few minutes, making sure it was completely silent in the hall and that Jules wasn't lurking in some dark corner, before leaning in, her voice dropping to a whisper. "Is this about him? Is it about Ale—"

"*Shhh.*" I slammed a hand over her mouth, my stomach flipping at the thought of him. "You can't say his name, Mia. Jules will go ballistic if you even mention him."

Her eyebrows shot up. "Oh my God. It *is* about him. I knew something was wrong when President Buzzkill called me and asked me to come over."

I sank onto the bed with a sigh, grabbing a fluffy pink pillow and slamming it over my face to keep from crying anymore. "It's bad, Mia."

"What happened? I thought you guys were doing great."

"We *were*."

I told her everything. Well, not everything—there were some details that should remain between me, Alek, and the things he made me feel in the shadows—but enough. I told her about all the flowers, the dates, and the protectiveness. I told her about Alek calming me down after my mental illness threw me into a spiral and how he took me home. And I was pretty sure that by the raised eyebrow she was giving me, she knew enough about what happened there.

But then I told her about the dinner, the feud I had no idea about, the grief Alek had been carrying for seventeen years. I told her about the guns and the bullet and the pain. Then, I told her about how Jules forced Alek away and locked me inside his home to force me to recover and get over my love for him.

My voice cracked when I told her about the two weeks of silence that felt like a slow suffocation, being buried alive as I watched more and more dirt shoveled onto me.

Mia listened without interrupting, ripping open two jelly face masks and applying them to both of our faces, her expression focused like this was one of Madame Germaine's debriefs.

"It's over, Mia," I sniffled, tears welling, and my nose clogged with gross snot that I wiped away with the tissue she handed me. "He's gone."

"He's not gone. That boy is obsessed with you. You are that man's personal drug, and he is addicted with a capital A. I saw the way he looked at you at the club. He's tweaking without you. I'm guessing he's doing everything in his power to get you back."

"But—"

"No buts, Eva. Trust me: I know men. And this one is starving without you. He's probably planning on how to steal you from your room and take you to his sex cave where he'll fuck you through all the positions in the Kama Sutra!"

Heat crept up my neck. "Mia."

"I'm serious. And second—" She glanced toward the door, then leaned in again. "Your brother taking your phone? Keeping you in this house? That's a problem."

I sighed. "I know. But he thinks he's protecting me."

"Yeah. From *joy*."

"And anyway, it never hurts to reduce my screen time," I said, ignoring her frown, my hands fiddling with the edge of the blanket. "I know Jules's methods are unconventional—"

"They're *barbaric*."

"—but he's my brother, and you know I can't stay mad at him. Maybe one day, things will go back to normal."

My normal before Alek.

The thought made me feel small.

Mia shook her head. "Don't worry. I already chewed him out for potentially ruining your dreams. That's what he gets for waiting weeks to call me and tell me you're sitting in this pit of sadness. He said you can go back to rehearsals on Monday."

Everything inside of me shot to attention, my heart picking up speed and my eyes widening. "He did?"

"Yup. I don't know how much you'll be able to dance without your arm, but he said you can at least come and watch. Madame Germaine has been letting the understudy train, but I think she still wants you if you're able to come back soon. So the good news is there's at least that. All you've gotta do is rest that arm up, and you'll be on the stage before you know it!"

"Yeah," I sighed, testing my arm. I could lift it a little—about shoulder height—but that wasn't enough to dance. My stitches had been removed a few days ago, so there was no worry there, but the tenderness of the area was my biggest concern.

Still, I could do it. Ballet was pain, after all.

I'd lived my life in a love-hate relationship with ballet. Many nights, my toes bled until I couldn't walk, and my feet were covered by calluses. Leaps and turns had the potential to ache me for days... yet I loved it. I would kill myself over and over for the dance. I would shove the knife in my own heart if it meant standing on the stage.

I was pretty sure most ballerinas felt like that.

Mia and I spent the rest of the day sprawled across the bed, whispering like teenagers to each other. She repainted my nails a soft ballet pink and fed me lots of candy and diet sodas she had delivered to the entrance, much to Jules's chagrin. We watched a terrible rom-com with the volume high, laughing so loud my brother came in four times to ask us to stop "cackling like witches." And when we finally heard his footsteps disappear down the hall, Mia would turn to me and ask me for more details about Alek. Like a lovestruck teenager, I happily handed them over, both of us squealing with every remembrance.

Maybe I shouldn't have been focusing on him, but to be honest, I was so happy to feel normal again that I let myself bask in the moment.

"What's the name he calls you? Sol-what?" she murmured.

"Solnyshka. It means little sun."

"Oh, like what the card had!" At my nod, she sighed dreamily. "That's so romantic. I hate him."

"You *hate* him?"

"Duh. I know he's going to end up stealing you away and whisking you off into the sunset with sex so mind-blowing that you completely forget about me."

I coughed on my drink. "I- I-... um... I mean..."

She laughed and wrapped her arms around me, squeezing me so tight that I could barely breathe. "I would say I'm kidding, but I'm not. That man is hot as hell."

"What does that have to do with anything?"

"You're so innocent. It's adorable." Mia pinched my cheeks. "It means he's going to break you on his dick. Split you apart like a pomegranate and feast on your forbidden fruit. But from the way you're blushing, I'd say he has already."

"Oh my *God*."

"I know. I want to hear every single detail."

"*No way.*" I giggled.

I took the pillow I was hugging and lightly hit her with it, making both of us erupt into a fit of giggles that were so strong, my stomach began to burn, and my cheeks ached from smiling. For the first time since the dreaded night, the house felt less heavy. Less like a cage and more like a temporary pause in my life.

"I love you, Mia," I said, curling into her chest.

"Aw, I love you too, Evie!"

"Can I be honest?" I bit my lip, and Mia nodded. "I really don't like that nickname."

She gaped, her hand flying to grip mine. "Eva, I had no idea! Why didn't you tell me? I would have stopped a long time ago."

"I don't know. It didn't feel important enough to say. You liked calling me that, and for a long time, I was fine if it made you happy, but lately... I don't know. Lately, I've been remembering how Alek has been trying to get me to stand up for what I want. I figured I'd start small."

His words from before bounced around my head, echoes of a life long since gone.

It's okay to ask for what you want, Evangeline. Demand it, even.

There's nothing wrong with being kind. But you don't have to sacrifice yourself for everyone. Anyone who deserves you won't ask that of you.

I am not frightened away. I am not leaving. I never will, Eva. You are mine. Nothing can keep you from me. Not even you.

A tear slipped down my cheek, but I wiped it away before Mia could notice.

She wrapped her arm around my shoulders and tugged me close. "I'm proud of you. And I'll stop calling you Evie *if you* promise to always tell me when you don't like something. We're besties. You can tell me anything."

I hugged her back, nodding into the embrace. "Okay. If only I could do that with Jules. But I can't... I don't know. I just can't."

Mia stroked my hair and sighed. "If only."

January 26th

ALEKSANDR

He will not be able to keep you from me for much longer, Evangeline.

I will come to you. And you will be mine.

For good.

ALEKSANDR
CHAPTER TWENTY-SIX

Murder. That was the only thing running through my mind—cold, hard murder. Killing the man who took everything from me, who thought he could cross the Reaper and *live*.

I would bury him alive if that was what it took to get her back.

I would crown him with his own blood, watch it fall down his temples while my lips found hers again.

I would burn everything and everyone he thought he could hide behind.

I would *destroy* him.

Two weeks had passed since Eva had been taken from me. Two weeks since I was knocked out in the Vallen house and dumped in a warehouse like I was fucking garbage. Nikolai found me shortly after I woke up, storming into the building, his gun raised. But I was alone, tied up in a pile of my blood, sweat, and drool. The only thing truly wounded was my pride.

"What the hell happened?" Nikolai had asked, helping me up, his face unusually serious.

And for once, I couldn't answer him. Because I didn't know. My mind couldn't think of anything but one word:

Eva.

I would do anything to get her back. *Anything*.

Because I was fucking obsessed with Evangeline Vallen. I didn't care about what kept us apart. Her brother, my dangerous life, our families' feud, anything.

Despite all of the rules, I wanted her. And I wouldn't stop until I had her.

This was merely a temporary setback. I had lost my Queen, but a King could still win the game. I just had to think through a strategy—after I slept away some of the ringing in my ears. Now that I'd gone fourteen days without my sunlight, the darkness was taking over my mind, my thirst for blood even stronger than before. It wouldn't be satisfied until I got her back.

"*Kill,*" the monster within me hissed. "*Fucking kill.*"

"Alek!" a voice shouted through my fog. "Alek, stop! You're going to kill him!"

Good, I thought. *I will fucking murder this city if I'm away from her any longer.*

I was becoming feral, the urges inside of me growing and growing. How dare Julian Vallen think he was enough to stop *me*? How dare Evangeline jump in front of that bullet for me? How dare the world think it could keep her from me?

"Alek! Jesus Christ, dude, *stop!*"

Two arms shoved me to the ground, a knee pressing down onto my back. I snarled, turning to face the person who thought they could restrain me.

Only to come face to face with my cousins' bright eyes.

"Dude, you need to fucking calm down," Nikolai said before gesturing to the bleeding man in the corner. "You could have killed Pavel."

I blinked a few times, my monster receding from the surface, simmering deep inside of me. Looking around at the ring I was standing in, the horrified faces around the room, I finally remembered what I was doing. Nikolai had brought me to the gym where many of my men practiced their hand-to-hand combat skills. I rarely came because I rarely needed it, but my cousin thought I should blow off steam.

Hence, the unconscious man who sat in a puddle of red.

The man blinked a few times, looking at me with fear.

"Sorry, Pavel," I said gruffly, though I didn't mean it. I was only sorry because I wished it were Julian Vallen I'd almost murdered instead.

Nikolai sighed, scrubbing a hand down his face like it would help wipe the tension from his bones. I knew he felt it. We all did. Everyone was uneasy, afraid I would decide enough was enough and go on a killing spree, uncaring of whether the men I was shooting were Vallens or Drakovs.

I was still toying with the idea.

"This isn't healthy," Nikolai said quietly. "You can't keep sending every man to the hospital. We're going to run out of people, people *you need*, by the way. And anyway, you can't keep fighting like this. This fire inside of you is going to burn you alive before you even get to her."

I rolled my shoulders, blood drying on my knuckles, my pulse still roaring in my ears. My body buzzed like I'd been plugged into a live wire, every nerve screaming for release.

"I don't care," I replied flatly. "If burning myself alive gets me closer to Eva, then I shall burn."

"Aleksandr, you know what I mean." He stepped closer, lowering his voice so the others couldn't hear. "You're not yourself right now. You're not thinking anything through. This is going to get all of us killed."

I laughed, sharp and humorless. "No. This"—I gestured vaguely to the rage still clawing at my chest—"is me thinking *very* clearly. Julian took something that belongs to me. There is only one outcome for that: his head mounted in my fucking living room."

Nikolai held my gaze for a long moment before exhaling deeply. My cousin rarely argued morality with me. We'd been raised in darkness, bathed in blood for as long as we could remember. Neither of us pretended we were anything but dangerous monsters lurking in the city's shadows.

But now, there was something cautious in his expression. Not fear of me—but fear of what came next. Fear of what I would be willing to do to get to her.

"You have to be smart," he said. "I'm all for getting her back. You know that. I like Eva, and when you told me who she was, my opinion didn't change. She's a sweet girl, and she brings out something soft in you that I haven't seen since Liza died. I want to help you get her back, but we can't do this if you don't have some sort of strategy, and storming the Vallen house, guns blazing, isn't the right one. It's going to get you killed."

"I don't care if I get killed."

And I meant it. Because this half-life I was living—this miserable existence spent clutching the pillow she slept on to my face, hoping to smell her shampoo again—was nothing. I would rather have died than move on without my Eva.

"You should care. Because right now, if I know Eva like I think I do, then she's just as miserable without you, pining and waiting for her Prince Charming to rescue her. But if you die, if you let your thick skull get yourself fucking killed, then she will be forced to move on with another man. And I'm going to guess you don't want that."

No.

No.

The thought of Eva with another man, smiling, laughing, kissing, *fucking*, drove me mad. She was *mine*. She would not marry another, would not fuck another, would not even *look* at another man. I would bury myself so deep into her soul that roots would grow. Any flowers she bloomed would bear the scent of me.

The darkness inside me roared. *Find her. Take her. Find her. Take her.*

Mine.

Mine.

Mine.

I slammed my fist into the ground, my jaw clenching. "There will be no other man," I growled, my voice colder than the Arctic. "*Never.*"

My cousin crossed his arms, lifting me off the ground and leading me toward the locker room. "I agree."

"She is *mine.*"

"I know." Nikolai leaned in and smirked. "So what are you going to do about it?"

The men flinched as I passed them, the air tightening with every one of my steps. But unlike before, my mind wasn't fogged with rage. It was clearer than ever, sharper than a razor's edge.

I showered in the locker room, watching Pavel's blood swirl down the drain, overlaying it with the memory of Eva's wound.

Fuck, I didn't even know if she was okay. I didn't know *anything*. All of my messages were going undelivered, and my attempts to drive past her brother's house were always swiftly thwarted by Nikolai. He'd sliced the brakes to my car, so that was currently sitting in the shop, waiting for a distant cousin of mine to pick it up.

Before, I'd debated killing him for all of his intervention. But now, I was grateful for it. He kept me from getting myself killed before I could come up with a better plan.

After I dressed in my signature suit—my plan solidified from the time spent standing in the hot water, letting the droplets fall down my spine—I found Nikolai waiting by the exit.

"So," he said, twirling his car keys in his hand. "What's the plan, cousin?"

"I need the Company's rehearsal schedule."

He smiled before reaching into the glovebox and shoving a packet of papers into my hands. "Already got it. Now what?"

"Now," I said, gritting my jaw, "I go to the damn ballet."

January 28th

ALEKSANDR

I'm coming, Eva.

EVANGELINE
CHAPTER TWENTY-SEVEN

I COULD BREATHE A LITTLE EASIER THE NEXT morning as I leaned against the mirror on the edge of the Company's practice studio, watching the other dancers move through the Dance of the Knights. In two weeks, they'd managed to make the number almost flawless. I was so proud to be part of such a theater, to be surrounded by some of the most talented dancers the city had ever seen.

The Montagues and Capulets moved across the stage in an elegant yet imposing dance. Mia swirled her invisible skirts, and I smiled at her as she twirled around a man who looked exasperated by her already. Meanwhile, Elsie looked calm and collected as she moved in time with Tybalt, her body light where he was strong.

It was one of the many reasons I loved this ballet—the push and pull, the back and forth, never knowing when Romeo and Juliet might rush off together and sneak a dance.

Madame Germaine slowly approached me, and my body stiffened, the movement causing my shoulder to ache.

"You have returned," she intoned, looking at me up and down. Her eyes paused on the bruise clearly visible beneath my tank top.

I nodded. "Yes, ma'am."

True to Mia's word, she had talked Jules into letting me return two days after she came over, though he'd promised to call Elsie to confirm my end times so I wouldn't try to sneak off and meet Alek. Though I wished I could have seen him, I had no way of doing that. Jules still had my phone, so I couldn't contact him. And even if I could have gone to see him, there was no guarantee that he would have wanted to see me. After all, I had brought this whole mess upon all of us.

"I have had Jeanine rehearse in your place," Madame Germaine said.

"I understand, ma'am." I looked down at the floor and pressed my feet together, desperate to relieve some of the tension in my stomach.

"Not perfect... Not perfect... Not perfect..."

A pair of fingers was placed beneath my chin, and Madame Germaine raised my eyes to meet hers. Her familiar expression was cold, betraying nothing. It reminded me of when she first did that during my auditions, the first time I wondered if I could belong here.

Now, I felt like I belonged nowhere. Not at the Company. Not at home. And not with Alek.

"I made you my Juliet for a reason, Evangeline," Madame Germaine said. "You shall stay late every practice and prove to me you remember the choreography. If you do, you shall dance as Juliet when March comes."

"But my brother—"

"I have already talked to that meddling male of yours," she muttered, not bothering to hide her disapproval. "He is aware you will be later than the other dancers. You begin today, Evangeline. Do not disappoint me."

And then she was strutting away, her cane clicking against the floors while she ordered the dancers to perform the morning awakening scene.

My heart fluttered in my chest. I still had a chance. I knew Mia had said Madame Germaine still wanted me as Juliet, but hearing it from Mia and hearing it from the director herself were two entirely different things. Maybe I did belong here, maybe my life *could* be somewhat normal.

But then I thought of Alek, and how the life I truly dreamt of could never be mine. And my heart sank again.

For the rest of the rehearsal, my mind buzzed both with the choreography I was running through and with the constant arguing in my head—one insisting that I could do this, that I had a little less than two months to continue rehearsing as Juliet, that my determination would see this through, while the other kept repeating one phrase.

Not perfect.

Not perfect.

Not perfect.

Not perfect.

Not—

Evangeline. You are so fucking perfect.

I gasped as his voice broke through the prison of my thoughts, filling that void inside of me with light. Every time my OCD tried to fight it, Alek's voice fought harder, repeating louder each time, *Evangeline. You are so fucking perfect.*

I held my hand to my heart and tried not to cry. I missed him. I missed him so much it hurt more than any bullet ever had. But what could I do? Romeo and Juliet's fairytale ended in death. It was naive of me to ever think our story would turn out differently.

When the practice finally ended, my mind ran in a million different directions, some destinations hopeful, most not. Mia unlaced the ribbons on her pointe shoes before bounding over to me, a wide grin on her face. "I'm so glad you're back, bestie."

"Me too," I said, double-checking to make sure my shoes were tied tight enough.

She grabbed her bag and frowned when I didn't move. "You're not leaving yet, are you?"

I shook my head. "No. Madame Germaine wants me to stay another hour and review the Juliet choreography."

"But I thought you couldn't dance until at least next week?"

"I can't. Maybe she just means I'm going to mentally review it? I'm not sure."

She gave me a crooked smile before kissing my cheek. "All right. But don't push yourself too hard. I'm proud of you for getting out of bed today."

My heart softened, and I reached out with my good arm and hugged her. "Thanks, Mia."

The rest of the studio cleared out while I sat on the floor in the center and waited for Madame Germaine to give me instructions. She walked over to me and said, "This week, you shall be reviewing on your own. Next week, when you begin to dance again, you will show me that you can still be my Juliet."

"Yes, ma'am," I said, already making a mental list of all the dances I would need to practice.

To be honest, I wasn't sure why she was having me stay here to do this, but it got me out of the house and away from Jules' hovering for a while, so I didn't argue.

Madame Germaine exited the studio while I took off my pointe shoes, wanting to give my feet a break since I wouldn't need them today. I groaned in satisfaction when I peeled them off, my toes practically singing in pure happiness. I began to massage the poor things, giving them the relief they desperately needed. A moan escaped my lips when I worked out a particularly painful knot.

A chuckle behind me made me freeze.

I stiffened, every part of my body aware that a dark presence had entered the studio, a predator waiting to feast on me. I stood just as a familiar hand gripped my waist and pulled me back into a hard body. "Now that's a sound I plan on hearing a lot today," a deep voice whispered into my hair.

I looked into the mirror in front of me.

And saw Alek's dark eyes looking back at mine.

January 28th

ALEKSANDR

Is she alone?

MADAME GERMAINE

Yes.

ALEKSANDR

Good.

ALEKSANDR
CHAPTER TWENTY-EIGHT

Eva's breath shook as her eyes met mine in the mirror, her pulse jumping against her neck, practically begging me to rip into her. And I wanted to—God, I *wanted* to. But I had one long hour planned with her, thanks to being a controlling investor in the one place she was allowed to go right now, and I planned on using that hour well.

"A-Alek," she whispered. "Is it really you?"

I scowled, my hand flying to her neck, arching her against me. "Were you expecting someone else, solnyshka? Have you already moved on from me?"

If she found someone new to replace me, if she thought she could fucking get away from me again, then she had no idea what I was capable of. I wasn't letting her go again.

Ever.

I didn't care if I had to crawl through the pits of Hell. If Eva went there, so did I.

"No," she moaned as I bit the tender spot by her collarbone, the monster within me ordering me to mark her, to show her fucking a brother that he could never get rid of me. But as much as I wanted to show the world that Eva was mine,

I had a plan to follow. I couldn't let my barely controlled lust ruin it.

"Good. Because you're fucking mine. And you better not have forgotten it."

"I haven't. I promise."

Keeping my eyes locked on hers in the mirror, I turned her to face me before my lips attacked her. I fought to kiss every inch of her—her hair, her lips, her cheeks, her neck, her shoulders, her eyes, her nose, all of it. It was all *mine*. I licked and sucked and bit her while Eva's body trembled in my arms.

"Mine," I growled, thrusting my hard cock into her behind. Her lip gloss smeared on my face, and I relished the taste of it. Of sweet, warm vanilla, of my even sweeter girl. "You are fucking mine."

I thrust my tongue inside of her mouth, my hand fisting in her hair while the other one tightened around her throat, loving the way her breath stuttered beneath my palm. Loving the way she submitted to my hold on her life.

My mouth devoured her. It was a savage claiming, one that would remind her of how thoroughly I'd ruined her. She belonged to me, and I would be damned if she let that fucking brother of hers try to keep us apart again.

Eva's hands grabbed onto my shirt, and for a moment, I worried she would push me away. That she'd forgotten my vow to her. But she stood on her toes and pulled me closer, letting me feel her warm body pressed against mine as I ravaged her to ruination.

"Alek," she breathed as I attacked her collarbone with hot, wet kisses that were sure to leave a mark from my teeth. "Alek... stop..."

"No."

"We don't have much time, Alek... If he catches you, he'll kill you."

I pulled back and stared into her chocolate eyes. "I was

dead the moment he shot that bullet at you. I won't fucking live without you, Evangeline. I *won't*." I slid my hand beneath her shirt and pinched her hardened nipple, loving the sound of her cries filling the practice studio. "Your body is mine. Your heart is mine. Your fucking *soul* is mine to take. Don't you dare try to push me away again."

And maybe she could sense the beast that was lingering beneath the surface, the one that wanted to throw her over my shoulder and lock her in my mansion until I could kill anyone who tried to keep us apart.

She'd said she loved me before. And if those torturous weeks apart had taught me anything, it was that love was a vicious obsession, a fiery storm of emotions men like me weren't meant to feel. Love was not always this tender thing found in fairytales. Sometimes, it had teeth and claws and wore the mask of a monster, forcing you to sign an oath made of your blood.

And I'd signed my name on the dotted line the moment I saw her pretty little face.

I ripped her tank top off her body, careful not to touch the bruise that I knew pained her. Her breasts bounced free, and I wasted no time taking the supple flesh into my mouth while my hands gripped her back.

Mine, mine, mine, something inside of me snarled. *My love. My sun. My girl.* Mine.

Eva cried out when I bit her nipple, her hands flying to my hair. "More, Alek. I need more."

I responded not with words, but with my hands pulling down her tights and all but ripping off her skirt. Her panties were more like little scraps of pink fabric, and I tugged them down, shoving them into my pocket for later. I wanted to suffocate in the smell of her pussy tonight when we were apart again.

Because as much as I wanted this to last forever, it

couldn't. I was an animal for her, my darkness snarling at the thought of giving her up again. But I would have to temporarily if I wanted Julian to remain ignorant of all the ways I was ruining his baby sister. The thought made my movements even rougher.

My cock was painfully hard as my lips found hers again. "Did you miss me, baby?" I murmured against them. "Was your pussy empty without me?"

"*Yes*," she moaned before a tear slipped down her cheek. It was a throaty sound, a desperate one. "I missed you so much, Alek. I thought I'd never see you again."

"Never. You will *never* get rid of me, Evangeline. I'm the fucking poison spreading through your veins. I'm the sickness you will never find a cure for. I'm the monster who has decided he likes the taste of you. And if you ever fucking think I will leave you again—" I thrust three fingers deep into her pussy, and Eva cried out at the sudden fullness. "—then I clearly haven't done my job in making you mine."

I slammed into her with an unforgiving tempo. I wanted to tear her apart, to break her open and stitch her back together so she would look at the threads of her soul and see me.

Her hands curled around my shoulders. And, fuck, I relished the sight of her chocolate eyes rolling into the back of her head. Eva wrapped her legs around my torso, opening wider for me to finger fuck her into oblivion.

As soon as I sensed the orgasm inside of her, my pace increased until she was biting her lip and seeing stars. She shouted my name as she fell undone, and I savored the feeling of her cum coating my fingers. While Eva came down from her high, I placed them on my tongue and sucked her lingering juices off, my taste buds singing from the sweetness.

An aching need built inside of me. The need to feel her move against me, to feel her writhe with pleasure, to own her.

Eva watched with hooded eyes as I unzipped my trousers and freed my throbbing cock. She licked her lips, and my gaze followed the path of her tongue like a compass pulling north.

"If I hadn't thought about that every day, I might have forgotten how big it was," she said before dropping to her knees and taking me in her mouth in one fell swoop.

"Fuck, solnyshka," I hissed, grabbing onto her ponytail while her tongue swirled along my shaft. My body tightened at the feeling of her touching me, licking me, sucking me. "Such a good fucking girl. I missed you so much."

As soon as she grabbed my balls with her free hand, I couldn't take it any longer. I let out a growl before I grabbed her throat, forcing her to stand along with me while I pulled her across the room to the two barres lining the mirrors.

Eva gasped as my hands turned her around, my cock brushing against her entrance while I bent her over and grabbed onto her hair.

"Hold on," I ordered, and she obeyed instantly, wrapping her small hands around the barre while I grabbed her hips and pulled them back, bending her over so her pert little ass was ripe for the taking. "Good girl. Does that hurt your shoulder?"

That fucking bullet wound. The sight of the bruise on her made me murderous, though I held it in, my anger buried beneath weeks of unspent lust.

"No, sir," Eva whispered.

"Good. Now stay there."

I gripped the base of my shaft, pumping it a few times while Eva's dark eyes watched me with anticipation. She rocked back once, and I responded by smacking her ass hard enough to make it red.

"I told you to fucking *stay*."

Eva whimpered. "I'm s-sorry. I... I really need you, Alek. It's been so long. I can't wait for you."

"You'll wait if I fucking tell you to wait, just like how you made *me* wait over two goddamn weeks to see you." My hands skated down her body before they reached her breasts. I pinched her sensitive nipples, groaning at the feeling of them hardening against me. "Did you enjoy hiding away from me, solnyshka? Did you sit in your ivory tower dreaming of another prince?"

She shook her head vehemently. "N-no. Only you. I only ever think of you. You've ruined me for all others."

"Damn right."

And then I rammed inside of her, my cock filling her to the brim while Eva's cry echoed through the studio. Her head fell forward, and I could practically taste her tears in the air as I slammed into her, stretching her despite her wetness. Her pussy clenched around me as if she was trying to keep me inside of her. But I moved in and out of her with brutal force, obsessed with punishing her, marking her, *claiming* her.

Mine. Mine. Mine. Mine. Mine.

"Alek," Eva breathed, one hand unwrapping from the barre.

"Keep it there," I snapped, and she listened instantly, returning it to its place.

"Alek... Alek, I—"

"I know what you need, baby. You need me to fuck you like the good girl you are. You need my cock filling you up and reminding you who you belong to. Because you might have thought I was done with you, but I never will be."

I wrapped Eva's perky little ponytail around my hand and used my grip to lift her eyes back to the mirror. Her tits bounced from the force of my body slamming against hers, and tears fell down her flushed cheeks. Eva's mouth was parted, her eyes practically black, as she watched me fuck her like an animal, rutting her into oblivion. My normally put-together and pristine girlfriend was falling apart, and imperfection had never looked so beautiful.

"You've never looked prettier to me," I whispered, my tone gentle despite the way I pounded into her. "My pretty, pretty girl. Look at how well you take my cock. Only you can do that. Only you can satisfy me. Only you are *mine*."

"Alek," she moaned. "Oh, Alek!"

My hand turned her head so she could look at every mirror lining the room. Watching myself fuck her at every angle was like a drug, making my head spin. I had to get one of these rooms put in my house so I could recreate this moment again and again, making her fall apart in every reflection.

"Look," I said, and I turned her head to the side so she could see the way her body bent over for me, watching my cock slide in and out of her. "So beautiful. So *mine*."

"Y-yours," she shuddered, her eyes widening at the view. At the sight of my flesh sliding in and out of her, at the sound of our skin slapping together brutally, at the heady smell of sex that filled the air.

And I watched through the mirrors as her lips parted and the orgasm took control of her. Her back arched, eyes rolling back while her fingers went white on the barre. One of my hands found her clit and pinched it to prolong her pleasure more.

A few more thrusts later, I was following after her. My cock tightened, and weeks without any relief spilled into her tender pussy.

"Eva, *fuck*," I hissed as my hands gripped her soft skin hard enough to leave bruises the size of her fingers.

I pulled out of her, some of my seed spilling onto her thighs as I exited her. I gathered it on my fingers and pushed it back inside her. Eva whimpered at the feeling of me re-entering her, her body probably sore after weeks without me.

But I didn't care enough to stop. I wanted to mark her in every way I could. I wanted her to walk around the city with my cum dripping from her, coating her thighs.

My obsession with her was an endless void. The depths were limitless.

"You can let go," I said, nodding toward the barre before bending to place a kiss on her ass. "Such a good girl, listening to me. Keep it up, and you'll be rewarded."

Eva's nostrils flared, and her eyes darkened in a way that I now realized reminded me of Julian. "Rewarded how?"

I wrapped my arm around her waist and pulled her closer, giving her one short but deep kiss. The taste of her still lingered on my tongue as it thrust inside her mouth before I pulled away with a wink. "You'll find out."

Her cheeks turned her favorite color. "So I'll see you again?"

I cupped her cheek. "They cannot keep me away from you."

Eva nodded before detaching herself from me. She grabbed her pointe shoes and walked over to her bag, her hips swaying naturally.

She bent down and rummaged inside before pulling out a pair of sweatpants and a large hoodie with the company logo. Her ass was up in the air as she did this, both her back hole and her glistening pussy on view for me.

I growled and couldn't resist palming her ass. Eva gasped as I rocked into it, already growing hard again. It would seem that I didn't need to recharge myself, not when I had her to tempt my body into wanting more.

"Where are my underwear?"

My hand flew to my pocket where the lacy pink satin had been stashed. Eva caught the movement and sighed. "You owe me new ones."

I grinned. She made such things natural, things like smiling, being happy. My little sun. My solnyshka. I thought I would have to go the rest of my life without this. I was glad my cousin helped me get my head out of my ass.

"My brother will be here soon," she said with a sigh. "I have to go."

Her brother. Her damn *brother*. That little fucker who kept getting in our way.

For now, I would play by his little rules to appease him. But not for long. I would find a way to make Eva mine for good.

She got dressed, and I pulled her to me, bending down to place a hard kiss on Eva's lips. She sighed and leaned into me, her hands coming up to grip my hair. When she started to pull on some of the strands, my composure faltered. I wanted to fuck her again. I *needed* to feel her against me this time while she shattered beneath me.

Brother and time limit be damned, I was going to have her again. I was going—

I grabbed the back of her neck and kissed her forehead before I let my beast take control of me. "I'll see you tomorrow, solnyshka."

Her brows furrowed. "Tomorrow? But, Alek, I—"

The sound of a car horn interrupted us. Eva's head looked toward the door before darting back to me, her body clearly warring with what to do. Follow his rules, or come to me.

I smiled to myself. It was only a matter of time before she broke free of her precious Julian, signing her soul to me instead.

I waved her off, and Eva took off toward the door. Before she left, though, she looked back at me one more time. "Bye, Alek."

"Tomorrow, Eva."

February 21st

MIA

One month until opening night!!!

Are you totally stoked?

Because I AM!!!!

EVANGELINE

A MONTH?

Oh no...

MIA

You are going to be so totally fine. You've been staying an hour or two every day after rehearsal, right? So you're going to be golden!!

EVANGELINE

About that...

MIA

Oh.

My.

God.

EVA, YOU DOG!!

EVANGELINE
CHAPTER TWENTY-NINE

Almost a month had passed since Alek and I reunited secretly. A month of stolen kisses in the shadows, a month of picnics on the main stage in the theater before Alek would push me down and eat me out, a month of learning all the ways I was as sexually depraved as he was.

Weekends were torture. Alek and I were only able to meet for an hour, sometimes two, after rehearsals. It was enough to satisfy the craving inside of me, but only barely. By the fourth week of sneaking around, I had become ravenous for him.

And if *I* was ravenous, then Alek was even worse.

He attacked me whenever I walked in the room, devouring me with kisses, thrusting inside of me like he couldn't go any longer without feeling me squeezing his cock. I'd become addicted to the sounds he made when he pushed me into the ground—the groans as he bit at my tits, the heavy breaths he made as he choked me into oblivion, the way he whispered my name like it was a prayer.

Eva... Oh, my Eva.

Things had changed between us, that was for sure. Alek was more vicious whenever he first saw me, his hands tearing at my clothes, running all over my body like he couldn't get to it fast enough.

But after, when his cum was drying inside of me, Alek would lie on top of me and be so tender that it made my heart ache. He'd stroke my cheek with his fingers and kiss each one of my freckles, whispering all the things he liked about me.

"My pretty girl," he'd murmur, kissing my nose. "My solnyshka."

So, despite his occasional brutality in sex, despite the anger that turned his eyes a cold shade of midnight blue whenever I had to leave, I couldn't help but feel like Alek and I were growing closer and closer, like our bond wasn't something that could be broken by distance or time apart.

It wasn't the relationship I'd imagined when I was younger. But it was *ours*, and I'd never been happier.

We lived in the shadows of sin and secrets, unable to communicate with each other beyond the stage. While Jules had finally given me my phone back, he took it each night, probably searching for signs that I added and unblocked Alek's number.

I was too afraid of what my brother would do if he discovered we'd seen each other again, so I resisted the urge to contact him, instead texting Mia occasionally. Our conversations avoided all mentions of him. She was now aware of our secret trysts along with Madame Germaine, who Alek had admitted to roping into his plans by using his position as primary investor in the ballet. Though he'd recently taken to joining our rehearsals, going over the blueprints for the theater's renovations while I danced.

"You deserve the most beautiful stage, solnyshka," he would say before kissing me gently. "I want you to have the best of everything."

But I felt like he already was giving me the best. He'd taken the time and effort to plan little dates for us after my rehearsals, learning my favorite foods and cooking them himself. He prepared an elaborate candlelit dinner for our first Valentine's Day, complete with one of the orchestra's violinists, and made gentle love to me atop the rose petals.

One time, his mom even sent pasta 'ncasciata for me to try, which Alek said was her way of bribing me to come over sometime. Apparently, all of the Drakovs were willing to set aside the war between families for their son's sake, caring more for his happiness than for revenge.

It was my brother who was the issue.

My feet burned as I practiced the quick steps of Juliet, bounding and leaping across the stage. We were rarely in the practice studio anymore, all of us needing the space the theater provided far more than the mirrors. It made everything feel more real.

I was the lead in the Company's production. Everything was riding on *me*.

Well, me and Raphael.

A bead of sweat trickled down my spine as I moved quickly. We were rehearsing the first act, which meant that I had to show Juliet's youthfulness through quick steps and turns, leaping and leaping and leaping and *leaping*. It was one of the more exhausting dances I'd ever done, though it was also one of the more fun ones, especially now that Mia had been made to be the nurse dancing with me.

She grinned as I jumped onto her lap and feigned a conversation with her, telling a story with my body like I'd done my whole life. That was the fun thing about dancing. I could communicate with words that never came to me. I could be strong, I could be assertive, I could be everything I wasn't in my reality.

Sometimes, when Raphael and I danced together, I pretended that it was actually Alek and me. And that made me breathe a little easier.

"Do you see what I see?" Mia hissed through a smile as I curled into her.

I shook my head, not willing to risk Madame Germaine's ire. Though the woman reassured me almost every day that I was her Juliet, that my weeks off hadn't ruined my chances, I still couldn't get it into my head. My imposter syndrome was too strong.

Though lately, it had been getting better. Every time that voice in my head tried to insist I wasn't perfect, I could picture Alek murmuring against my neck, "*Evangeline. You are so fucking perfect.*"

And for a moment, I would forget all of the reasons I was not, and my heart would fill with so much love I didn't know what to do with it.

"Out there. Back row," my best friend whispered. "Look when you get a second."

"Mia Renford, you better not be talking on my stage!" Madame Germaine snapped, grabbing her cane. Every other dancer flinched, though Mia didn't seem to care. Maybe she wasn't subjected to the same fear that we all were when we were younger—our teachers bringing out a stick to use whenever our turns were not on relevé.

Or maybe Mia was truly fearless.

As Madame Germaine stopped the dance to chew my best friend out—snapping her cane on the floor to punctuate each word—my eyes went to the audience, where a shadowed silhouette sat, watching me. I gulped as his dark eyes glistened. I could practically feel his hunger radiating, a burning need that only made mine stronger.

"Alek," I whispered under my breath, my hand reaching out of its own accord as if to pull him to the stage.

"What was that, Eva?" a voice from behind me asked.

I turned to find Elsie looking at me with concern. Ever since my shoulder healed, she'd stopped staying with us, though she still kept an eye on me during practice. I wasn't sure if it was because my brother had asked her to report back to him or if it was out of her own concern.

"Oh, nothing," I said, smiling at her before it fell as I remembered Alek once telling me not to.

If you aren't happy, don't pretend to be.

Elsie frowned. "Are you sure? You don't look like it was nothing."

I shook my head. "I'm fine. Really. I'm just thinking about rehearsal."

Her frown deepened, though she thankfully said nothing. Elsie was extremely smart. I highly doubted she believed my half-lie. But maybe she remembered the fact that I still hadn't told Jules about her plan to retire and possibly move away. Maybe she decided to help me keep a secret of my own.

My suspicions were all but confirmed when she spoke again.

"I hope you know what you're doing. Be careful, Eva. There are more ways than one to get your heart broken," she finally said before walking off the stage.

I frowned. What did that mean?

I turned back to the silhouette and gave him a soft wave. To my delight, the darkness waved back, greedily watching as I turned back to the stage and resumed my dance.

March 3rd

NIKOLAI

Are you back at the ballet today?

ALEKSANDR

Yes.

NIKOLAI

Right. Dumb question. You always are.

Will you do me a favor while you're there?

ALEKSANDR

No.

NIKOLAI

Can you put in a good word with blondie?

I'm trying to get a ballet beauty too. 😏

ALEKSANDR

No.

NIKOLAI

WHAT?

Why not?

ALEKSANDR

Out of every ballerina there, she is the second least likely to accept you.

NIKOLAI

Second least?

Who's the least?

ALEKSANDR

Mine.

EVANGELINE
CHAPTER THIRTY

"Ow!" I hissed as a pin struck me in the side. I turned to the costumer, who looked at me unapologetically, a bunch of other pins held between her teeth. "That hurt!"

"Beauty is pain," she said in a thick Russian accent that reminded me of the one Alek got whenever he was in a jealous mood—all angry that Raphael had to touch me while we danced. I guessed it was a good thing that he hadn't been present for any of the balcony scene rehearsals.

Yet.

Because it was only a matter of time before Madame Germaine made Raphael and me actually rehearse the kiss. We'd gotten away with forehead touches up until this point, but she was insistent upon a true declaration of love for the show, which was less than three weeks away.

Alek was going to go ballistic.

"Beauty doesn't have to be pain," I muttered. Spa masks, bubble baths, a cute new shade of lip gloss. None of *those* were painful.

"It does when you are Juliet," she snapped right back, stabbing me with another pin as she placed a bit of embellishment on the bodice. I resisted the urge to scowl back at her.

If you aren't happy, don't pretend to be.
Damn it. I *did* scowl. And it felt good.

A few minutes later, I was finally out of the costumer's closet and in the theater. I could practically feel Alek's nervous energy subside as I stepped into the stage lights. He hated going long without seeing me, which meant that our hours apart were basically torture for him.

I moved next to Raphael and waited for Madame Germaine's orders, my eyes going out to the seats to find him.

I found him in the back of the audience, his body once again shrouded in shadows. I waved once before the sound of the cane on the floor snapped my attention back to the rehearsal.

People were scurrying about in half-finished costumes while sets were being placed, and a tech crew practiced the lights.

We were preparing for next week's full dress rehearsal after our sitzprobe earlier this week, which was the rehearsal where we ran the show with the orchestra for the first time. There were a few kinks to work out still—playing with a large group of live musicians was much different than our one accompanist, who feared Madame Germaine more than she feared God—but overall, it went pretty well.

Madame Germaine said I'd more than exceeded her expectations, probably because I spent most of my evenings in my house practicing as a way of avoiding Jules.

I'd broken my silence—it was almost impossible for us to go over a month without speaking to each other when we lived together—but not by much. Our dinners were filled with stifled pauses and awkward conversation, and any attempts to bridge the gap on his end were met with a RBF Mia would be proud of.

Jules seemed to expect me to forgive him a lot sooner, but I was holding out. He needed to learn that my crush on Alek was more than just a fleeting fancy that could be shoved aside with an order. I loved Alek now more than ever, and I was determined to let my stubbornness win out over my brother's.

"We will practice the balcony pas de deux," Madame Germaine said. She gave Raphael and me a sharp look. "In full."

I gulped. I knew what that meant, and judging by the stiffness in his posture, so did Raphael. The director expected us to kiss.

Raphael gave me a nervous look. To his credit, he didn't want to kiss me as much as I didn't want to kiss him. Neither of us was the other's type. I wasn't a male, and Raphael wasn't Alek.

But I think the biggest reason for his hesitation was Alek. Everyone knew of my boyfriend's possessiveness. Despite never showing his face in our rehearsals, he'd made it known with the flowers he gifted me before things all went wrong and the notes he still left me now, usually containing the words "mine" in some form.

Plus, I had a giant hickey on my neck from where he bit me yesterday.

Thankfully, Jules believed my lie about it being a curling iron burn from rehearsal. Maybe Elsie stood up for me, or maybe the makeup I threw on under my hoodie actually hid it. Considering the way Raphael's eyes kept flashing to it, I doubted it was the latter.

"It's okay," I said softly, hoping that was true.

Raphael didn't look convinced, but he went off to the side of the stage anyway as Madame Germaine ordered, "Begin."

The orchestra began to tune up, and I took my first position. The music was soft and slow—a stark contrast from the chaos I could hear backstage—as I began to dance alone as Juliet in her room. My dress flowed with the rest of my limbs as I moved like water, flowing and shifting in time with the rise and fall of the music.

The director hummed as Raphael darted on and off the stage until he appeared in front of me, his arms outstretched as the music became even more emotional and romantic. I ran on pointed toes, enveloping him in a soft hug that made Mia roll her eyes at me backstage.

I pushed Raphael away, running away from him, pretending to be worried while he chased me. For a moment, I was reminded of Alek and me—of our circumstances forcing me to leave him while his obsession with me fueled him to find me.

It was Alek I thought of as Raphael and I came together and began our soft dance. Alek who my heart swelled with love for while my body moved in a rhythm of romance. The pas de deux was so much more than a simple loving dance. It was an innate conversation between hearts and souls, the comfort of knowing and being known, the feeling of pleasure as two slowly began to move as one.

And maybe that was why the others gaped at me from behind the curtains while Raphael and I danced: because the whole time, I was thinking of the man I *truly* loved.

Alek.

The dance was filled with tender moments—pirouettes, arabesques, lifts. We moved with the sweeping music, portraying a story of young, budding love kept apart by tragedy.

Raphael's fingers continued to find the hem of my dress, Romeo showing his longing for Juliet. And every time he picked me up into the air, his hands trailed down my body, fingers brushing against my lips.

I could feel Alek's anger as I arched my back and reached for the sky, my face a perfect portrayal of a yearning woman. But it was *Alek* I was yearning for.

It was always him.

Still, I understood why his jealousy began to weigh down the air. Raphael and I were doing an incredible job of capturing the emotions in the dance. It would have been easy to believe we were truly in love. And I *was* in love.

Just not with Romeo.

By the end of the dance, Raphael kneeled to the floor. My steps were light as I crossed the stage to him. Raphael stood and grabbed my waist as I went up onto pointe. And with my heart thundering in my ribcage, he cupped the back of my head and spun me in a close circle. My hands fell against his jaw as Raphael pulled me in for a soft, open-mouthed kiss.

"STOP!" a voice boomed from the back of the theater.

My heart dropped.

The silhouette was standing now, stalking down the aisle with his fists clenched, walking like some dark god hell-bent on making every sinner suffer. And right now, the two biggest ones were sitting center stage for him, displayed like a feast.

I gulped as I took a step away from Raphael, muttering under my breath, "Rapha, if you want to live, go. *Now.*"

I wasn't sure if it was the seriousness of my tone or the air of darkness hovering around Alek, but Raphael listened, running backstage before Madame Germaine could force him to come back.

"Yes?" Madame Germaine said, holding up her chin. But even she appeared to tremble under the weight of his aura.

Alek stepped halfway into the light. The muscles in his jaw were clenched, and his eyes were completely black. And maybe there was some part of me utterly ruined, because my core tightened with need at the feral expression in his eyes.

"Everyone. Out," he growled lowly. The authority in his voice was enough to bring a wave of fresh goosebumps to my skin. His rage sounded barely controlled, an unhinged beast gnawing at the bars of its cage.

One wrong move, and it would break free.

The other dancers turned to Madame Germaine, who nodded before exiting the stage. Maybe the director would have fought more if we hadn't been nearing the end of rehearsal anyway. We might have even gone a little late because of how long it took for me to deal with the costumer—who pinned me extra for complaining.

Soon, the theater was empty, and we were alone.

"Alek," I whispered, my voice cracking in the middle. I could feel his anger from the front row. It both frightened and exhilarated me.

Alek ascended the staircase to the side of the stage, each step mimicking the echo in my heart.

Boom.

Boom.

Boom.

Boom.

By the time he reached me, I was already a wet, quivering mess, my body aching to have him again. Twenty-four hours was too long.

I was tired of this—of this half-life without him. I wanted a full relationship with Alek. A real one where I could bring him over to dinner without worrying about who would be the first to fire a gun. I wanted to see him in the audience at all of my shows and go out to the club with him and Mia. I wanted to go on normal dates outside of the Company, I wanted to wake up next to him each morning, and I wanted to fall asleep wrapped in his arms.

And one day, I wanted to marry him.

Alek gripped my chin and lifted my eyes to his. The darkness in his expression practically turned me into a puddle. Some sick part of me answered the sick part of him—and I liked it that way. I liked knowing we made each other better and worse.

Maybe Jules was right. Maybe I didn't really know what love was like. But I couldn't imagine it looking any different than this.

"When were you going to tell me you had to fucking kiss him?"

"I..." But I had no good answer.

Alek pulled me closer and bit my neck harshly, a mirror to the bright red hickey. I gasped, my back arching into his.

"Have you forgotten that you're mine? That every inch of your body fucking belongs to *me*? These lips are mine to kiss and suck. This neck is mine to bite and choke. These tits are mine to pinch and squeeze. And this pussy is mine to fuck however I want."

He snarled, already ripping at my dress, hands holding me hard enough to bruise. He quickly undid my pointe shoes, tossing them across the stage. Fabric tore, and the cold air from the theater instantly filled my body as he destroyed the rest of my clothing, including my underwear.

A distant part of me knew that the costumer would be even more furious than before at my ruined dress, but an even bigger part of me didn't care. I didn't like it anyway. It didn't feel right for Juliet, for *me*.

And anyway, it was in his way.

"This cunt," Alek growled, shoving two of his fingers inside of me and curling them against my G-spot, "is *mine*. And if you ever think about letting someone get that close to it again, I will show that miserable soul why they call me the Reaper."

"*Alek*," I hummed, letting his fingers work their magic inside of me. It was a slow, torturous rhythm, one that made me forget whether this was a punishment or not. Every touch felt like a gift. I wanted more, more, *more*.

"Alek, I didn't want him... It was for the show. I pretended it was you."

He stilled inside of me. I whimpered when his fingers exited me, the emptiness in me even more apparent. I felt hollow without him, like I would never be truly filled until I had a taste of him again.

"You did?"

I nodded, my breath shaky. When he got this look in his eyes—the hungry one, like he was about to eat me alive—he was hard to predict. Would he slam me against the ground and thrust into me from behind? Or would he gather me in his arms before making slow, tender love to me?

Or would he do both?

"Such a good girl." His gaze studied me with a dark lust that made my pussy tingle, his touch soft where his eyes were not. "My Evangeline."

He cupped my neck with his large hand, and my fingers found his hair to anchor myself in the dark strands. The veins popped out in his tanned forearms as he studied me with fascination, completely enraptured while his thumb stroked my quivering pulse.

"My pretty, pretty girl," Alek murmured, almost as if in a trance.

Then, he blinked, and the hardness was back, his dark irises filled with embers of a fire that constantly burned inside of him.

"*My* pretty, pretty girl," he said again before squeezing my throat. I coughed as my vision went black around the edges, though instead of asking him to stop it, I sank into the feeling. Into the pleasure that came with losing control to him.

Every thought exited my mind, even the ones of the unbearable heat between my thighs coupled with the dripping wetness soaking the skin. All I could think about was air. I needed air.

No. I needed him. Only him.

Alek was the air I breathed. He was my life, not oxygen or dancing or anything else.

It was only ever Alek.

"You were made for me," Alek said as he released my throat, keeping his grip on my neck but letting me catch my breath.

I barely had time to prepare myself before he was reaching behind me and cupping my ass, lifting me in the air, and sheathing himself inside of me.

"*Oh*," I moaned, tipping my head back and letting the pleasure run through me. But unlike his fingers earlier, Alek's thrusts were now brutal, each one meant to punish me for kissing another man.

I bit my lip to keep from crying out at the savagery, some carnal part of me enjoying being fucked like I was just an object to him. Like I was a possession.

Like I was his.

The scent of my arousal filled the air, but Alek did not stop to savor it. He pushed harder and harder, breaking me apart with his cock and putting me back together with every squeeze of his hand on my throat.

He slammed his lips against mine, and I moaned against him. His tongue pressed into me, licking my mouth, dominating my tongue, fucking me even harder than his cock. This was too much. Every sensation brought me to an edge whose cliff became higher every time we fucked. I chased the sensation, letting myself succumb to this pas de deux of pleasure.

His eyes were hooded as he pulled back, lips swollen from our kisses. My saliva and lip gloss were smeared on his face, but Alek didn't wipe it off, instead savoring the sight of my essence over him. Small, erotic grunts slipped past his lips as he thrust, each one sounding more and more like my name.

"Eva. Eva. *Eva*."

I felt like I was going insane, like any moment my heart

would crack open, and he would see the way his name was signed in permanent ink. But if I was going to sign myself over to anyone, I was glad it was Alek.

Alek squeezed my neck one more time, and as soon as the air left my body, I fell over an edge of pleasure into a pit made of an entirely different feeling.

Love.

All I could think about as the orgasm overtook me was how desperately in love with him I was.

Alek roared before spilling into me, and my pussy greedily drank every drop, loving the feeling of him coating me from the inside, claiming me.

"Mine," he murmured as his chest heaved. "*Mine.*"

I lifted one hand from his hair and pushed a dark strand out of his eyes before kissing his sweat-covered forehead. "Yours," I said with a soft smile. "I am all yours, Aleksandr Drakov."

Alek exhaled once before he whispered, "I love you, Evangeline."

My heart stopped and restarted in my chest, the absence of a beat making my whole body clench around him. "W-what?"

His cock slipped out of me. Alek set me gently onto my feet, careful of my tender toes. He had spent many days after rehearsal massaging my bleeding and sore feet, an unfortunate side effect of putting them through hell in the name of ballet.

Alek kissed me once, saying against my lips, "I love you, Evangeline. I never thought I could love anyone, yet you walked into my life, proving me wrong with your pink ribbons and bright smile. I'm so glad you ran into me and stole my scarf."

"Hey! You said I could keep that." I grinned, wrapping my arms around his neck. "But I love you too, Alek."

I felt like I was flying, like I was floating amongst the stars, thanking them for all of my dreams coming true.

Well, almost all of them.

We still had to sway Jules, but Alek reassured me daily that he had a plan that needed time to work properly. He promised me that he wouldn't hurt my brother, so all I had to do was trust him and hope that things worked out. In the meantime, I enjoyed getting to know him—both emotionally and physically.

Alek helped me get dressed in my costume, eyeing the broken straps on the pale gray dress meant to be my nightgown for the balcony scene. "You look much better in pink, anyway. I'll speak to the costume department."

I thanked him profusely for that because, honestly, the woman scared me more than Madame Germaine. At least Madame Germaine didn't have pushpins that she stuck into me to make me a human hedgehog.

He tucked my panties into his suit pocket and rolled my tights up my body, smirking at the cum drying on my thighs. He kissed my shaking legs. "I love you."

And because I was a glutton for those words on his lips, I slipped on the torn dress and leaned forward, smiling against him. "Say it again."

"I love you." Alek tugged me onto his lap and ran his hands through my hair.

"Again."

"I love you." He tilted my head up, and his warm breath skated across my lips.

"Again," I whispered, my voice much softer now.

"I love you." And then he pressed his lips to me, kissing me slowly, tenderly, while whispering, "I love you, Evangeline. I love you. I love you. *I love you.*"

"I love you too, Al—"

But before I could finish and kiss him again, a strong arm was pulling me back into a furious body.

Alek rose, enraged, his fists already clenched and his hand

pulling out his gun, pausing when he realized who he was pointing it at.

Jules.

My brother held me tight to his body, and I felt all of the blood leaving my flushed face.

"Jules," I whispered, trying to fight his grip but stopping when his brown eyes flashed to mine, his dark anger more than evident.

"I fucking told you to stay away from him," he hissed. Shame filled me from head to toe, but, surprisingly, not shame for disobeying him. No, it was shame for not telling him sooner. Shame for not realizing that I could never hide my love for Alek, not truly.

"Jules, I can't. You know I—"

"No, Evangeline, I don't feel like I know you very well at all." He turned to Alek, and his anger became murderous.

But Alek didn't back down from the challenge, instead squaring his shoulders and bringing himself to his full height. His jaw was hard, and his eyes were darker than the universe. All traces of the gentle man I knew were gone.

If Jules was murderous, then Alek was the coldness of Death in the flesh, ready to destroy the world for taking away his light.

I longed to run to him, to tell him that I wanted to pick him, not my brother, but Jules held me tight.

"And *you*," Jules seethed. "You should be fucking ashamed of yourself. Your fight has always been and will always be with *me*. Filling a young girl's head with lies and nonsense as part of your fucked up game is despicable. The knowledge that my little sister will be safe from your poison will warm me until I am rotting in my grave."

"That day will be much sooner than you think if you don't fucking unhand her," Alek snarled. His eyes flashed to me, and they softened a bit. "Evangeline. What do you want?"

This was it.

This was my chance to prove to Jules what I really wanted, to voice the conflict that had been in my heart for weeks.

It would have been so easy. *Jules. I want to be with Alek.* That was all I had to say.

But when I looked up at my big brother, at the man who would do anything to protect me, I froze. My love for Alek was strong, so strong, but was it enough to sway him?

Was *I* enough?

My self-doubt cost me dearly. Jules smiled smugly as Alek's face shuttered. My heart broke at the dejection written there, but before I could correct myself, Jules slung me over his shoulder and carried me out of the theater without saying a word.

"I hope you enjoyed your freedom, Evangeline," my brother said as he took me to his car parked in front of the curb. "Because it's all gone."

But I said nothing, because all I could think about was the look on Alek's face and the horrible knowledge that I was the first girl he'd ever allowed himself to love. The first girl he opened his heart to, ever since it shattered at the death of his sister. The first person he allowed himself to be vulnerable with.

And like everything else, I ruined it.

March 6th

MISSED CALL FROM NIKOLAI
NIKOLAI

Dude, wanna hang out?

I got a new video game that has lots of blood and death and all the things you like.

MISSED CALL FROM NIKOLAI

...

Alek?

Alekkkkkkk?

Aleksandrrrrrrrr?

MISSED CALL FROM NIKOLAI

Are you at the ballet today?

Did you get your girl back?

MISSED CALL FROM NIKOLAI

Alek?

ALEKSANDR

It's over, Nikolai.

NIKOLAI

Says who?

I've never met a Drakov who gives up before. We're annoying little cockroaches.

Emphasis on the cock. 😉

ALEKSANDR

It's over, Nikolai.

Done.

MISSED CALL FROM NIKOLAI

> Leave me alone.

NIKOLAI
Oh fuck.

This is bad.

Don't worry, cousin!

Help is on the way dearie!

MISSED CALL FROM NIKOLAI

Fuck, if you're not threatening to punch me, this really is bad.

Did you seriously fucking block me? You little shit.

EVANGELINE
CHAPTER THIRTY-ONE

THE SILENCE CONTINUED FOR THE NEXT FEW DAYS. But instead of feeling hollow like before, now I was only angry.

Actually, I was furious. Both at myself and at Jules. The feeling sat in my chest like a second heartbeat. It was hot, restless, impossible to ignore. I was so used to happy feelings, *pink* feelings, that this darkness inside of me surprised me.

How dare he? How dare he barge into my life and try to control it—try to control *me*? How dare he try to tear me away from Alek?

And how dare I let him?

Jules tightened the reins around me. He'd confiscated my phone again and started posting guards outside my bedroom door. Neither Mia nor Elsie was allowed to come over all weekend, and I was also forbidden from returning to rehearsals. Jules didn't care that I'd worked my entire life to get the role of Juliet. All he cared about was keeping me away from Alek.

Every rule felt like another hand at my spine, pushing me into a position I hadn't chosen.

But he didn't realize that every one of his actions only strengthened my resolve.

Something in me had already tipped past the point of return. I needed to take control of my own life, not let my older brother boss me around. But I also had to be smart about things. I couldn't blow up on Jules while he was still fuming. That risked him getting even angrier and doubling down on his efforts to punish me.

So I bided my time. I hid out in my bedroom and thought about how I could ever make things right with Alek. Every time I closed my eyes, I pictured the shuttered look on his face, the disappointment coupled with the lack of surprise that I had picked another.

But that was the thing: I hadn't picked my brother. And I hadn't picked Alek either. I was finally picking myself, the girl who liked who she was when she had a man who lifted her to new heights. If only Jules understood that.

I hadn't chosen my brother that day in the theater. I had merely been shocked at the fact that he'd caught us and asked me to fight on the spot for Alek when it was a battle I was destined to lose. And I knew my brother well enough to know that no matter what I said then, he wouldn't have accepted it.

Jules was a stubborn wall of fire and flames. If I pushed him too hard too quickly, he would simply consume everything around him. So to be successful, I would need a slow, steady stream of cooling water—not more heat.

I avoided him. I took my meals in my room, and I refused to look him in the eye. He was not the loving brother I knew well. He was a man overrun by fear.

If only I had a way to show him that there was nothing to fear. That I was strong enough to handle myself.

By the time Monday rolled around, Jules was furious. I'd gone days without speaking to him, and it was clear that I had no intention to break that. Before, I'd at least deigned to look at him. Now, I didn't give him the luxury.

So I wasn't surprised when, as I was putting sweatpants over my leotard and skirt, Jules barged into my room, fists clenched at his side and his eyes like molten chocolate. "Where the fuck do you think you're going, Evangeline?"

"To rehearsal. I've already missed enough practice," I said as I moved to step into the bathroom so I could tie my hair back into a bun.

My brother blocked my path. His arms pressed against the doorframe, and his jaw hardened. "Evangeline, you don't seem to understand that you're not fucking leaving. And you're especially not going to go somewhere that *he* owns."

A familiar anger rose, the same one that had been simmering for weeks ever since Jules tried to pull us apart. Instead of shoving it back down to that box inside of me that I kept locked tight, I let myself feel the unfamiliar emotion, let it bubble in my veins while my inner voice kept repeating one thing.

"How dare he?"

And then another one, a richer, deeper, stronger one that said, *"I love you, Evangeline."*

It was time, for once, to let love win.

"No, Jules," I said coolly, and it shocked even me how steady my voice sounded. I tossed aside my need to please everyone for once in my life. Instead, I focused on *my* pleasure, what *I* wanted.

Alek.

"You don't seem to understand that I am going to ballet rehearsal. We are running the whole show today, and I am going to be there. I am going to dance as Juliet, and then I will *maybe* consider coming back if you actually start speaking to me with respect like a fellow adult instead of a kid."

While Jules stood, slack-jawed, I ducked under his

shoulder and began to work on my hair. My bun wasn't perfect, but for once, I didn't feel the need to make it that way. I was happy with how I was, perfection be damned.

He opened his mouth to speak, but I cut him off with a wave of my hand. I grabbed my duffel bag and slipped on my sneakers before narrowing my eyes at him.

"And another thing," I continued, my tone harder than it had ever been. "Alek makes me happier than I've ever been, and he's never asked me to change who I am to fit into a cage. But I don't know if I can say the same thing about you right now. So Alek and I are going to be together. So you can either accept that and stand by my side as my brother, or you can live the rest of your life knowing you lost a sister because of the choices *you* made."

And then I walked out the door, feeling lighter than I ever had in years.

March 7th

EVANGELINE

Alek?

MISSED CALL FROM EVANGELINE

...

I understand why you might not want to talk to me. I wouldn't want to talk to me either right now.

But I had to tell you that I stood up to him. I stood up to Jules, I got my phone back, and now I'm headed to the theater. And I feel free, Alek. So, so free.

So if you'll still have me, I want to be yours. I choose you. I love you, Alek. No matter what.

I'm going to rehearsal now, but after, can I come over? I really want to see you. Just let me know x

ALEKSANDR
CHAPTER THIRTY-TWO

I'd had a bad feeling ever since I woke up. Not anger or even depression, like I'd been feeling on and off for days, but a wrongness. It was low and persistent, like pressure behind the eyes that continued to build into a migraine. The feeling crawled under my skin and refused to leave me, no matter how much I ignored it.

Something bad had happened. But I didn't know what. It was hard to tell when everything in my life felt so wrong.

My office was too quiet. The silence grated on my ears. I sat behind my desk, my chin resting in my hand, my paperwork untouched. The city stretched beyond the windows in an array of glass and steel, both alive and indifferent. This was one of the few offices, meant for my property development firm, that reminded me the least of Evangeline, which was why it'd been the one I was working in the most since she'd left.

Normally, I liked the silence up here. It gave me a chance to think. It made men nervous, reminding them who they were standing in front of—the Reaper of the city.

But today, the office just felt empty.

My thoughts were filled with visions of Evangeline. Eva with snow in her hair, her cheeks flushed from the cold. Eva smiling as I brought her the largest bouquets of pink flowers I could find with every date. Eva laughing as my nose nuzzled her neck. Eva moaning as I thrust into her. Eva. My beautiful, beautiful Eva.

I ground my teeth and shoved my thoughts of her away. Why was I pining for her? She chose Julian, not me.

Because you love her, something soft inside of me whispered. But I pushed that voice away, too.

I picked up my pen and tried to work on some paperwork for the updates to the ballet theater. Despite my inability to step into the building without my chest tightening at thoughts of our last moments together, I still wanted to update the theater. It was an investment, and Drakovs didn't back away from things once they began.

But the theater needed a *lot* of work. The electrical wiring was old, the plumbing was barely holding itself together, and some of the aesthetics were desperately in need of an update. I should have been able to finish a lot of the preparation for my crews to begin in the off-season, but instead of being productive, my mind kept replaying Eva's and my last moments. I couldn't fucking escape them.

She'd chosen her brother. Chosen safety. Chosen the cage she'd been raised in over the danger of me.

And I didn't blame her for it. But that didn't mean that every second without her wasn't agony. Every one of our precious memories turned sharp and ugly as soon as I recalled the look on her face as Julian pulled her away from me.

Disappointed. Like all the fight in her had left. Like I wasn't worth it.

I felt... empty. Tight in the chest, like something vital had been scooped out and left me standing upright, running on pure spite and depression at this point.

But I forced myself to keep moving. I was Aleksandr

Drakov. The Reaper. I didn't pine. I didn't chase women who didn't want me.

A part of me knew that was a lie. Eva wanted me. Eva was the first girl who wanted me, who I wanted, too. And that was the cruelest part.

A knock sounded at the door, interrupting my lamentations. "Go away," I ordered.

But Nikolai let himself in anyway, because of course he did. He was like a stubborn dog following a grumpy master.

"You look like shit," he said mildly, dropping into the chair across from my desk. "Like dead shit, which is impressive considering you usually have this air of a corpse with money, but you've somehow made it worse."

I gritted my jaw. "What do you want?"

"To talk to my favorite cousin, of course." He studied me for a second, too perceptive for my liking. "You heard from her?"

"No."

"That's not an answer."

"What the fuck are you talking about? Of course it's an answer."

"Not to *you*. Aleksandr Drakov doesn't take silences or rejections."

"He does now," I mumbled. "There are too many rules, Nikolai. You wouldn't understand."

He arched a blond brow. "You think I don't?"

"No. Because you haven't followed a damn rule in your life."

"And you've never played a game without changing the rules to win."

He leaned forward, blue eyes boring a hole into my head. I ignored him, turning back to the view of the city behind me. I couldn't bear to see anyone right now. They all reminded me of Eva, of the girl I was missing.

"Where's your phone, Aleksandr?"

I glanced back at the top drawer of my desk, where the device sat, powered off. I'd thrown it in there earlier when I realized she wasn't going to call me. Staring at a blank screen only made the hollow feeling in my chest worse, like every minute I went without hearing from her reminded me that she wasn't coming back.

I didn't respond.

He sighed. "Alek—"

But my cousin was interrupted by the harsh ringing of sirens from the city below.

A lot of them.

The sound was distant at first, soon rising to a roar, building and building, their echoes passing through the streets and up to the window of my high-rise.

Something in my chest tightened, the ugly feeling growing. I looked across the city and found thick, black smoke rising into the air from several blocks away. A fire, a large one by the looks of it. Red lights were racing to get to it, hoping to prevent a catastrophe. But by the growing size of the smoke, that wasn't possible.

Wait.

That fire was downtown. It was near—

"Where is it?" I snapped, and Nikolai froze as I turned back to him, bracing my hands on the desk. "Where the fuck is the fire, Nikolai?"

He frowned, already pulling out his phone, typing a few things before scrolling. Then he went still.

"Where is it?" I snapped, some inner part of me already knowing the answer.

He looked up at me, exhaling a ragged breath. Something uneasy flickered across his face. "The ballet theater."

The room tilted on its axis, my vision blurring.

No.

No, no, no—

"Multiple alarms. Heavy smoke." Nikolai's eyes flicked back to his phone. "There's an evacuation in progress, but they were in the midst of a busy rehearsal. It sounds like they're worried a few may be stuck inside."

"That's not—" I shook my head. "She's not there."

She couldn't be. After catching us about to go for round two, there was no way Julian Vallen was going to let Eva out of his sight.

My heart slammed so hard it hurt.

The feeling

That fucking *feeling*.

I ripped open my desk drawer and snatched my phone, my fingers clumsy as I powered it on. The screen lit up, revealing mostly missed calls and messages from Nikolai, but one from Eva, too. And texts. She texted me *this morning*.

My breath caught as I scrolled through them.

I feel free, Alek... I want to be yours. I choose you. I love you, Alek... I'm going to rehearsal now...

The world narrowed to a single, brutal point, every part of me focused on that one little word.

Rehearsal.

"No," I breathed, the word tearing out of me like stitches on a wound. "Fuck. *No.*"

I clicked the call button, my heart pounding in my chest with every long second without an answer. The phone rang and rang and rang, haunting me with the silence in between. Finally, I heard a click, and my body loosened.

Until I heard the words, *"Hi, you've reached Eva. I can't come to the phone right now—"*

I called her again, but the same thing happened again. And again. And the texts I fired off went unread and unanswered, too.

"No," I snarled, already running for the door. "Pick up, solnyshka."

I didn't remember getting to the car. Didn't remember Nikolai sliding into the passenger seat, his face as determined as mine. Didn't remember starting the car and whipping out of the spot in front of my building. All I knew was the sound of my own heartbeat drowning out everything else as I tore through the city like a bat out of hell.

My mind could only think of one thing. Her name repeated like a prayer to a god I didn't fully trust to keep her alive.

Eva.
Eva.
Eva.
Eva.
Eva.

I blew through the streets, ignoring every red light, every vehicle in my way. My fingers were repeatedly pressing the call button by Eva's name, hoping she would pick up and reassure me that she was already.

But the dark feeling inside of me only grew stronger.

If something happened to her, I would never forgive myself. If I had seen her texts, I would have rushed over to the theater. I could have gotten her out myself. But I was sulking, too convinced that I had lost the girl that somehow managed to sneak past every one of my walls.

I could smell the smoke from three blocks away. Black. Thick. *Wrong*.

It covered the air like a blanket, making it impossible to see. I skidded the car to a stop and rolled down the window, coughing through the ash.

Sirens screamed, and police officers directed the crowd away from the burning building. In the distance, firefighters scrambled to the theater, which loomed ahead, its beautiful old stone blackened, bleeding smoke into the sky.

I growled under my breath before parking the car and ordering Nikolai to take care of it. I couldn't fucking sit still while waiting for the news on whether Eva made it out okay. I had to be there amongst the chaos. I couldn't rest until I knew she was in my arms again.

I sprinted to the front of the building and found a large group of ballerinas in sparkling costumes huddled together, their faces covered with soot. I scanned the group, praying that I found my petite girl among them. But she wasn't there.

No.

No.

Where the fuck was she?

A hand wrapped around my wrist, and I turned, knowing I was wearing a murderous expression, only to find a sobbing Mia in front of me. Mascara ran down the front of her cheeks, and her bun was disheveled. The fury that someone was stopping me slowly leeched out as my hope restarted. Maybe Mia knew where Eva was. Maybe she was coming to bring me to her.

And then she opened her mouth, and the hope inside me died.

"A-Alek," she sobbed. "It's Eva. No one knows where she is. She was on the stage with Raphael, and he said they got separated. You have to f-find her. I-I know you will."

Everything in me snapped to attention. She was still inside the fucking theater.

"Where is she?" I all but roared, my inner beast clawing, fighting for control. It's a suffocating feeling, this need to get to her.

Mia pointed at the burning building.

I turned, about to run up the stairs inside, when I saw him.

Julian Vallen stepped out of his car, his face white with both fury and terror. Chocolate eyes, the same color as Eva's, locked onto me.

"You," he roared, crossing the distance in seconds. He grabbed me by the collar and slammed me back against one of the stone columns. "You did this. You sick fuck. You tried to hurt her—"

"Get the fuck off of me," I said, shoving him off me so hard that he stumbled, eyes widening.

I didn't want to hear the rest of his anger. My eyes were too focused on the entrance, on the smoke pouring out the doors. That's where Eva was.

My light. My life. My love.

My solnyshka.

My feet were moving before my mind was. I ran past the firefighters, past their erected barriers. I ran past the fear clawing up my throat and the cold terror in my bones that threatened to outweigh the stifling heat.

"You're not getting away from me that easily, Evangeline," I hissed under my breath, letting just enough of the monster bleed through my facade. "You cannot fucking escape me. If you die, I will follow right after you."

And then I ran into the flames.

March 7th

EVANGELINE

Alek?

Are you there?

I think my phone is broken... Nothing is delivering... But if you can see this, I'm trapped on the stage. I can't move this piece of the set off of me.

I think this is the end of us, Aleksandr.

I love you.

EVANGELINE
CHAPTER THIRTY-THREE

"Help!" I screamed, my voice raw from both my cries and the excessive smoke I'd inhaled while lying on the stage floor. "Help me!"

But no one was coming. I knew that with chilling certainty. I was alone, waiting for my body to be eaten by the flames.

The fire didn't start like they did in movies. There was no sudden explosion, no dramatic imagery of flames licking up the walls. It began quietly, insidiously—an acrid smell that cut through the familiar scent of rosin and sweat and old velvet curtains.

At first, I thought something had blown, an old lightbulb or something. It was a historic theatre, and nothing in the main area seemed to be out of order. But then, someone in the scene shop screamed.

Smoke poured in from the wings, thick and gray, curling along the ceiling like a living thing. The music cut out mid-measure, the abrupt silence somehow louder than the orchestra ever was.

"Fire!" someone shouted.

The word cracked the room open.

Everything happened at once after that. Dancers bolted in every direction, slippers skidding against the stage, bodies colliding as panic took over. Madame Germaine was yelling, voices overlapping, chaos swallowing every attempt at order.

"Come on! To the exit!" Raphael shouted, grabbing my hand and guiding me to safety.

I ran with him, my feet burning from my pointe shoes. My heart was pounding so hard it felt like it was trying to escape my chest. Smoke burned my eyes. I coughed, the movement making my throat tighten. Ash rained down like snow, clinging to my costume, tangling in my hair.

We didn't make it far.

Crack!

The sound split the air above us. Wood snapped, something giving way. I barely had time to look up and let go of Raphael's hand before a part of the grand set broke loose and fell to the ground.

Pain exploded through my body as I hit the floor, and the breath was knocked clean out of me. Something heavy pinned my legs, pressing into my ribs. I screamed, the sound swallowed immediately by the roar of the fire.

"Eva!" Raphael yelled, dropping beside me. He tried to lift the beam, his face reddening with strain. But the wood didn't move, not even when I tried to help him lift it. "I... I can't—"

"It's okay," I gasped. Smoke filled my lungs, every breath shallow and sharp. "Go. Get help."

"I'm not leaving you."

But I wouldn't let him die with me. "You have to. *Please.*"

Another crash echoed through the theater, closer this time. Raphael hesitated, terror written all over his face.

"Go," I whispered, nodding to the door.

"I'll come back," he promised, his voice breaking. "I swear."

Then he was gone, disappearing into the smoke. And I

knew that no matter how noble Raphael was, he would be breaking that promise. The firefighters would never let him back in, and that was *if* he didn't collapse as soon as he escaped. These moments were probably my last.

Flames darted out from the growing wreckage, licking at my skin before deciding they liked the taste of me. The heat became unbearable, the air thick and choking me. My vision blurred, spots dancing in front of my eyes.

I tried to move, to push the weight off me, but my body shook uselessly beneath it. I'd never lifted weights a day in my life, a decision I was regretting now.

I was regretting a lot of things. But the biggest was how my relationship with Alek had ended.

There were so many things I should have said, so many things I should have done differently. I'd wasted so many moments by being afraid of who I truly was inside, denying the part of me that belonged to him. But I should have gone to him, I should have run after him and told him I loved him sooner.

It hurt knowing that I'd finally been brave. That I'd chosen him, yet I hadn't even gotten the chance to tell him how I felt. He would never know how sure I was about him, about us. I was ready to burn my old life down to stand beside him.

And now I was burning alone.

Tears streamed down my cheeks, mixing with ash.

"I'm sorry," I whispered to no one. To Jules. To Alek. To myself. "For everything."

My eyelids fluttered, the world dimming. The heat and smoke began to finally pull me under—

"*EVANGELINE!*" a deep voice roared into the dark.

At first, I thought it was my mind fracturing, smoke playing tricks on me. But then I heard it again.

"*EVANGELINE!*"

My heart stuttered. Either I was just hearing things or...

Or he had come for me.

"Evangeline! I can feel you here, baby, where are you?" Alek shouted.

"I-I'm over h-here," I croaked, forcing my eyes open so I could try to see him. They stung, but I kept them open, coughing several times until I was sure I was going to throw up from the force.

The smoke was slowly suffocating me. Every breath brought me less and less relief, the ashen taste settling on my tongue.

I spotted a large shadow across the stage, swiftly moving toward me. It solidified into a man wrapped in smoke and flame. Alek's face was streaked with soot, and his eyes were wild and glowing like an angel of death.

He dropped to his knees beside me, hands already gripping the fallen beam.

"I've got you," he said, voice raw. "I've got you, solnyshka."

I tried to help him, but my movements were weak. I wasn't sure how he was going to get it off of me when Raphael couldn't even make it move, and he'd inhaled far less smoke than Alek probably had in his search for me.

But Alek rolled up his sleeves, exposing forearms I'd thought about many hours late into the night, and shoved the set piece off of me like it weighed nothing. His arms were around me a second later, crushing me to his chest while I tried to breathe through the pain in my body.

"You're okay," he breathed, his body trembling. He whispered the words over and over like he was trying to convince himself more than me. "You're okay. You're okay."

I clutched his shirt as a thick sob escaped me. My body curled into him like he was the only real thing left in this world, the only thing standing between me and death.

"I love you," I whispered. I cupped his cheek with a soot-covered hand. I wanted to kiss him so badly, but I knew this wasn't the time, not when the set was collapsing around us and we risked becoming trapped. "I thought I lost you. I thought I ruined everything."

He pressed his forehead to mine as the smoke swirled around us. "Never," he said fiercely. "I would burn this world to ash before I let it take you from me. Because I love you, Evangeline. And I will stop at nothing to give you the happily ever after you deserve."

Alek scooped me up into his arms, holding me tight as he turned toward the exit. He must have been able to see better than I could, or he knew his way around the theatre better from studying the blueprints so much, because his steps were swift and sure as he led me to safety. The flames roared behind us like they were angry he'd stolen me back.

The cold, late winter air hit me like a ton of bricks as we escaped the burning building. We were suddenly rushed by a swarm of people—firefighters, paramedics, other dancers. I spotted Madame Germaine's stern but worried gaze amongst the crowd, and I even thought I saw the auburn locks and brown eyes that belonged to my brother.

But all of my attention was on the man holding me.

I turned to face him, looking up into his dark blue eyes. They looked like sapphires, only more beautiful.

They were the last thing I saw before everything went black.

March 8th

NIKOLAI

Hope little Eva is okay, boss. She looked pretty rough when you pulled her out.

ALEKSANDR

The doctor said she'll be fine. Bruised ribs and smoke inhalation, but no major injuries and her burns are pretty minor. She's hooked up to oxygen, and the doctor gave her a sedative to help her sleep so she's out now.

NIKOLAI

That's great!

Is her brother going to let you live?

ALEKSANDR

I'll die before he tries to keep me away from her again.

NIKOLAI

Fuck, dude. That's intense.

ALEKSANDR
CHAPTER THIRTY-FOUR

My body was stiff as I pulled the chair from the side of the room closer to the bed where Eva lay fast asleep, an oxygen mask over her face. I wanted nothing more than to wrap my arms and hold her close, but I didn't want to risk hurting her, so I settled for the feeling of her hand in mine.

Fuck. It was so limp.

I was running on fumes at this point, but no part of me wanted to sleep in that uncomfortable hospital chair. Every time I closed my eyes, I pictured her frail body pinned beneath a column designed for the set. Her expression had looked so lifeless before I showed up, her eyes closed and her mouth slightly parted.

I never wanted to see that look on her again.

Whenever the visions threatened to stop me in my tracks, I reminded myself of her answering me in a room filled with smoke, her in my arms, her whispering that she loved me, her looking at me as if I was both her dark horse and the white knight atop it.

My girl. Mine.

I squeezed her hand and was delighted by the slight squeeze back, as if even in sleep she reached out to me. I brought her fingers to my knuckles and gently kissed all of them. "I'm sorry I wasn't there earlier, Eva. But I'm here now. I always will be."

"Is that so?" a voice rasped from across the room.

I startled. Normally, it was impossible to surprise me, but with the love of my life attached to a ton of fucking wires on a hospital bed, I wasn't exactly at my best.

There was a dark figure in the corner, lurking in the shadows of the room. Julian Vallen stepped into the dim, fluorescent lighting.

"Fuck," I hissed under my breath. "How long have you been there?"

"A long time." Julian's voice was laden with torture. He sounded like *he* was the one who went through hell, not Eva and me. But I couldn't blame him too much. He was the first one to greet me at the door when I walked out with her in my arms, the first one to usher us both into the waiting ambulances where they tried—and failed—to separate me from Eva. Everyone else had made it out much quicker than we did, so we were swarmed with medical attention. I'd lost Julian in all of the chaos.

The Vallen King's brown hair was sticking up in a million different directions, and his matching eyes were bloodshot. Dried streaks of silver tears sat atop his sunken skin, his under-eyes dark and purple. Julian looked like he might cry at any moment as he looked at his sister sleeping next to me. The vulnerability surprised me.

"You saved her," Julian murmured.

I scoffed. "Of course I saved her."

"She would have died if you weren't there." His voice was hollow as if he was still trying to process it himself.

"But I was there. I always will be." I softened as I looked down at Eva sleeping peacefully before looking back at Julian, at the unreadable expression on his cold face. "I won't fucking leave her. And if you try to make me, I will make sure my bullet hits where I aim it."

It was a low blow—it would take an idiot not to notice the guilt he wore like a badge of disgrace—but Julian frowned, his eyes darting between the two of us. "You really love her?"

"Yes," I replied without hesitation.

"This isn't some game or form of sick revenge using my sister? This is actually love?"

"I don't know what to tell you, Vallen. I'm not going to pretend to be an expert on love and other fucking emotions because I've never been in it before. All I know is that from the moment I met her, she's been my entire world. And when I see her, everything looks a little bit brighter, and I feel a little less alone. If that's not love, it's damn near close."

I looked down at Eva before smiling to myself. "Plus, anyone who spends three minutes with that girl would find themselves as enamored as I am. No matter who her family is."

Julian sat down at the edge of the bed and looked at his sister, grabbing her other hand. "She has a way with her. She's spent her whole life being completely ignored, so she doesn't know the power she has to draw people in. I know my parents' methods were unconventional, but they were only trying to protect her. I tried my best to be there for her, to protect her in my own way, but I know I wasn't enough." He looked at me, his eyes darkening. "She seems to think *you* are enough, though. At least that was the impression I got when she essentially told me to fuck off earlier tonight."

I couldn't help the grin that flooded my face. God, I wished I could have been there to see that. She was probably brilliant.

My eyes fell onto her face, on the ash the nurses hadn't yet cleaned off, on the small bruises forming on her cheekbones. And I was torn looking at her in that hospital bed.

One part of me knew that Eva was probably better off

without me. I'd known her for almost three months, and she'd been hospitalized twice. My world was a dangerous one, and while my greatest enemy was sitting across from me, there were others. What if something worse happened to her? What if I didn't make it in time? What if she *died*?

I couldn't live in a world without her. I would crawl to the pits of hell myself if she left me alone in this realm. So maybe I should have left her, if only to keep her safe.

But the other part of me was a selfish beast. I couldn't imagine a life without her walking the halls of my mansion or my townhome. I couldn't imagine traveling the world without her by my side. I couldn't imagine a future where I didn't wake up every morning with her sweet face next to mine, and I didn't fall asleep every night with my cock coated in her cum. I wanted to cook for her, I wanted to spoil her, I wanted to fucking *marry her*.

Maybe we had only been together for three months. But those three months were the best of my life.

"I don't like you," Julian said.

"And I don't care."

"You don't deserve her."

"No one ever could. But I'm the bastard who will try to deserve her every day."

Julian sighed. "But I believe you love her. You went into a burning building for her, for fuck's sake. I have a feeling that if this were another one of your plans, you wouldn't have done that. You keep her happy, and you clearly keep her safe."

"What are you saying, Vallen?"

"I'm saying that I don't like this at *all*... but I'm not going to stop it, either."

I exhaled slowly. Something in my ribcage shifted, settling into place.

I looked down at Eva, at the steady rise and fall of her breath and the soft curve of her mouth, even in sleep. She looked untouched by the chaos she'd endured, like the world hadn't nearly swallowed her whole.

Then, I turned back to Julian, my gaze hard, silently accepting the responsibility. Because Julian Vallen wasn't just handing me his permission.

He was handing me *her*.

Julian's face contorted as he muttered under his breath, "Don't make me regret this, Drakov."

"I can't promise that." Mainly because Julian was probably *already* regretting this.

But it was too late to change his mind. Eva was mine. He couldn't take her back from me.

Both of us looked over at the girl lying in the bed. The girl who had somehow managed to bring two enemies together for the first time in twenty-three years.

Eva.

March 8th

NIKOLAI

So... Do I still have a living cousin?

ALEKSANDR

Yes.

NIKOLAI

YAY!

Does this mean we can play Xbox later?

ALEKSANDR

No, Niko.

NIKOLAI

Reuniting with little Eva, huh? 😏

😏😏😏

ALEKSANDR

Shut the fuck up.

EVANGELINE
CHAPTER THIRTY-FIVE

When I came back to reality, my whole body was sore. It wasn't an unbearable pain like after I'd gotten surgery on my shoulder, but I was aware of every little movement I made and the way it sent aches throughout my body. Every time I took a breath, every time my shoulders rose and fell, my torso lit up with pain.

I groaned, stretching out my sore muscles and coughing once. That was agonizing, and it took me several deep breaths to finally inhale without feeling like my lungs were on fire, coated in ash.

The fire. Right.

I shoved aside all my memories of that event, not wanting to relive it. Even the thought of those flames trying to get me made me want to hide under the hospital bedsheet.

You're okay, I reminded myself. *Alek got you out. He saved you just like a Prince Charming.*

Yes, Alek was my Prince Charming. And he was my villain, too.

But most of all, he was mine.

My eyes slowly fluttered open. I winced at the bright light, a slight whimper slipping past my lips without meaning to.

"Shh, solnyshka," a soft voice murmured. A warm hand caressed my cheek, stroking it with his thumb.

Alek.

I tried to open my eyes even more, tried to move in the bed so I could see him, *hold* him. A pair of hands held me against the bed. "You're all right. No need to rush."

"Al... Alek," I said, coughing a few times.

"I'm right here, baby. Take it easy."

I focused all my attention on the places he touched me, grounding myself in the feeling. I inhaled and exhaled several times. "That's it. Good girl."

Hearing those words drove me wild. I knew I should have been focused on the pain, on my slight difficulties breathing, on anything other than how badly his hands pushing me into the bed made me want him. But after going a few days without him, I needed him. I needed *more*.

My eyes opened once more, and the world came into focus. It took a few seconds to adjust to the brightness of the hospital room. There was a slight beeping noise coming from a monitor behind me, and I was covered by a thin bed sheet and an even thinner dress. The room smelled like antiseptic, cleaner, and a faint whiff of musk.

My gaze found him last, his body stiff in a small chair, leaning toward the bed. Alek's hair was mussed as if he spent hours running his fingers through it. He wore his signature black suit, only instead of being pristine, it was rumpled, some of the buttons undone to reveal his tattoos. His eyes were dark, and his jaw was tight until I whispered, "*Alek.*"

"How are you feeling, baby?"

There was something guarded in both his tone and his expression, like he almost expected me to wake up and push him away. But I would never do that. I meant what I said before the fire. I wanted him.

I tried to sit up further, but my movements were

constricted by the IV in my arm and the mask over my nose. I pulled that off and set it to the side. Then, I grabbed Alek's lapels and pulled him to me, crashing our lips together.

His tense body softened against me. Alek brought his hands to my waist and my hair, his tongue thrusting inside of me. I moaned at the taste of him, at the feeling of his tongue practically making love to mine, always dominant.

"I love you," I murmured against his lips, surrendering to the feelings churning inside of me.

"I love you too, Evangeline," Alek said before pulling back with a groan. "But *fuck*. We can't."

I stuck my bottom lip out in a soft pout. "Why not? Don't you want me?"

He slammed me into the bed, his hand wrapping around my throat, and his teeth biting my earlobe. "Of course I fucking want you."

Alek wrenched himself back, staring at his hand in almost horror. "I could have hurt you. Fuck!" he cursed, shoving himself off the bed. His chest heaved as he placed his forehead against the wall, clearly trying to calm himself.

It took a few tries to stand up, my legs wobbling as if they were still asleep, but eventually, I made it out of the bed, the IV dragging behind me. I felt better than I expected to, which was a welcome surprise. Alek stiffened when I placed my arm on his forearm and pulled him back to me.

"You would never hurt me," I whispered before grabbing him by the back of the neck and pulling him into me.

Alek didn't fight me much as our lips met in a gentle kiss that quickly deepened. Heat flared between us like the most natural thing in the world, building low in my core before spreading out to the rest of my sore limbs.

He kissed me like he'd been starved. Slow at first, reverent, his mouth moving against mine with a careful restraint that trembled at the edges. His hands slid to my waist, thumbs brushing the thin fabric of the hospital gown, as if reminding himself I was alive. That I was here with him, never going anywhere again.

I whimpered into his mouth, my fingers tightening in his hair. "I need you, Alek. I need to feel you in me."

His grip tightened, and he pulled back. His lips traveled across my face with tender kisses. "Evangeline... I can't. You're in the hospital for fuck's sake. Your brother went to take a call."

"Because *you* saved me. I wouldn't be here if it weren't for you." I tilted my head, pressing a kiss to his jaw, then his throat, breathing him in. Smoke and steel and something unmistakably Alek.

My hands wandered, slow and sure, relearning him. Feeling the tension coiled beneath his skin. Our time apart was too long. I wanted to memorize the look on his face as he came in me. I wanted to taste the devotion on his tongue.

"I want to feel you. I *need* to."

He shuddered when I kissed the corner of his mouth again. "Eva," he warned, voice rough. "We shouldn't—"

"Alek." I pulled back enough to look at him. I tried to display every emotion on my face so he knew this was what I wanted, what I *needed*.

"Please," I whispered.

And that was enough.

Something dark and hungry flickered across his face before he mastered it, ice cracking under pressure. He cupped my cheek, thumb brushing under my eye with a tenderness that didn't match the fire burning in his gaze.

"I will not fuck you now, solnyshka."

I opened my mouth to protest again, but Alek placed a gentle finger on my lips. "I will not fuck you now. Not while you're hooked up to all these machines, not while we're on a bed with fucking wheels, and not while you're still recovering.

I won't risk hurting you right now. But I will make you feel so good, baby."

He guided me back toward the bed, his movements controlled, where my breath was not. He helped me gingerly lie down before following after me, settling between my legs. His presence was a familiar weight I welcomed as he braced himself over me.

Alek's lips traced a path from my mouth to my jaw and down my neck, pausing to bite his favorite spot. Everywhere he touched, he left goosebumps.

My fingers dug into his shoulders as he kissed lower, slower, pausing at my breasts long enough to make my open legs quiver. Alek pulled my hospital gown up to reveal my bare pussy, sucking in a breath at the sight.

He stared at it for several moments, his gaze appreciative. I could already feel the wetness drenching my thighs the longer my anticipation lasted. The world narrowed to the sound of my pounding heart and the steady, devastating focus in his eyes when he looked back at me.

"You're mine," he said darkly. "That's not a promise. That's a threat."

And I knew with unwavering certainty the hidden meaning in his words: that my brother would not stand in our way. That these flames had somehow burned our fairytale ending into the storybook. That we would finally be together again.

So I nodded and said, "I know. And you're mine."

"Yes," he said, blue eyes piercing me. "I am."

The darkness in his eyes made my pussy throb, and by the way his jaw clenched, Alek knew it.

He lowered his head without warning, dragging his tongue up my slit. I arched at the sensation until one of Alek's hands pushed my stomach down, the other gripping my thigh as if to anchor himself to me. Then, he returned, burying himself inside of me, his breath hot and heavy while he tasted the most intimate parts of me.

"Mmm," he hummed, and the sound sent a vibration up and down my spine. "You taste so fucking sweet."

My hands went straight to his hair, tugging at the messy strands with so much force that it probably would have brought him to his knees if he weren't already on them.

"Alek! Oh my God, *Alek*," I moaned as he hungrily ate me out.

He worshipped me with his tongue, licking and biting and sucking me into oblivion. I writhed on the bed, the beeping of the monitor suddenly lost in all of the sensations.

"When I die, I want my head to be buried between your legs," Alek growled. "I want to meet death with the taste of you still on my lips."

He latched onto my sensitive clit before his tongue darted out and stroked it with a rhythm so fast it almost seemed impossible. My cries died in my throat when one of his hands snaked up my dress to pinch my nipple while the other one buried two fingers deep in my pussy.

The rush of sensations was almost too much. Alek removed the hand from my breast and brought it to my abdomen, where he used it to push me deep into the bed while his fingers' pace increased. They pumped harder and harder while his mouth leisurely moved against my clit.

"Feel me inside of you. Feel me all the way in your fucking stomach, Evangeline, because that's where I'm going to be for the rest of our lives."

"Alek... I need... Alek, *please*."

"Shh," Alek murmured. "I know what you need, solnyshka. You're taking me so well. Such a good girl. Now come for me."

I did instantly, my body obeying his every command. My mind was empty of everything but the sparks traveling through my veins. Alek lapped up every ounce of my cum, sighing in pleasure at the taste of my utter satisfaction.

I collapsed against the bed. Normally, Alek would have brought me over the edge multiple times in one night. But I had a feeling that I wasn't going to be able to push him any farther. Not until I was out of this stupid hospital.

Alek pulled himself next to me and kissed me softly. The smell of my juices on his lips made me dizzy, and I attempted to deepen the kiss before he pulled back with a grin, his eyes bright for the first time in a long time.

"You're not going to kiss your way into a second round, Evangeline."

I shrugged, the movement tugging at the still-tense parts of my body. "It was worth a try."

"You have plenty of time to try later. *After* you've healed."

"Wow, it's amazing... I think I'm healed already! Full recovery," I said, a small smile playing on my lips as I ran my hands over my body, hoping it enticed him enough to dive back into me.

Alek groaned. "*Eva*. You're killing me. I can't keep resisting you."

"So then *don't*. I want you, you want me, and I'm healed enough to have you. What's there to resist?"

He shook his head, but he was already settling himself atop me, fingers toying with the hem of the hospital gown. "There's no rush. We have forever, baby."

I leaned up and kissed him, smiling when he let me pull him back down. "So let's start our forever now."

June 21st

JULES

Do I have to sit by him, Evangeline?

Surely there's any other seat in that blasted theater of his. He built it at least double the size of the last one.

EVANGELINE

Yes, you do. It's my closing night, and you have to do what I say. You two are going to bond whether you like it or not.

JULES

I DON'T like it. I don't like HIM. That's the point.

EVANGELINE

So then learn to like him. Easy!

EVANGELINE ADDED ALEKSANDR DRAKOV TO THE CHAT

JULES

No.

EVANGELINE

He's not going anywhere, Jules. Might as well accept that.

ALEKSANDR

No. I am not.

EVANGELINE

:)

EVANGELINE
CHAPTER THIRTY-SIX

My chest was tight as I stood backstage, preparing to walk on. It was the closing night for *Romeo and Juliet* at the City Ballet Company theater.

Well, the new one.

Three months ago, this place had been filled with ash and ruin. Beams were charred, balconies had collapsed, and the grand chandelier had shattered upon the floor. It was a ghost of the place I once considered home.

Now, it was breathtaking.

The new Drakov Theater rose around us in gold and velvet, reborn into something even grander than before. The new chandelier scattered warm light like stardust, its crystals catching every light onstage. Freshly carved balconies curved along the walls, and the restored frescoes glowed softly overhead.

With such extensive damage, it would have been impossible to rebuild the theater in enough time to finish the season. But Alek had done it. He'd pulled every string he could, hired the best companies in addition to his own, and he'd rebuilt the place I loved all so that I could be here, ready to bask in the glow of the stage.

The air smelled of chalked silk shoes, roses, and something else. Something electric.

Anticipation.

The music swelled, filling every corner of the theater. I walked over to the funeral pyre, preparing to dance the final pas de deux, one made not of shared moves, but a back and forth of dances as Romeo and I greeted our deaths. I settled as the curtains were pulled backward, revealing a grieving Raphael and me. And then our bodies moved before our minds could catch up, and we danced together.

My feet barely touched the stage as I stood atop my Romeo, who clutched a bottle of the fatal poison in his white-knuckled fist. The choreography lived in my muscles, but the emotion—*that* came from somewhere deeper.

Romeo and Juliet. Love and loss. Devotion written in blood and sacrifice. I'd felt it all over the past few months. Yet here I was, dancing.

Not just with Raphael, but with every scar I carried. With the marred flesh of the bullet wound on my shoulder. With the memory of fire and smoke that still sometimes haunted me in the night—and the way Alek had carried me out of hell without hesitation. With the certainty that I was alive in a way I never had been before.

I danced with a love that had survived it all. A love that chose each other every day.

I poured that love out through my body, hoping the audience saw it as Juliet's love for Romeo. But I knew the truth:

It was for Alek.

I spun around, and my gaze flicked instinctively to the wings, where Madame Germaine stood beyond the curtain. Her hands were clasped tightly in front of her, her sharp eyes following every movement. When our eyes met, her severe expression softened into something rare and radiant.

Pride.

The director's lips curved in a small, approving smile. I was her Juliet, and I was doing well. My throat tightened before I turned away.

And then, my eyes found *them*.

They were in the private box to the right, so close to the stage that I could almost make out their smiles in the stage lights.

I spotted Nikolai first, his attention flicking across the room. Jules was next to him, his jaw tight, his attention fixed on the stage. He watched me, but sometimes his eyes darted to the curtains as if trying to spot someone else. There was something protective and fierce in his posture that almost made me chuckle. Alek looked at me like that.

Jules had begrudgingly accepted my relationship with Alek. He didn't like it at all, and he made that clear often, but he didn't try to stop me from seeing him. Sometimes, he even agreed to have dinner all together, though I limited how often I asked that for everyone's sanity.

They had learned, the two of them—learned that loving me meant not tearing each other apart.

I was still trying to figure out a way to tell my brother that I wasn't renewing the lease on my apartment because Alek had asked me to move in with him after the show. I'd said yes, of course, but Jules?

Jules would be enraged.

And then he would get over it because he loved me.

Besides, based on Elsie's confirmation that she was still planning to retire after this show and the little sparkle she got in her eyes when I asked her if she still wanted to open her bakery, I had a feeling that my brother had bigger things to worry about soon.

And at the other end of the balcony, his body partially hidden by the shadows, sat the love of my life.

My gaze kept falling to him as I moved through the pas de

deux, and though Alek's expression was ice-calm, I knew his eyes were shining with pride as he watched me. I knew the way his shoulders softened when I landed a difficult turn. I knew his body followed mine like gravity. I knew the way his eyes darkened with silent obsession. And suddenly, my heart felt too full for my body.

The music slowed, sorrow threading through the notes, a foreshadowing of the darkness to come. But at that moment, I felt only lightness surrounding me. Lightness and love and all of the emotions I'd been searching for as I settled into the final pose.

For half a breath, there was silence.

Then, the theater erupted. Applause thundered through the hall, rising like a wave, crashing over the stage. Flowers rained down at our feet. Bravos echoed from every direction.

I felt every joyous noise as I held my stance, lying atop Raphael, my body collapsed with sorrow. I let the heady feeling settle into me before raising my head and looking back at the box.

Alek stood, a small smile on his face as he clapped for me just like he did months ago. I pressed a hand to my chest, emotion overwhelming me as I took a final bow.

Because for the first time, *my* voice—not Alek's—silently whispered, "*Perfect.*"

June 22nd

JULES

Eva.

Where is Elsie?

ALEKSANDR
EPILOGUE

ONE YEAR LATER

I felt her presence as soon as I stepped into our mansion. After a long day at the shipyards trying to figure out what the fuck was going on with one of our missing shipments—and a long night spent killing the people responsible—I craved her light, the feeling of sunshine that followed her no matter where she went.

"Solnyshka, where are you?" I called out, but I was met with silence. I frowned as I shrugged off my suit jacket and handed it to one of the staff who was always home whenever I was not.

"Solnyshka?"

Nothing.

My worry might have worsened had the maid not turned to me and said, "She's in the studio, sir."

I let out a long breath of relief. It had taken me almost two years to learn how to leave her in our home alone without having a panic attack. Every time I stepped out of the door, I was crushed by the weight of my anxiety. Oddly enough, it took Julian coming over and sitting with her for me to get some damn work done.

He still came over from time to time. So did Mia and Nikolai, unfortunately. My parents had even taken to visiting her, their smiles wide as they accepted her as if she were their own daughter. It had taken many hard conversations to uncover the truth about Liza's death, but my family never once held it against Eva. How could they? She was a four-year-old girl, and my sister's death was truly a tragic accident. But it had taken many visits to convince Eva that they didn't hate her.

Quite the opposite, actually. My mother kept asking when she could visit again, filling my girl and my fridge with far too much food.

But Eva kept reassuring me that she didn't need anyone to babysit her, and I'd finally learned to give her that space to grow. It wasn't that I didn't trust my Eva to handle herself, but after Charlotte's situation last year, it was hard to trust the world with someone so beautiful.

Soft music floated down the hall from the ballet studio I'd built for her in one of my spare rooms. It was the first renovation I'd done. I wanted Eva to have a space that felt like her own, a room to symbolize my house becoming ours.

And I also wanted a place where we could fuck in front of the mirrors again. Which we did.

Many times.

I leaned against the doorway and watched her move through her familiar rhythms. I'd learned them long ago. The way she warmed up slowly, methodically. The way she favored her left side when she was tired. The way her breathing changed when she forgot anyone else was watching.

The studio was quiet except for the soft brush of her bare feet against the floor. Sunlight spilled through the tall windows, catching dust motes in the air and turning them gold.

Eva moved through the room with an ease that knocked the air from my lungs. It was the off-season for the theater, and this dancing felt different. There was no orchestra, no costumes, no stage lights, and no audience except for me. There was only Eva wrapped in pale pink fabric, her hair pulled back by a matching ribbon, while her body moved like it was always meant to.

Freely.

My gaze drifted, unbidden, to her left hand, where a large diamond sent sunlight scattering across the room. The thing that officially marked her as *mine*.

I'd given it to her months ago on the closing night of last year's performance of *The Nutcracker*, where my Eva danced as the Sugar Plum Fairy for the whole city to see. I was so damn proud of the way she'd moved up to principal. The prima ballerina of the show. And my heart.

Now, we planned our wedding, a beautiful affair set for next spring. I couldn't wait to see her in a white dress, her soft smile tucked behind a veil, before she became mine in the only way she was not.

Evangeline Drakov, my wife.

I smiled at the thought of that.

Sometimes, my thoughts drifted to the future, to a time when we'd have children with her soft eyes and my stubbornness. Mornings filled with soft chaos and nights with my family surrounding me while I succumbed to sleep, exhausted and happy. I wanted her barefoot and laughing in the kitchen as much as I wanted her commanding a stage.

Eva and I had many conversations about this, but we both agreed that she should enjoy her career for now. I would support Eva in any way I could, including taking on parental duties so she could dance, but Eva wanted to linger in this phase of our lives a little longer, and I was a patient man.

And selfishly, I wanted her to myself a little longer.

Eva finished a turn and finally noticed me, her lips curving when our eyes met. "How long have you been standing there?"

"Long enough to appreciate how beautiful you look today."

Her cheeks turned a treasured shade of pink. She walked toward me, steps unhurried. A bead of sweat trickled down her exposed back, and warmth radiated from her skin.

Eva held out her hands to me, and I took them, brushing my thumb over the ring. "I'm going to marry you," I murmured, kissing the stone and the gold band.

Her smile widened. "I love you."

I pulled her closer, pressing my forehead against hers. I breathed in the smell of vanilla and strawberries, still my favorite scent in the world. "I love you too, solnyshka."

Our kiss was soft, unrushed, and full of certainty. Certainty that our lifetime together was going to be the most beautiful thing in the world, full of many days spent like this, right in each other's arms, choosing to stay.

"I'm glad you weren't watching where you were going, Alek," Eva said, echoing her words from years ago. "And I'm glad you found me."

I smiled. "I always will."

"Is that a promise?"

"No. It's a threat."

ALEKSANDR
BONUS EPILOGUE

TEN MONTHS LATER

My wife. My wife. My wife. My wife. My. Wife. My *wife. My* wife. *My wife.*

Mine.

That was all my mind could repeat as the night went on, a night filled with dancing and drinking and a cake with way too much fucking frosting. A night spent celebrating the day I'd just had—a day where I'd married the love of my life.

A day when Evangeline Vale had become Evangeline Vallen.

My wife.

Mine.

I held onto her waist as I followed her throughout the room. Well, I'd tried to. Eva had picked the poofiest goddamn dress I'd ever seen, a large ballgown with a corset bodice and little embroidered flowers all along the sparkly tulle. She looked like a princess, smiling and flitting about the room while people gushed over her bridal beauty and the giant ring on her finger.

A photographer snapped a photo while I blinked,

momentarily stunned by the flash. At first, I'd been annoyed by the way he kept getting in the fucking way—I wanted to consummate our marriage, which was impossible when he was *always there*—but now I was grateful for him. Because I needed these pictures. I needed something tangible to prove that this day actually happened, that Eva actually married me.

That she was really my wife now.

The party began to wind down now, and Eva started to sway on her feet, her eyes drooping to reveal sparkly lids that had probably taken Mia all day to do.

She turned to me, a love-drunk smile on her face. It was my favorite look on her, I decided.

"What do you want to do now, husband?"

I grabbed her waist again, not giving a damn if I was squishing her dress this time. At the dark look in my eyes, Eva bit her lip. But I bent down and used my teeth to tear it away.

"That's mine to bite, wife."

Fuck, I loved calling her that.

Eva shuddered, her breath coming in quick stutters as she said, "Yes, sir."

Oh, the sound of her submission was music to my ears. Despite the fact that I had snuck into her bridal suite this morning, I needed her *now*. I could never get enough of Eva. She was the craving that could never be satisfied.

Never.

I groaned before dragging her out of the banquet hall, where the grand reception was held. Then, when she kept tripping on the tulle, I swept her into my arms, one hand squishing all the fabric under her knees while the other splayed across her back.

The crowd cheered, and a few people patted my back in congratulations, but I paid none of them any mind. My eyes were locked on the woman in my arms, her eyes wide as she looked at me like she wanted to eat me alive. I'd let her. I'd let my wife do just about anything to me right now.

"So... you want my cock inside you? You want my hands on you and my lips tasting you? You want to scream my name like the good girl that you are? You want to start our honeymoon night early?"

Eva nodded quickly. I grinned as our car pulled to the curb. My driver got out and held up the door, and I all but barreled inside, hungry to be inside of her.

My lips crashed against hers, my hands struggling to find her thighs in all of the fabric. So instead, my fingers found my zipper and unleashed my cock—which was already agonizingly hard, ready to be inside of her—while I kissed down her neck, sucking and biting whenever she arched for me.

"How attached are you to this dress?" I asked. My voice was so rough it sounded like sandpaper.

Eva frowned. "Very."

I sighed. "Fine."

Gathering all of the tulle in my hands, I hiked the skirt over her waist. It was heaven to find her without underwear—as if she knew I wouldn't be able to go all night resisting her.

I gripped Eva's hips before adjusting her position on my lap. And then I slammed her onto my cock.

Eva's mouth parted as her body curved into me. Her chocolate irises rolled to the back of her head. There was no foreplay, not today, and the suddenness of my actions had her so shocked she stilled. Her cheeks turned a delicious shade of pink under my heated gaze, her pussy clenching around me.

I thrust upward, practically spearing her in two with my impatience. A moan filled the car, and I was thankful that there was a thick divider between my driver and us. These noises were only for me.

"My wife. My beautiful wife," I murmured while kissing her neck, my hips rocking inside of her. "All mine."

Eva blinked a few times, her lids hooded with pleasure. She leaned forward and kissed me softly, so at odds with the harsh force of my cock inside of her. "Yours, Alek."

I savored the feeling of my brand new wife, her pussy clenching around me. It took everything in me not to rip into her. Now wasn't the time for rough fucking. Now was the time for lovemaking, for giving my wife everything she needed and more.

My wife.

Fuck, after years together, she still felt so tight. So fucking good, made for me and only me.

Slowly at first, I moved inside of her, thrusting in and out while rocking my hips in a way that I knew would hit the spot that made her moans get higher.

"Faster, Alek. Faster," she panted, her fingers flying to my hair. I'd learned over the years that she liked gripping the dark strands, liked the way my jaw tightened whenever she pulled to the point of pain.

I couldn't resist her, not even as I was trying to be gentle. The slapping of skin echoed in the car as I pounded into her from below, savoring Eva's soft whimpers like they were gold. My hands flew up to cradle her body closer to me, one of them sheltering her head from the roof of the car while the other arched her into me. It was like all my fantasies came true.

"You're my wife," I growled, teeth finding her neck while my cock pulsed into her with each word.

"Your wife," she breathed. Eva tried to pull me impossibly closer while my tongue slid across her quivering pulse.

"My wife."

Thrust.

"*My* wife."

Thrust.

"My *wife*."

Thrust.

"My—"

Thrust.

"—fucking—"

Thrust.

"—*wife*."

There was something about looking down at me while I fucked her into oblivion—her eyes rolling back into her head while her moans were loud and her pussy was tight—that made me easily fall apart.

Add that to the fact that I was the happiest I'd been in ages, and I was in heaven.

"Alek… Alek, I'm about to…"

But Eva didn't get to finish her sentence before she spilled over the edge with a scream.

And I did, roaring as jet after jet of hot cum coated her insides. "Fuck, solnyshka," I said with a thick exhale. "You are spectacular."

Eva seemed to still be high up in the clouds, so I sat back, content to just cup her cheek and wait for her to join me back on Earth. She was too beautiful for words. I had no idea how I got lucky over three years ago, running into her on a snowy night in the park. But despite some of the pain that followed, that night was the kickstart to the best thing that could ever happen to me.

I wouldn't change a thing. Well, maybe her injuries, but in a sick, twisted way, every time I looked at that now-faded bullet wound, I remembered the way she fought for me. The way she chose *me*. Like Life loving Death. And I fell in love with her all over again.

Everything we went through, all of it, got me *her*. My wife.

I still couldn't get over those two words together.

Soon, her breathing evened out, and she curled into my chest, my cock still inside of her. To be honest, I didn't want to remove it. Not if I didn't have to.

"I love you," I murmured against the soft skin of her neck. "My beautiful wife."

She smiled. "My husband."

Then, she giggled, which had me quirking an eyebrow. We just made love and she was *giggling*?

"You were quite gentle," Eva said.

I growled. "It was our first time as husband and wife. Did you want me to whip and choke you?"

I expected her to blush or sputter, but she surprised me, holding my gaze, her own darkening. "You are more than welcome to, sir. You're the one in charge."

Contrary to how it appeared, I didn't plan on fucking my wife in the backseat of a car. I'd had a romantic plan to take her to the penthouse suite of one of my many hotels where we would make love as husband and wife surrounded by rose petals.

I should have known that Eva, as much as she claimed to want a Prince Charming, liked me best when I was a villain.

"Oh, I love you," I said, turning her around so she was lying across the backseat with me on top of her. I smiled as I lowered my face to hers, my cock already moving inside of her again. "My pretty, pretty wife."

Want more from Lina Harper? Subscribe to her newsletter now for updates on future books, bonus scenes, and more!

<u>Authorlinaharper.substack.com</u>

A Sneak Peek...

Keep reading for a sneak peek at Adagio, a dark mafia/ballet romance starring Elsie Farrow and Julian Vallen, featuring:

- Childhood friends to lovers
- One-night stand gone wrong
- Groveling
- Second chance romance
- Chronic pain rep
- Eating disorder survivor rep

Releasing Summer 2026.

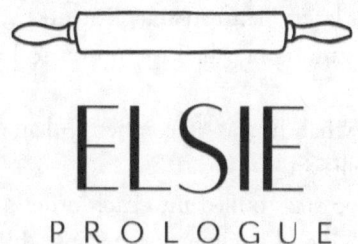

ELSIE
PROLOGUE

I swear to you this: I will find you, Elsie Farrow. And you will be mine.

- Julian Vallen

BEFORE I DROPPED OUT OF HIGH SCHOOL, MY favorite subject was surprisingly science. I liked how elements acted in predictable ways, how everyday occurrences were like magical marvels. It fascinated me, and I spent a lot of my free time—what little of it I had—in my room curled underneath my duvet, reading nonfiction science books. Maybe in another life, I would have gone to college for it. But I liked the way mine turned out.

For a few weeks, I was in a huge astronomy phase. This was when I was slowly starting to realize that my relationship with my mother was not only toxic, but emotionally abusive as well. I liked knowing that I could look up in the sky and take comfort with little balls of light that contained entire worlds—worlds far, far away from mine.

One time, I read about this phenomenon called neutron star collisions. Two neutron stars in a system together could get caught in each other's gravitational waves, causing them to circle each other. As they spiraled faster and faster, gravity would force the stars to merge, colliding at almost the speed of light. The resulting explosion had the power to either form a black hole or a larger neutron star. But no matter what, the light from the gamma rays had the power to bring worlds to their knees.

That was what it was like when Julian kissed me. A neutron star collision.

We were two stars pulled into each other's gravity fifteen years ago, circling and circling and circling, thinking we were never going to collide. But tonight, thanks to a little bravery on my part and a *lot* of whiskey, we were.

And I hadn't yet figured out whether this would result in my love for him turning into a black hole that enveloped everything in darkness or a star larger than ever.

Julian smashed me against the wall, his hands already flying to my back, fumbling with the bra hook. "Fuck," he said, his voice slurring a little. "How do you get this off?"

"Let me."

I pushed him back, much to his clear annoyance, and undid the bra before slipping my soaked panties down my legs. Julian quickly followed my lead, throwing his boxers across the bedroom. His cock looked like it was throbbingly hard, so large that my mouth watered again. I wanted to run my tongue along the veins, taste the bit of dried precum on the reddish tip. But I couldn't, because that would delay him getting inside me, and I couldn't wait any longer.

And apparently neither could he, because his lips were consuming me again in a frantic rhythm, licking and sucking and biting mine. He devoured me like I was his last meal—and, in a way, I was.

Because this was a goodbye. I couldn't let myself forget that. In the morning, he would be here, regretting all of this, and I would be far away, ready to start my new life.

That's all this was. A goodbye.

But it was hard to think about while Julian was palming one of my breasts, stroking the underside before rolling the nipple between his fingers. Goosebumps traveled along my spine from his tongue.

My arms gripped onto his broad shoulders just as Julian thrust his pelvis into mine, sending shockwaves that spread throughout my entire body. His hard erection rubbed against my clit while his lips kissed their way down my jaw.

"Julian," I whimpered. "Please."

Within half a second, Julian Vallen was buried inside of me. He groaned as he thrust all the way, both of us too eager to take it slow. I gasped at the fullness. My hands flew to his shoulders while my legs wrapped around my waist, allowing him to thrust deeper, *harder*.

The world shook. Two neutron stars had finally collided.

And soon, I would have to deal with the black hole.

Acknowledgments

This book would not exist without a whole slew of people who I cannot name without outing myself. I will do my best with what I have, but if you are not named, please know that your love and support are appreciated regardless.

First, to my husband: thank you for supporting this dream of mine through all of the ups and downs. And thank you for being willing to test out some scenes with me—though I'm sure you don't mind at all.

To my dog, for sitting on my lap as I wrote this book and giving me lots of cuddles and kisses.

To my family, for their unwavering support. They will no doubt read this book, and that thought alone fills me with shame.

To all my writing groups, many of you will not know that this story is me. If you do, you have no doubt supported this throughout its entire journey from crazy, mid-panic attack thought to publication. You all pushed me to make this book happen. And for that, you have my gratitude. And if you don't, I still appreciate you for making me into the writer I am today.

To my friends, you have no idea this exists, but I love you anyway.

To the authors that came before me in this genre, your work inspired me and showed me that darkness can still be beautiful. For that, I thank you.

To Wattpad, who paved the way for my fiery love for all things dark romance. And KU, for stoking it.

To Eva and Alek, for existing in my head for many months and not leaving, even when I thought I couldn't tell their story.

And lastly, to the readers, who picked up this book, giving a chance to someone they may not know. I appreciate you down to the last page.

With love and death,
    Lina

About the Author

Lina Harper is a dark romance author who occasionally writes things completely unserious. She began writing long ago under her true name, but got frustrated with publishing and decided to write privately for fun. Her stories are filled with obsession, sarcasm, and spice that'll have you taking a cold shower contemplating whether to read the next one or not (spoiler alert: you should).

She's spent her whole life learning to manage her mental illness and neurodiversity, and enjoys writing characters who struggle with some of the same things. When she's not writing, she leads a private life in the United States with her husband and dog.

https://www.authorlinaharper.com

www.ingramcontent.com/pod-product-compliance
Lightning Source LLC
LaVergne TN
LVHW030315070526
838199LV00069B/6469